The RETURN of THARN
By HOWARD BROWNE

When Tharn set out to rescue his beloved Dylara, he did not dream the whole Cro-Magnon world opposed him

TRAKOR, youthful member of the tribe of Gerdak, moved at a swinging trot along a winding game trail that led to the caves of his people. Through occasional rifts in the matted mazes of branches, leafs, creepers and vines of the semi-tropical forest and jungle, rays of the late afternoon sun dappled the dusty elephant path under his naked feet.

His slim young body, clothed only by the pelt of Jalok, the panther, twisted about his loins, was bathed in perspiration, for both heat and[Pg 42]humidity were intense here in the heart of primeval jungle. From time to time he transferred the flint-tipped spear to his left hand while he rubbed dry the sweating palm of his right against his loin cloth; for a slippery spear shaft could mean the difference between life and death in a battle with some savage denizen of this untamed world.

Trakor was beginning to worry. There was less than an hour of daylight remaining and he was still a long way from home. The thought of spending even a small portion of a night alone in a territory that abounded in lions, panthers, leopards and the other fearsome creatures of forest and plain, sent shivers of dread coursing along his spine.

And there was no one but himself to blame for this predicament! A boy of seventeen had no business attempting a task that would have given an older, more experienced warrior pause. Only a fool, he told himself bitterly, would have gone forth alone to hunt without having first gained experience by many trips in the company of seasoned hunters, thus learning the habits of the wild creatures.

It was all Lanoa's fault! In the soft fragrance of midnight hair curling about the tanned oval of her lovely face, in the smoothly rounded perfection of her slender body, in the golden depths of her clear, glowing eyes, were the seeds of madness that had sent him forth on a fool's errand! Before coming under her spell he was content to spend his days learning from old Wokard the art of painting scenes of tribal life and the hunt on the walls of the caves of his people.

Not until he watched Lanoa's other suitors displaying the trophies of the hunt did young Trakor make his decision to lay aside his paints and venture out in search of game. For it was easy to see how greatly Lanoa was impressed by the boastful tales of the other young men.

But where they hunted in groups, for safety's sake, Trakor would go out alone after Neela, the zebra, or Bana, the deer. And when Lanoa saw him return to the caves of Gerdak with the carcass of Neela across his shoulders, his heavy spear trailing from a casual hand, then would she realize that of all the young men of the tribe it was Trakor who was best suited to be her mate!

Thus the stuff of dreams ... and how different the reality! Since early morning of this day he had wandered through the forest and across wide stretches of prairie, seeking any of the various species of succulent grass-eaters that served as the principal fare of the Cro-Magnons. And while he had caught sight of grazing herds on several occasions, his utter lack of experience in the art of stalking prevented him from coming anywhere near enough for a successful spear cast.

Now he was slinking back home empty handed to face the gibes of those he had thought to impress, while the light of day gradually waned and the dark shadows of the jungle grew heavier across his path.

But the boy's wounded pride began to trouble him less as the certainty that he must spend a night in the open became increasingly evident. The everyday noises of the jungle, so nerve-wracking to those unable to interpret them, yet unnoticed by the jungle-wise, kept him in a constant state of apprehension while his fertile imagination pictured lurking shapes crouched behind the wall of tangled underbrush lining either side of the trail.

WITHOUT warning, the narrow path debouched into a fair-sized clearing, through the center of which moved the sluggish waters of a shallow stream, its low banks covered with reeds.

[Pg 43]

Compared with the dull half-light of jungle depths, the glade seemed bright as midday, although the sun had already dipped behind the towering rampart of trees to the west. Trakor's heart swelled with renewed confidence and his step was almost jaunty as he moved through the knee-deep grasses and rustling reeds to the river bank.

Now he knew exactly where he was. Another hour at a half-trot would bring him to the caves of Gerdak. The jungle wasn't such a fearsome place after all! He had spent an entire day in the open and not once come across anything more dangerous than monkeys and birds. Tomorrow he would go out again to hunt, nor would he return empty-handed a second time.

Dropping to his hands and knees at the river's edge, he drank deeply of the brackish waters. Rising, he took up his spear, waded the ankle-deep stream and trotted lightly onward, his goal the break in the opposite wall of trees which marked the continuation of the same trail he had been following.

Thus did young Trakor betray his abysmal ignorance of the jungle and its inhabitants. No experienced wayfarer of the wild places would have approached that opening without the utmost caution; for it is often just such a setting the great cats choose as a place to lie in wait for game.

The slender youth was within a few feet of the bole of a mammoth tree that marked the trail's entrance, when a sudden rustling amid a clump of grasses to one side of the path brought him to a startled halt.

Before Trakor could recover from his initial shock, those trembling grasses parted, and with majestic deliberation, Sadu, the lion, stepped into the trail less than twenty paces from the paralyzed youngster.

Huge, impressive, his sleek, tawny coat and bristling mane shimmering in the fading sunlight, his tufted, sinuous tail moving in jerky undulations, stood the jungle king, his round yellow eyes fastened hypnotically on his intended prey.

Trakor knew that only seconds remained for him in this life, that within fleeting moments he must go down to a horrible death beneath rending fangs.

And with that knowledge came a fatalistic courage—a courage he had not dreamed he possessed. With icy calmness he closed the fingers of his right hand tightly about the shaft of his spear and brought it up level with his shoulder, point foremost, ready for a cast when the great beast should charge.

Slowly Sadu crouched for the spring, his giant head flattened almost to the ground, massive hindquarters drawn beneath him like powerful springs, his long tail extended and quivering.

Voicing a thunderous roar, Sadu sprang.

RACING across the plains and through the jungles of a savage world, moving with unflagging swiftness by night and by day, came Tharn, mighty warrior of an era already old twenty thousand years before the founding of Rome—an era which witnessed the arrival to recognizable prehistory of the first *true man*.

Somewhere to the south of this Cro-Magnon fighting man, separated by endless vistas of primeval forest, grass-filled plains and towering mountain ranges, were the girl he loved and the men who had taken her.

Still fresh in Tharn's memory were the events of the past few weeks: the battles in Sephar's arena; the bloody revolt engineered by Tharn and his friends; the arrival of his father and fifty warriors of his tribe; the ascension of his close friend, Katon, to the kingship of Sephar; the finding of his own mother, long given [Pg 44]up for dead after disappearing from the tribal caves ten summers before; the stunning shock upon learning that Jotan had taken Dylara with him when he and his party of fellow Ammadians began their journey back to far-off Ammad, mother country of a civilization and culture far in advance of the Cro-Magnon cave dwellers.*

* "Warrior of the Dawn", December, 1942-January, 1943, *Amazing Stories.*—Ed.

The thrust of a knife from the cowardly and treacherous hand of Sephar's high priest had come near to costing Tharn his life on the eve of his departure in quest of Dylara. As it was, an entire moon passed before the caveman was able to leave his bed.

Pryak, the high priest, had died horribly in payment of his treachery; but Tharn suffered a thousand deaths from enforced idleness while the girl he loved was being carried farther and farther from the one person who possessed the ability to effect her rescue.

And then, over a moon ago, Tharn bade farewell to his mother and to the father whose name he bore, and plunged into the heart of the unfamiliar territory south of Sephar, taking up the trail of those Ammadians who held Dylara.

NEAR sunset of this particular day, Tharn awoke from a nap, as it was his practice during the baking heat of mid-afternoons. By thus conserving his strength during the more trying portion of the days, he was able to spend many hours after nightfall, when the air was cooler, in pursuit of his quarry.

Rising to his feet on a softly swaying branch a full hundred feet above the jungle floor, Tharn flexed the mighty muscles of arms and legs, his naked chest swelling as he drew in great draughts of humid atmosphere. The slender fingers of his strong, sun-bronzed hand pushed back the shock of thick black hair crowning his finely shaped head and strikingly handsome features, while the flashing, intelligent gray eyes roved quickly over the mazes of foliage surrounding him.

Nor was it his eyes alone that probed those curtains of growing things; ears and a nose keen as those of any jungle dweller were no less active.

2

He was on the point of descending to the game trail below when Siha, the wind, brought to his sensitive nostrils the scent of man commingled with the acrid smell of Sadu, the lion.

For the space of a dozen heartbeats he stood there, high above the hard-packed earth, while his keen mind rapidly analyzed the message his nose had picked up. From the strength of those scents he knew both man and beast were not far away, while the direction of the breeze told him their position.

Since the day Tharn, the son of Tharn, set out in search of the girl he loved, he had encountered men on several occasions and always those meetings were unpleasant. The Cro-Magnon tribes inhabiting the mountain ranges between Sephar and the land of Ammad were distinguished by their ability as fighters and an unflagging suspicion of strangers. Were it not for Tharn's tremendous strength and incredible agility, he would have died long ere this.

Consequently his first reaction was to let Sadu and the unknown man settle their impending quarrel without his own intervention. But a basic part of Tharn's character was his ready willingness to come to the aid of the underdog, to champion the cause of the weak and oppressed. It was a trait which had brought him to the brink of disaster more than once; but Tharn, were he to have given the matter any thought at all, would not have had it otherwise.

Thus it was that the caveman altered his course to the east and he set off through the trees, swinging [Pg 45]among the branches with the ease and celerity of little Nobar, the monkey. Now and then, with the agility of long practice, he sent his lithe body hurtling across some gap between trees, to grasp with unerring accuracy the limb his quick eye had selected. Yet notwithstanding his seemingly reckless pace his passage was almost soundless; and though the tangled verdure appeared as a solid wall, only rarely did his flying figure scrape against the riot of vegetation hemming him in.

A few minutes later the giant Cro-Magnard swung into the branches of a tree at the edge of a large circular clearing. Even as he reached the broad surface of a bough extending over the floor of the open ground, he caught sight of his old enemy, Sadu, the lion, crouching in the trail almost directly beneath him. Simultaneously he saw Sadu's intended prey: a slender Cro-Magnon youth, some four years younger than Tharn himself, who was standing stiffly erect, facing the lion, a flint-tipped spear poised in his right hand.

Tharn felt himself thrill to the boy's unflinching courage even as he recognized its futility, since no human could thus withstand the iron-thewed engine of destruction that was Sadu, the lion.

Tharn was given no opportunity to make use of his arrows or grass rope; for even as he observed the two figures below, the lion's tail shot stiffly erect, a shattering roar split apart the jungle stillness and Sadu charged.

As a swimmer dives from a springboard, so did Tharn launch himself into space, his right hand snatching the flint knife from the folds of his loincloth as he left the branch.

NEVER before had the cave lord thus attacked the king of beasts; but never before had he sought to wrest Sadu's prey, unharmed, from the animal's fangs and claws. As it was, he landed full upon the lion's back, crushing the beast to earth only inches short of its goal.

Voicing a startled shriek, Sadu rebounded from the forest floor like a tawny ball and turned to rend his foolhardy attacker.

Tharn, however, was not on the ground. His mind, trained from birth to function with lightning-like rapidity, had chosen the only way to prevent his unplanned act from resulting in certain death for himself. And so it was, as his diving body crushed Sadu to the ground, he passed his strong left arm about its neck, locked his powerful legs about its loins, and plunged his flint knife into its side, seeking the savage heart.

Roaring, snarling and spitting in a frenzy of rage, Sadu reared high and toppled back upon the human leech. But Tharn's legs locked only the tighter while the heavy knife, backed by biceps like banded layers of steel, sank home again and again.

Had the battle endured seconds longer the outcome might very well have been reversed. But before then Tharn's weapon tore twice into that untamed heart, and Sadu, with a final fearsome shriek, collapsed to move no more.

As Tharn rose to his feet, his calm gray eyes met the awed, half-mesmerized gaze of the boy whose life he had saved. At sight of the incredulous expression on the young face, the cave lord's firm lips curved in a winning smile that lighted up his strong, noble features.

As for Trakor, he could not have moved or spoken had his life depended on it. There was no doubt in his mind but that he was in the presence of one of the gods old Wokard often described. Who else but a god could slay Sadu with only a knife; who else but a god could possess such a combination of inhuman strength and unbelievable agility? The noble poise of that handsome head above broad [Pg 46]shoulders, the soft sinuous curves of that straight and

3

perfect figure, the unclouded bronze skin, the calm dignity of bearing and manner—all those things were attributes of the benign gods who watched over and protected the people of Gerdak's tribe.

Tharn's smile broadened as he guessed something of what was running through the boy's mind.

"Do you," he asked, "hunt often for Sadu with only a spear?"

Trakor shivered. "I would not hunt him with a forest of spears! When he came out of the grasses my blood turned to water and my toes crawled under my heels. Now I know what it is to be afraid!"

"You should have taken to the trees while I fought with Sadu," Tharn said. "Had he killed me, he would have slain you as well."

"Even Sadu cannot kill a god," the boy said simply.

Tharn blinked. "A god? I am no god. I am Tharn, a man of the caves, like you."

Trakor, while tremendously flattered at being compared with the stranger, was far from convinced that Tharn was telling the truth.

"A caveman could not slay Sadu thus," he declared, pushing a bare toe gingerly against the dead beast's back. "No, you are a god, for gods have been described to me many times by old Wokard, who knows all about such things."

The giant Cro-Magnard shrugged, smiling, and sought to change the subject. "Who are you?" he asked.

"I am Trakor, of the tribe of Gerdak."

"The caves of your people are nearby?"

"An hour's march in that direction," Trakor said, pointing.

Tharn's eyebrows lifted in surprise. "So far? Do you often go alone this deep into the jungle?"

Whereupon Trakor found himself telling the forest god the whole story: how the raven-haired Lanoa had shown, by her admiration for the young hunters of the tribe, that she would never become the mate of a man who did not excel in the hunt; how he was determined to prove to her and to the others of Gerdak's tribe that he too was a great hunter.

Tharn listened with grave attention, and while there were times when he was tempted to smile at some unconscious revelation of the boy's character, he resisted the impulse. It required courage to venture alone into the forest armed only with a spear. The soul of an artist, as revealed by Trakor's love of painting, had clashed with the hot blood of youth and a desire to appear to advantage in the eyes of a lovely woman. Older and more conservative men than Tharn would have named Trakor's act sheer lunacy; but Tharn was neither old nor conservative. Under the circumstances he would have done exactly the same thing.

WHEN Trakor was finished, Tharn said, "There will be other days for hunting. Unless you are willing to travel the jungle at night, you had best start for the caves of Gerdak."

Trakor sought to hide his apprehension as he looked about the dusk-filled glade and back to the dark hole which marked the game trail entrance.

"You are right," he said, turning to the cave lord. "I am grateful to you for saving me from Sadu, mighty Tharn. Who knows but that someday I may be of help to you."

"Who knows?" Tharn repeated gravely.

He remained standing there as Trakor turned and walked briskly toward the wall of foliage to the south. The boy's shoulders were squared and his brown-thatched head erect as he moved away, and Tharn felt a warm glow of admiration at the fierce pride that would not let its owner ask for[Pg 47]further protection. For he knew that secretly Trakor dreaded the thought of traversing the final stretch of night-shrouded jungle.

Purposely he waited until the youth was nearly out of sight, to learn if, at the last moment, Trakor's step might falter or his head turn for one last appealing glance. But the boy forged steadily ahead....

"Wait, Trakor," Tharn called.

The youth turned quickly and watched as Tharn gathered up his bow, quiver of arrows and grass rope from where they had fallen when he leaped to do battle with Sadu. With his weapons restored to their usual places, the caveman rejoined Trakor at the forest's edge.

"Since my way lies in the same direction," Tharn said, "I will go with you for a time."

"Good," Trakor said laconically. He might have said more, but he doubted the steadiness of his own voice, so great his relief.

Side by side they moved briskly along the winding trail, while the gloom of early night grew amidst the semi-tropical depths of forest and its inextricably tangled maze of branches, vines and creepers.

4

In some way these two members of the first race of *true men* to trod the globe were much alike; in others, as different as day from night. In age Tharn was no more than four years beyond his companion; in height perhaps an inch taller. Both were darkly tanned and each was clothed only by a loin-cloth of panther skin.

But there the similarity ended. Where Trakor was slender and with muscles not yet fully developed, Tharn's bronzed body was sheathed in supple sinews that rippled like steel cables beneath smooth skin. There was an undefinable surety, a boundless confidence, reflected in the graceful majesty of his expression and bearing. Unconsciously Trakor sought to carry himself in a like manner, for he was deep in the throes of hero worship.

"Tell me, Tharn," Trakor said diffidently, at last, "are you not truly a god?"

"It might be," Tharn said lightly. "Since I have never met a god, I would not know."

Trakor thought over the answer for a while. It did not seem that a real god such as old Wokard described would speak so of himself. Could it be that his new found friend, for all his superhuman abilities, was actually an ordinary man, just as he had claimed from the first?

Well, man he might be, but never an ordinary one!

"I am glad you are a man, Tharn," he said finally. "I do not think I would like to know a god."

"Nor would I," Tharn agreed soberly.

THEY moved rapidly ahead for a time, neither speaking. Suddenly the thunderous challenge of a lion rose from the depths of jungle not far to their right. Trakor shivered slightly and shot a quick glance at his companion. It was too dark for him to make out Tharn's expression but he seemed entirely unmoved by the sound of Sadu's voice.

A moment later Trakor heard the rustle of something moving in the undergrowth beside the trail, and a prickly sensation crawled along his spine. Sadu was hunting again! He would have liked to call Tharn's attention to the faint sound but hesitated to do so lest he appear overly nervous. Again came the slight rustle.

"It is Gubo, the hyena," Tharn said unexpectedly.

Trakor gasped. "How do you know that?" he demanded, both relieved and bewildered.

"He is upwind from us."

"Upwind? You mean you can scent him?"

"Yes."[Pg 48]

The young man from the tribe of Gerdak nearly betrayed his skepticism. Never before had he heard of a man whose nose could receive and interpret a scent spoor. It smacked of a kinship with the animals themselves.

"Are you sure?" he asked uneasily.

Tharn's quick ear caught the undercurrent of incredulity in the boy's voice, and he smiled under the cover of darkness. It was not the first time his unique ability had been doubted. He drew Trakor to a halt.

"Watch," he said.

Lifting his head the cave lord gave voice to the hunting squall of a leopard. So perfect was his imitation of Tarlok's cry, so fearsome the sound, that Trakor shrank back in quick alarm.

As the harsh scream rose on the night air, there was a sudden flurry of motion among the tangled foliage to their right, a blurred figure skidded into the trail ahead of where they stood and disappeared around a bend of the path. In the brief moment in which it was visible, Trakor recognized the animal as Gubo.

Crestfallen, Trakor could think of nothing to say. Never again, he resolved, would he doubt any statement made by this god-like stranger. There were many questions he burned to ask, but an aura of reserve seemed to surround the man—an aura he hesitated to intrude upon. At last he could contain his curiosity no longer.

"Where lie the caves of your people, Tharn?"

"Nearly two moons' march to the north," the cave lord replied readily enough.

"You came so great a distance alone?"

"Yes."

"Why?"

Tharn did not at once reply. During the moon since he had set out from Sephar in search of Dylara this was his first opportunity for a friendly word with a fellow man. On the several occasions that he encountered hunting parties of Cro-Magnon warriors, he had been regarded as legitimate prey to be hunted down and slain. Tharn expected no different attitude; it was the way of his own people when they came across fighting-men of other tribes. Consequently he gave such groups a wide berth, fighting against them only when given no other choice.

5

Long periods of silence, however, were no hardship to Tharn. Since boyhood he was accustomed to spending most of his days and many nights alone in the jungles and on the broad plains of this savage, untamed world, finding his greatest pleasure in matching his courage, cunning and strength against the denizens of forest and prairie. And because none of the other young men of his father's tribe was so highly developed mentally or physically, he made no intimates among them.

It was the kind of life which tends to develop a reticent nature in any man; and while Tharn was in no way morose or antisocial he was given to saying little beyond what must, of necessity, be put into words.

UNDER the warmth of Trakor's awed respect and undisguised admiration, however, Tharn's customary reserve began to thaw and he spoke at greater length than he intended.

"Two moons ago," he began, while they moved steadily along the twisting elephant path, "the girl I wanted as my mate was taken by a group of men who called themselves Ammadians. These men came from a great territory that lies south of your own caves. Ages ago many hundreds of the Ammadians left their country and traveled into the north, stopping finally in a high valley only a few marches from where the caves of my people now are."[Pg 49]

"Here they built many strange caves on level ground by piling heavy slabs of rock together, surrounding them all by a great wall of stone. They named this place Sephar and spoke of themselves as Sepharians."

"From time to time bands of Ammadians cross the plains and mountains and jungles between Ammad and Sephar. The leader of one of those bands, an Ammadian named Jotan, saw Dylara and wanted her for himself. Not long before this, Dylara had been taken from me by a hunting party of Sepharians, and she was held captive by Sephar's chief until he gave her to Jotan."

"Soon thereafter Jotan's party set out on the return journey to Ammad. Because of a wound, it was an entire moon before I was able to set out in pursuit of those who hold Dylara."

So engrossed was Trakor in the other's story that he quite forgot his uneasiness regarding the night-cloaked jungle about him. His imagination was fired by Tharn's adventures, and his ready sympathy went out to the cave lord in his romantic quest.

"Then you must enter the land called Ammad and take Dylara from those who have her?" he asked.

Tharn nodded. "At first," he said, "I hoped to overtake Jotan and his men before they could reach Ammad. But several times I lost their trail for days on end. Once a raging fire swept over a great stretch of grasslands I was crossing and I was forced to spend many days circling the burned section before I was able to pick up the signs of their passage. Then, ten suns ago, I lost the trail completely; since then I have been guided only by the directions given me when I left Sephar."

For a little while Trakor did not speak. Then: "Are these men you call Ammadians not so large as the people of our tribes? Do they cover their bodies with a strange kind of skin that comes from no animal? And do they wear strange coverings on their feet? And do they carry a strange length of branch with a tight length of gut tied to each end and many small spears such as you are carrying?"

Tharn, his pulses suddenly beginning to pound, seized the boy by one arm, bringing him to an involuntary halt. "Such are the Ammadians," he said tensely. "What do you know about them?"

"I have heard the warriors of my tribe speak of them," Trakor said. "There have been times in the past when we fought them. But they are brave and good fighters and we do not have the gut-strung branches which throw the small spears so straight and so far. So now we seek no quarrel with them unless they come too near our caves."

"Why, it was no more than five suns ago that Roban, son of Gerdak himself, watched a large party of them as they made their way up the great cliffs not far to the east of our caves. I heard him tell about it at the cooking fires that same night."

"Did he speak of women being among them?" Tharn demanded.

Trakor scratched his head. "I do not think so. As I remember it now, I did not hear the whole story; for Lanoa walked away from the fires and I followed her before Roban had finished."

Tharn's hand dropped from the boy's arm. "Come," he said, and once more they set out along the path.

CHAPTER II
CRO-MAGNON HOSPITALITY

AS the two Cro-Magnon men rounded an abrupt bend in the elephant path, the jungle and forest ended sharply at the edge of a wide clearing before a sheer cliff, its surface dotted with many cave entrances. Near the escarpment base a dozen cooking fires blossomed against the [Pg 50]darkness, and the shadowy forms of members of Gerdak's tribe moved about them.

For a moment Tharn and his companion remained standing at the forest edge watching the activity. The cave lord's acute sense of caution, without which few dwellers of this savage world lived long, kept him motionless while his sharp eyes took in every detail of the surrounding terrain. This business of approaching a village of strangers—and therefore enemies!—was a move not lightly to be taken, even when accompanied by one of its inhabitants.

Trakor tugged at his arm. "Come, Tharn! Come and receive the gratitude of my father and my people for saving me from Sadu. When they hear how you slew him with nothing more than a knife they will worship you as a god!"

His vague reluctance still with him, Tharn permitted the youth to urge him into the open. They were well into the clearing before one of the men about the fires caught sight of them and gave a warning shout.

Instantly a score of warriors caught up their spears and formed a bristling line facing the newcomers, while others piled dry branches on the fires sending flames shooting high to illuminate the scene with almost midday brightness.

"Put down your spears!" cried Tharn's companion, laughing. "It is I—Trakor, son of Kygor. Where are your hunters' eyes that you do not know me?"

But the line of spear heads did not waver. Now, moving from behind the formation of fighting men came Gerdak, chief of the tribe. Short, squat and very ugly was Gerdak. Set nearly flush on his broad sloping shoulders was a bullet-like head, almost hairless as the result of an old scalp infection. Firelight reflected in his pig-like eyes made them glow like burning sparks as he glowered from beneath shaggy brows at the tall stranger at Trakor's side.

"Who is he?" growled the chief, jerking a grimy thumb at the cave lord.

"He is my friend," Trakor said, and there was the beginning of anger in his tone. "His name is Tharn. In all the world there is no greater fighter."

Nothing changed in Gerdak's expression. "He is not one of us. Tell him to go at once or I will kill him!"

Trakor stiffened. Suddenly his anger flamed into the open—flamed with such intensity that he completely forgot the object of his wrath was his own chief.

"YOU will kill him! Ha! There are not fifty among you who could kill him! With only a knife he slew Sadu—leaping upon him as though Sadu were no more than Bana, the deer. He comes among us as my friend—treat him as such!"

As he spoke Trakor, beside himself with the hot anger of the young, had advanced until he was standing directly before the burly chieftain. With his last words the boy so forgot himself as to shake a fist in the other's face.

With a lightning sweep of one knotted fist Gerdak struck the infuriated boy squarely in the face. So terrible the force of the blow that Trakor's feet completely left the ground and he fell, unconscious, a full ten feet from where he had been standing.

EVEN as the boy's body was falling Tharn acted. With a catlike bound he reached the chief, fastened a hand about the man's bull neck and lifted him into the air. Holding the dazed Gerdak in a grip of steel he began to shake him until bones creaked in protest and his senses fled and he hung, limp and lifeless, in the circle of those mighty fingers.

As Gerdak crumbled to the ground, his spellbound warriors came to life. With shouts of rage they leaped for[Pg 51]ward to close upon the stranger who had dared to lay hands on their chief. But the agility and muscles that had brought their owner through countless jungle battles were more than Gerdak's warriors had reckoned with.

With a panther-like leap Tharn reached Trakor's prone figure. Snatching it from the ground to a place across his shoulder the cave lord turned and raced for the safety of the forest. Behind him came a shouting, cursing mob of raging fighting-men, brandishing spears and knives of flint. Had they thrown those spears within the first few seconds, the outcome would have been certain and Gerdak avenged. But they did not, and seconds later Tharn and his burden were lost among the shadows of overhanging trees.

For more than an hour Gerdak's warriors ranged the vicinity in search of the pair, thrusting their spears among the tangled undergrowth and racing along the game trail on the chance their quarry was following it. Finally they reluctantly abandoned the hunt and returned to where the body of their chief still lay on the clearing floor. Discovering a spark of life yet remaining, they bore him to his cave and after a while succeeded in bringing him back to consciousness.

It would be many suns before Gerdak fully recovered from his experience, but deeply planted in his dull-witted mind were the seeds of fear—fear that the mighty stranger called Tharn might return.

A WEAVING, bobbing sensation was Trakor's first impression as his hurt brain struggled back to consciousness. Beneath him was warm smooth flesh, and now and then he felt the brush of leaves or a vine against his back and sides.

When he opened his eyes he found himself being borne at a rapid pace through the forest top. For a moment he was unable to grasp the meaning of his strange position, then a familiar voice said, almost in his ear:

"Lie still for a little while. We are almost there."

It was Tharn's voice and with it came the memory of what had transpired before Gerdak's fist struck him unconscious. With a sigh, Trakor let the tenseness leave his body and he lay quietly across his new friend's broad shoulder.

Onward went Tharn, threading his way among the tangled labyrinth of branches with practiced ease. Broad boughs bent alarmingly beneath the double burden as he neared their tips while passing from one tree to another; but always he found the next before the weight proved too heavy. Yet so accustomed to such jungle highways was the cave lord that he seemed fairly to be flying through the trees.

Finally Tharn came to rest upon a wide branch high above the ground. Gently he deposited Trakor to a sitting position beside him, permitting the boy to rest his back against the tree's bole.

So intense was the darkness about them that Trakor was barely able to make out the form of his rescuer although he was only a few inches away. Trakor grasped a small branch to insure him from slipping from his high flung perch and for a little while said nothing, waiting until he could be sure the words would come out without a quaver.

"Where are we, Tharn?" he said finally, pleased at the matter-of-fact tone he was able to muster.

The darkness hid Tharn's understanding smile. "A short distance from the caves of your people."

"They are no longer my people," Trakor said hotly. "Even when I told them you were my friend they were against you."

He was silent for a moment. Then: "What happened after Gerdak struck me?"

Briefly Tharn told him of what [Pg 52]transpired in the clearing. When he was finished, the boy was thoughtful for a little while. The realization was strong that never as long as Gerdak lived would he be able to return to his own people. That alone did not cause him to regret what had happened; it was the knowledge he might never again see his father and mother that was hard for him to bear. As he was still hardly more than boy quick tears stung his eyes and he was thankful the darkness prevented his companion from seeing these signs of weakness.

The turn events had taken within the clearing had hurt Tharn, too. Lost was his opportunity of questioning Roban, son of Gerdak, about the party of Ammadians Trakor had mentioned. He broke the momentary silence to say:

"Have you any idea where the Ammadians scaled the cliffs you mentioned?"

Not until now did Trakor recall the reason his new friend had sought out the caves of Gerdak. The realization that his own unthinking anger was largely responsible for Tharn's failure to get the information was galling and he said so at length.

Tharn halted the flow of self recrimination. "Gerdak," he pointed out, "would not have allowed his son to tell me anything. I hardly expected any other reception so we have lost nothing.... Do the Ammadian travelers who pass this way scale the cliffs at the same place each time?"

"No," Trakor replied sadly. "There are many places that afford a way over them."

"And you recall nothing Roban said which would indicate the place this last party used?"

"No, Tharn. It could be any one of ten." When the man beside him made no reply, he added: "What do we do now?"

TRAKOR'S use of the word "we" brought the realization to Tharn that he was now faced with two problems. The first, of course, was to locate the trail of Dylara's abductors—and already his keen mind had hit on a short cut to that end. The second problem showed every indication of being a great deal harder to solve: What was he going to do with Trakor?

To permit the boy to return to the caves of Gerdak was unthinkable. The chief would be sure to blame him for what had happened; and while he might not actually kill Trakor he would certainly make his life unbearable. Nor could he leave this inexperienced youngster to face the jungle alone. Sadu or Jalok would be feeding on his soft flesh before two suns were gone!

The only alternative was to take the boy with him on his search for Dylara. It would mean slowing his pursuit of the Ammadians to a relative crawl—a thought galling to the cave lord....

"What do we do now?" Trakor said again.

Tharn shrugged lightly, his decision made. "We wait awhile. Now we shall sleep for an hour or two."

"Up here?" Trakor's voice faltered a little.

"Would it be better to sleep on the ground?" Tharn asked with grim humor.

As though to underscore the question, the distant scream of a panther came to their ears. Trakor shivered. "The tree is better," he admitted. "It is only that I have never slept in a tree," he laughed uncertainly. "I suppose I can get used to it."

"Lean your back against the trunk," Tharn said, "and allow your legs to drop on either side of the branch you are sitting on, resting your feet on the branches directly below. That way you will not fall, no matter how soundly you sleep."

The boy obeyed, and while he found the position less restful than the heap of pelts in the cave of his father, it was bearable. He knew he would not[Pg 53]be able to sleep, for already the chill of the jungle at night was creeping into his bones.

Seconds later he was sleeping soundly, while above him Tharn too slept in a fork of the same tree.

A HAND shaking his shoulder awoke Trakor with a start. Crouching on the branch beside him was Tharn, his magnificent body faintly discernible in the diffused light of Uda, the moon.

"Come," Tharn said. "It is time we set about locating the path used by the Ammadians in scaling the cliffside."

"At night?" Trakor asked wonderingly. "Would it not be better to wait until there is enough light to pick up the trail?"

"I have another plan," Tharn replied evasively. "Here," he added, stooping. "Place your arms about my neck."

Although he did not understand the reason behind the order Trakor followed his companion's bidding. An instant later he was swept up and out into the maze of branches while borne in Tharn's arms.

Where before much of the passage through the middle terraces of the trees had been hidden from Trakor by darkness, now the way was lighted by the moon, disclosing to the youth's horrified eyes the awful depths beneath. Gradually Trakor's fears grew less as he observed the unfailing sureness with which Tharn trod this high-flung pathway, and in its place came an abounded admiration of his agility and strength. Never before had he heard of a human who used the same avenues as little Nobar, the monkey—and used them with the same nimbleness and speed. Occasionally warriors of his tribe lay in wait for game among tree branches, but such climbing was as nothing when compared to this.

That uncanny instinct which so often had guided Tharn through unfamiliar territory did not fail him this time, and within half an hour he and his burden were gazing from the safety of a high branch at the deserted cliffside containing the caves of Gerdak.

At the sight of the familiar scene a great weight seemed to press against Trakor's heart. Was his new-found friend deserting him—returning him to certain suffering at the hands of short-tempered Gerdak? Did not Tharn know that never again would he dare to return to his own cave—that the chief would make him pay a thousandfold for championing the giant stranger?

Dreading the reply, he asked: "Why have we come back here, Tharn?"

"You told me Roban, son of Gerdak, knows the route taken by the Ammadians," said Tharn. "I am going to ask him where I may find it."

"But you cannot!" cried Trakor. "The instant Gerdak and his warriors see you their spears will cut you to pieces!"

"Then I must keep from being seen," Tharn observed lightly. "Point out to me the cave where Roban sleeps. I will enter and get him, bringing him here that I may question him in peace."

Trakor was horrified by the suggestion. "It is impossible! Mighty as you are, you could not hope to enter and leave the chief's own cave without being caught. Always several warriors sleep just within the entrance, for there are several among the tribe who hate Gerdak and he fears assassination while he sleeps."

For a long moment Tharn seemed lost in thought and Trakor was congratulating himself upon his success in talking the cave lord out of his mad scheme. But Tharn's next words showed his silence had been prompted by another reason altogether.

"Describe Gerdak's cave to me," he said, "telling me, if you can, where in it Roban is most likely to be sleeping."[Pg 54]

For a second Trakor was tempted to disclaim all knowledge of the subject. But then the realization came that Tharn would go ahead with his plan with or without the information he sought.

Carefully he told all he could about the chief's cave, describing in minute detail its layout and plan, together with such information as where the guards were likely to be sleeping and the probable location of Roban's sleeping furs.

Roban, he said, would not be difficult to pick out. He was about Trakor's own age but very skinny, with long legs and arms and a peculiarly shaped head, the crown rising almost to a point. He was an unpleasant youngster, sly and cunning, and generally disliked.

Tharn listened attentively; and when his new friend was done, he unshipped the quiver of arrows from its place on his back and handed it and his spear to Trakor. The grass rope he left coiled across his shoulder and under the opposite arm, and his flint knife remained in the folds of his loin-cloth.

"Wait here for me," Tharn said. The boy nodded, not trusting himself to speak, and watched the other slip easily through the branches to the ground at the clearing's edge.

BROKEN cloud formations dotted the midnight sky and Tharn waited patiently until one of them could obscure the full moon long enough for him to gain the foot of the steep scarp a hundred yards away. Several times small clouds blotted out Uda's radiant beams; but not until a sizable one moved into the proper position did Tharn leave the protecting shadows of the tree.

With great bounding strides, silent as the shadows themselves, Tharn crossed the clearing to the cliff's base. For a few moments he skirted its edge until he located a series of man-carved ridges which formed a rude and perilous ladder to the cave entrances above. With the sure-footedness of long practice he swarmed lightly upward, past cave after cave, until he came to rest a few feet below the yawning hole marking the entrance to Gerdak's dwelling.

He crouched there motionless, his ears straining for some indication that those within were still awake. But other than a faint sound of someone snoring, he heard nothing.

With infinite stealth he drew himself onto the ledge outside. To his unbelievably sensitive nostrils came the assorted smells of a Cro-Magnon shelter. Through the medium of scent he established that five men and two women were within, all of them his ears said were sound asleep.

Suddenly the cloud was gone from the moon's face and silver effulgence bathed the cliffside, leaving Tharn exposed to possible discovery. And so, crouching, the naked blade of his flint knife held ready, Tharn entered the lair of Gerdak, chief of a Cro-Magnon tribe.

As Tarlok, the leopard, stalks the wariest of grass-eaters, so did Tharn make his way into that black hole. No human ear would have been able to mark his passage as his naked feet, seemingly endowed with eyes of their own, threaded their way past one sleeping body after another.

Two warriors lay athwart the entrance; these Tharn stepped across, so close he could feel the animal heat from their bodies. Past a stack of spears piled against a side wall, avoiding a block of stone on which were piled several baked clay pots and dishes, skirting a heap of furs where an old woman slept, mouth open and the breath whistling between toothless gums ... these were danger points along the way.

At last he reached the rear wall of the cave—and there he found the object of his search. A lanky length of tanned human lay face up on a pile of skins, breathing heavily, arms thrown [Pg 55]wide. A few feet away, near a side wall, lay the stocky form and hairless pate that belonged to Gerdak, the chief.

The time had come for the high point of danger in Tharn's plan. Crouching beside the sleeping form of Roban, Tharn tightened his hold on the hilt of his knife, swung his arm in a short savage arc and brought the butt of the knife hard against the young man's skull!

There was a single violent upheaval of limbs which Tharn smothered instantly beneath his own weight, a sobbing cry which died unborn as a mighty hand pressed against the parted lips ... and Roban lay senseless.

Swinging the unconscious youth to his shoulders, Tharn turned to make his way back to the cave entrance. Three cautious steps he took ... and then a muscular hand closed about his ankle!

10

CHAPTER III
SADU ATTACKS

SADU, the lion, pacing slowly and majestically through the velvet blackness of a jungle night, came to a sudden halt as Siha, the wind, brought to his sensitive nostrils the acrid scent of burning wood.

For several long minutes the great cat stood as though turned to stone, his broad nostrils twitching nervously under the biting fumes. Sadu was unpleasantly familiar with the red teeth that ate everything in their path, for it had been scarcely a moon ago that he barely escaped the fangs of a forest fire.

Had it been smoke alone which Sadu smelled, he would have turned away and sought his night's food elsewhere. But commingled with the scent of fire was another smell, and it was the latter that finally sent him slinking ahead.

After the lion progressed another several hundred yards in this manner, the winding game trail debouched abruptly into a large natural clearing bordering the reed-covered banks of a wide shallow river.

Standing amid the impenetrable shadows cast by a great tree at the clearing's edge, Sadu surveyed with slitted eyes the bustle of activity about the open ground. There were at least fifty men there, some of them tending a blazing windrow of branches arranged in a large circle to encompass a considerable section of open ground where were heaped several mounds of supplies. Others were preparing the evening meal, bringing water from the river and performing the other duties which go with establishing camp for the night.

It was the scent of these men that had brought Sadu here. Ordinarily he would have passed up the two-legged creatures for the more satisfactory flesh of zebra or deer, but there had been an absence of such meat lately because grass-replenishing rain had not fallen in many moons and the grass-eaters had strayed away from the vicinity in search of fresh pastures. Too, Sadu had found man easy prey when he was alone—in numbers he was dangerous, particularly when backed by burning brands and sharp-pointed sticks.

The circle of fire with which these men had surrounded themselves gave Sadu pause. Only the pangs of hunger kept him from turning about and seeking less complicated prey. Slowly the heavy lips rolled back, baring the great fangs, and from the depths of the cavernous chest came a series of grunting coughs.

As the dull, rumbling challenge reached the ears of those within the camp, men straightened from their tasks and looked fearfully into the heavy darkness beyond the light from the fires. A few unslung their bows and tested the strings, while others made sure their heavy war spears were within reach.[Pg 56]

In the center of the camp itself, a group of five people—two girls and three men—broke off their conversation as the first notes of Sadu's voice reached them, and looked nervously at one another.

"Sadu is hungry too," one of the girls observed lightly as she turned her attention back to the freshly grilled meat on the clay dish before her.

"Will he attack us?" the other girl asked unsteadily, her dark eyes round with fear. Her slender, softly rounded body was covered with a knee-length tunic of some coarse, woven material and a cloud of black curls framed the delicate features of her olive-skinned face.

"I do not think so, Alurna," the first girl said, without taking her eyes from her food. "Sadu fears fire; he would have to be close to starving to brave the flames."

One of the three men, a slight, small-boned man whose round, full-fleshed face habitually wore an expression of slow-witted amiability, moved a little closer to the fire. "How do we know," he said anxiously, "whether this lion is not that hungry?"

The first girl shook back her wealth of reddish brown hair and looked at the speaker, her brown eyes sparkling with laughter. She said, "We *can't* know, Javan—not until he either springs through the fire or turns around and goes away."

If the words brought any comfort to Javan, his actions failed to show it. Once more he shifted his position until he was close to sitting in the burning branches and the fingers of his right hand were trembling uncontrollably as he groped for his flint-tipped spear.

"Dylara jests, Javan," the tall, broad-shouldered man next to him said. "There are too many of us for even several lions to attack."

"You say that, Jotan," Dylara said, "because you do not know Sadu as I know him. Often he will charge a hundred warriors through fires far larger than ours, yet at times several lions have run away from one man walking alone in the jungle. More than any other beast, Sadu is a creature of moods, and no one can say for sure what he will do."

11

THE third man in the group rose now to scrape the remaining food on his plate into the fire. He said, "We are certainly in no position to dispute with Dylara the habits of animals." There was a subtle note of condescension in his voice that only Jotan and the princess Alurna noticed. "You must remember that Dylara is different from us. Most of her life has been spent among the people of the caves, and there can be no doubt but that the barbarians know the jungle and its life far better than we can ever hope to."

Jotan's pale blue eyes frosted over and the hard, firm angle of his jaw tightened. For nearly two moons now he had endured Tamar's gibes at his love for a girl who had been a barbarian slave of Sephar's court. Many times during those sixty suns had Tamar said that no member of Ammad's ruling class, as was Jotan, had a right to take as mate some half-savage cave girl. There was such a thing, argued Tamar, as *noblesse oblige*, and Jotan was not only alienating his friends by this mad passion but breaking the laws of his class and his country.

Not that Tamar had anything personal against Dylara. On the contrary, he thought her beautiful and as gracious and regal as Alurna herself. But there was the matter of birth and blood—barriers too great for acceptance as the noble Jotan's mate.

All this was in Jotan's thoughts as he answered Tamar's last remark. "Perhaps it would be better for us," he observed lightly, "if we had a little of Dylara's knowledge of the jungle creatures and their ways. Perhaps then we would be spared such terror [Pg 57]at the sound of Sadu's roar."

He made the statement while looking full into Tamar's eyes, and was rewarded by seeing a tinge of red creep into his friend's freshly scraped cheeks. And because no man likes to be called a coward, no matter how indirectly, Tamar sought to hit back ... in the one way that would cut Jotan the deepest.

"It is unfortunate," he said mildly, "that we could not have brought along with us the wild man who came to Sephar seeking Dylara. I'll wager he would not turn a hair were Sadu to charge among us at this moment."

As though in direct challenge to the statement, Sadu, in the darkness beyond the camp, again lifted his voice in the hunting roar of the king of beasts.

This time the hot blood of anger welled into Jotan's face and a biting retort formed on his lips. But a glimpse of Dylara's suddenly stricken expression checked them there, unuttered.

In the brief silence that followed Tamar's words, Dylara was aware that the others were watching her as though to learn if Tamar's edged comment would goad her into a response.

And so she made answer; and while the words were directed to Tamar, it was Jotan whom they hurt.

"You are right, Tamar," she said proudly. "Tharn, more than any man I have ever known, is free of fear. How could he know fear when there is no man or animal that could match his strength, agility or quick mind."

"Had you seen him, as I did, crush the skull of a full-grown lion with a single blow of his fist, had you seen him close in battle with Tarlok, the leopard, with only a stone knife to use against Tarlok's teeth and claws, had he carried any of you through the highest branches of the forest top—then you would know why I am sure he came through the battles in Sephar's arena! That is why I know that even now he is on his way to take me from you."

"And when he does come, neither you nor all the warriors with you can keep him from his purpose. You are children—all of you!—when compared to Tharn!"

THE nails of Jotan's fingers were biting into his palms. "And would you go with him, Dylara?" he asked between stiff lips.

The girl's lovely brown eyes softened as she saw the pain under his carefully expressionless face.

"Yes, I would go with him," she said gently. "All of us know that I am no more than a prisoner among you. All of you have been kind and thoughtful and friendly toward me. Yet there is never a moment that I am not under the eyes of a guard. That is why I say that, given the chance, I would escape and return to the caves of Majok, my father."

Alurna shuddered. "You would not get very far, Dylara. The jungle beasts would get you the first night."

"I think not," Dylara said matter-of-factly. "You keep forgetting that I am not a Sepharian. The jungle and plains are not to me the horrible places they seem to you who have spent your lives behind the stone walls of your cities."

"How can you think of returning to such a life, Dylara?" Jotan said, almost pleadingly. "It is no way for a girl to live—in constant danger day after day, living in cold, damp holes in a cliff, wearing only an animal skin."

"Wait until you have seen the city of Ammad! As wonderful as Sephar must have seemed to you, it is crude and barbaric when compared to the splendor of the cities of my country. And in all the world there is no palace so lavish as that of Jaltor, king of all Ammad. Why, a few days among the glories and comforts of life among my people and the thought of returning to your caves would be hateful indeed!"

But Dylara was shaking her head. [Pg 58]"No, Jotan. Tamar is right when he says I would not fit into such a life. I was taken to Sephar as a slave to the Sepharians; and, as considerate as you have been, I am being taken to Ammad while still a slave."

"Not as a slave!" Jotan protested. "You are to become my mate. You will be shown the same honor, the same respect that I am given. I am a noble of Ammad, Dylara. Jaltor, ruler of Ammad, is my father's closest friend. He—all Ammad—will be at your feet the day we go before the high-priest of the God-Whose-Name-May-Not-Be-Spoken-Aloud and he makes you my mate."

The conversation clearly had gotten out of hand. Both Jotan and Dylara, so hard did each strive to make the other see his side of the argument, were putting into words things they ordinarily would never have said in front of those with them.

And all during the exchange, Alurna, princess of Sephar, sat there and watched them, her head bowed slightly and a hand shielding her face that none might see the hatred and jealousy mirrored there.

For Jotan was hers! Whether he was aware of that as yet was immaterial. Men had been blinded by beauty before and still brought to their senses before it was too late. As lovely as the cave girl was, Alurna knew that her own beauty suffered little by comparison—something that Jotan would have seen long ago were his eyes not blinded by a mad infatuation.

There was little else to do for the time being, Alurna realized, except wait. Tonight or tomorrow or a moon from now the opportunity for ridding herself of her brown-haired rival would come along. She had almost arranged the girl's death in Sephar, but Dylara had slain the hired assassin. Next time the result would be different. Fortunately it was not something that had to be done in a hurry. Dylara gave no indication of willingly becoming Jotan's mate, and being a person of high principles, Jotan would have her no other way. The only danger, really, was that his unfailing courtesy, thoughtfulness and complete adoration might succeed in winning the cave girl's love.

SADU, the lion, standing beyond the circle of light cast by the fire, raised his voice in a challenging roar that cut into silence the encampment of humans. His hunger was growing with the passage of time and the sight of the many two-legged creatures behind the leaping flames.

Again, Sadu's majestic voice rolled out, filling the clearing with spine-tingling sound, and from the depths of night-shrouded jungle behind him came an answering roar. A moment later the foliage parted and a second lion slunk through the shadows just beyond the periphery of light. The newcomer was a great, tawny-maned beast even larger than the first. He eyed the blazing piles of branches and the men beyond them with slitted eyes for a long moment, then uttered a series of low, coughing grunts. In response to the signal, three more lions—a female and two full-grown males—emerged from the undergrowth to join their leader.

The first lion eyed the strange family and bared his great fangs, warning them with a low rumble that he would permit no interference in his hunting. They stared at him silently with a kind of dignified reserve, then turned their attention toward the humans beyond the wall of fire.

Two full hours dragged past. Within the camp the larger part of the caravan was sleeping soundly, huddled against the chill night air in sleeping furs. The normal guard of ten warriors had been doubled against the possibility of attack by the great cats.

Suddenly one of the lions rose to its feet and with regal deliberateness stalked into the open ground bordering the line of fires. Slowly the jungle king strode along the unsteady line [Pg 59]of burning wood, his lithe sinews rolling beneath the shimmering hide, the sinuous tail moving in graceful undulations. Soundless were his padded paws on the turf and the mighty voice was silent.

Several minutes passed before one of the guards caught sight of the single lion. The man lifted a loud shout of alarm and several more of the sentries hastened to join their companion. When he pointed out Sadu less than a spear's cast outside the fires, the others readied their weapons for the attack they expected at any moment; while Sadu, seeing the flurry of motion among the hated manthings, lifted his mighty head and gave voice to a thunderous roar. "... Dylara! Dylara!"

The cave girl awakened instantly at sound of the frightened voice. She sat up and threw back the folds of her sleeping furs. In the flickering reddish glow of the night fires she saw the slender form of the princess Alurna bending over her.

"What is the matter?" Majok's daughter demanded.

"The lions!" Alurna moaned through chattering teeth. "Listen!"

13

Fully aroused by the other's panic, Dylara rose from the ground and tried to pierce the velvet wall beyond the light. Most of the camp's sentries were grouped at a point near the line of fire, fingering their spear and bows nervously and staring at something between them and the jungle.

... Sadu ceased his uneasy pacing, his tail lashing now in brief, jerky movements. Too long had he put off feeding. The fearsome fires were dimmer now; let them die down just a little more and he would leap across them and take his food.

Elsewhere among the sheltering trees the other lions watched him with unblinking attention. By now there were fully a score of the mammoth brutes lying among the tall grasses and reeds. In two's and threes—even one family of six—they had assembled, drawn to the scene by the voices of the first arrivals.

Again Sadu threw back his head and poured out his rumbling roar, seeking to build up his confidence sufficiently to brave the fires protecting his prey. Cautiously he began to inch his way toward the flames, his hindquarters held low, his majestic head extended and flattened until his nose was close to the ground.

While behind him other lions, made bold by his move, also began to creep toward the circle of fire.

DYLARA stiffened as Sadu's august voice echoed through the clearing. Her brown eyes, keener than most, began to pick out points of glowing yellow among the black shadows of the trees—bits of light that she recognized instantly as the eyes of lions. Even as she was conscious that there were many of them, she became aware of their growing size.

The cave girl waited no longer. Pushing past the fear-ridden princess, she went quickly to where Jotan slept nearby beneath a mound of furs and began shaking him urgently by the shoulder.

The Ammadian opened his eyes. "What—what is it? Dylara? What is wrong?"

"The lions!" Dylara said hurriedly. "Many of them. They are preparing to charge us!"

Flinging aside his furs, Jotan leaped to his feet and raced among the sleeping warriors, arousing them with a prodding foot and a few urgent words of explanation. Meanwhile, Dylara hurried to where the sentries were keeping watchful eyes on the first lion.

"Quick!" she exclaimed. "Throw some of the burning branches among the trees. There is still time to drive Sadu away!"

... Sadu, at sight of the rapidly awakening camp, halted his slow advance. For a moment he hesitated, his highly strung nerves twitching [Pg 60]with indecision. And when several of the men dragged burning branches from the fires and threw them, like blazing spears, in his direction, he snarled uneasily and drew back. Already a few of the other lions had turned tail to flee back into the jungle. In another moment the retreat would become a rout and Sadu must seek elsewhere for food.

And then there occurred one of those unpredictable turns of fate which none can foresee. One of the blazing brands, propelled by a strong arm, struck full against the flank of a retreating lion. There followed a puff of smoke as hair burned away a wide patch and seared the skin beneath.

Sadu's uncertain temper blazed with the flame. With a startled roar that paled to nothing the surrounding chorus of growls, screams and curses, he wheeled about and bore down upon the camp, roaring as he came. A few feet short of the flaming stockade, Sadu rose in a mighty leap, cleared the flames easily, and landed squarely among the startled Sepharians.

Instantly pandemonium raged. The men scattered wildly from Sadu's flailing claws and glistening fangs, only to encounter other lions who, emboldened by the success of the first, had turned back to leap the barrier. Already a dozen of the tawny, sinuous bodies were sowing death among the ranks of Jotan's followers.

The princess Alurna huddled among a heap of furs and sought to close her eyes against the horrors of the growing massacre. But not seeing at all was infinitely worse than reality, and so her eyes remained open and staring.

Suddenly a huge, yellow-maned monster bounded toward her. A lithe spring brought it atop a mound of supplies scarcely ten feet from where she lay paralyzed with fear. Slowly the lordly head swung in a menacing circle and the savage eyes fixed upon her shrinking form. The small ears twitched back until they lay tight against the sleek skull, the mammoth maw parted to disclose awesome fangs and a low growl rumbled low in the deep chest.

Jotan, shouting orders in an effort to rally his scattered men to some semblance of order, caught sight of the doomed princess as Sadu rose in his spring toward her. Careless of his own safety, he drew back his strong right arm and launched his heavy war spear. The keen blade

14

flashed across the intervening space and caught Sadu squarely in the chest, knocking him to one side and killing him instantly.

WHILE all this was taking place, Dylara, daughter of Majok, had remained crouched close to one of the heaps of burning branches where she knew Sadu would be reluctant to approach. She saw man after man go down beneath the ravaging cats, and twice she saw lions leap back into the darkness, carrying the limp corpse of some unfortunate Ammadian. She witnessed, too, Jotan's rescue of the princess Alurna, and despite the awful carnage about her, she smiled grimly as Urim's daughter ran forward and threw her arms about the tall Ammadian noble.

At the moment it abruptly dawned on Dylara that this was her opportunity to escape from those who held her an unwilling captive. She turned her head and stared out into the open ground between camp and forest edge, seeing the long shadows cast by the flickering flames. If she could but cross that ribbon of grassland safely and gain the safety of the trees!

Even as she silently voiced the wish, her mind was made up for her. From behind one of the piles of supplies emerged a tawny shape. Two blazing eyes caught sight of the cave girl, and heedless of the nearby fire, the giant cat began to slink toward her.

Dylara, wise to the ways of the jungle, acted. Without a second's hes[Pg 61]itation she whirled about and raced through a narrow break in the circle of fire, heading for the darkness beyond. Even as she acted, she knew this might be merely exchanging one peril for another: there could easily be ten lions between her and the safety of the trees.

With an earth-shaking roar, Sadu gave chase.

Her heart pounding wildly, Dylara shot across the open ground like an arrow from a bow. Behind her, gaining ground as though his frail quarry were standing still, came the lion, its jaws widely distended, low growls welling from its throat.

The low-spreading branches of a forest tree loomed ahead of the fleeing girl. Sadu was only a few feet behind her ... already he was launching the last leap that would crush the girl to earth just short of her goal.

IN the camp itself, Jotan's bellowed commands were beginning to take effect on the disorganized warriors. Those still alive and unwounded managed to form a spear-bristling phalanx, standing shoulder to shoulder, while the blood-hungry cats moved slowly around them. Twice, a lion charged that square of flint spear-tips, only to fall back with roars of rage and bleeding from wounds. For a few minutes longer the beasts continued to circle warily about the men, now and then feinting charges in an effort to draw them into breaking ranks.

But the warriors, heartened by the confident bearing of their leader, held fast in spite of the fearful nearness of distended jaws and gleaming fangs.

At last, as though by some strange understanding, the lions began to withdraw, dragging with them some of the torn bodies of warriors who had died during the battle. Only the sharp commands of Jotan himself prevented the others from an attempt to save their fallen comrades from so horrible a fate—Jotan who was realist enough to know that any such foolhardy action— no matter how noble the purpose—could only result in further casualties.

When at last the lions were gone, Jotan set about restoring the broken defenses of the camp. Fires were increased in number and size, scattered supplies and weapons were reassembled and the wounded cared for.

Not until all this was done did Jotan learn of Dylara's disappearance. At first he was nearly frantic with worry, picturing her as being dragged away by one of the marauders. It was not until he questioned the wounded that the true story came out.

"No, Sadu did not get her. Not in the camp anyway." The warrior, wincing from the pain of a long gash in one arm, pulled himself into a sitting position as he replied to Jotan's questions. "She was crouched down near the fires until one of the lions began to creep up on her. She wasted no time in doing something about that!"

"What *did* she do?" Jotan demanded impatiently.

"The only thing she could have done: slipped through the fires and ran for the trees."

The young Ammadian noble glanced toward the Stygian gloom of the distant jungle and a faint shudder coursed through him. "What a mad thing to do!" he said, half to himself. "I would rather face Sadu here in the light than plunge into those shadows." To the wounded man he said, "Did you see her reach the trees?"

The other man shook his head. "My eyes are not that good. The lion chased her into the darkness and I lost sight of them both. She had a good start and she ran very swiftly."

"Which way did she go?"

The warrior waved an arm toward the south. Jotan picked four men who, carrying spears and torches, accompanied their leader in that direction.

15

They reached the fringe of trees and jungle to the south of the camp, [Pg 62]and walked among the tree boles, calling out the cave girl's name. But only the voices of disturbed bird life and the distant scream of a panther answered their cries.

"Sadu must have gotten her after all," said one of the four.

"I don't believe it!" Jotan snapped. "She knows the jungle beasts too well for that to happen."

"Then why," asked another of the men, "does she not answer our calls?"

Jotan ignored the question. "Return to the camp," he said through a strange lump in his throat. "When morning comes, we will take up the search for her."

Alurna, still weak and shaken from her recent experience with Sadu, watched the five men enter the camp. She saw Jotan dismiss the others and come over to where she was seated between Tamar and Javan. When there was no sight of Dylara, and when she noticed Jotan's grim expression, her heart bounded with a wild and horrible hope.

"Well, Jotan?" Tamar said quietly.

HIS friend spread his hands in a helpless gesture. "There is no trace of her," he admitted, and in his voice was a note of such intense suffering that Tamar's heart went out to him.

Javan, blinked stolidly at the stricken man, put into words the unvoiced question of the others. "The lions...."

Jotan shook his head. "I don't believe they got her. There were no signs of a struggle. No ... bones." His voice faltered on that last word, and he threw his hands wide in sick bewilderment. "I don't know what to think!"

The princess Alurna spoke up suddenly in silken tones. "Have you forgotten so soon, O noble Jotan, the cave girl's own words?"

Jotan stared deep into the faintly mocking gray-green eyes of Urim's daughter. "What do you mean?" he said stiffly.

"Did she not say: 'I would escape and return to the caves of Majok, my father'? Did those words mean so little to you?"

Harsh lines deepened at the corners of Jotan's lips. "Yes, she said that. But she would not try to get away at night. Especially tonight, when there are the God knows how many lions roaming about the camp. The hardiest warrior would not dare that, let alone a frail girl."

"How long," Tamar broke in, "will you go on thinking of Dylara as a 'frail' girl? Can't you understand that she is not our kind of woman? She does not fear the jungle: all that she needed was a chance to get into it without our seeing her, and tonight she was given that chance. You have Sadu to thank for that."

For several long minutes Jotan sat there without speaking, his gaze fixed unseeingly on the leaping flames of the campfire. What strange currents and cross-currents, he mused, had been set into motion by his love for the girl of the caves. There was the steadily widening rift with Tamar—Tamar whose only flaw was his stiff-necked pride in lineage and noble blood—Tamar, who was his closest friend, his almost constant companion since boyhood. Together they had learned the arts of hunting and fighting, together they had served as fellow officers in Jaltor's armies, together they had crossed those interminable stretches of jungle, plain and mountain between Ammad and far-off Sephar. Could he afford to risk an almost certain break with Tamar by pursuing further his mad infatuation for the missing cave girl?

There was another complication, too—one leaving him open for repercussions even more unpleasant than the loss of a friend. There was no doubt in his mind but that the Princess Alurna was in love with him. He knew that in the eyes of his family and friends she would make any man a mate to be proud of. From the stand[Pg 63]point of beauty alone she was almost as lovely as Dylara. More than that, however, Alurna was the niece of Jaltor, monarch of all Ammad and a personal friend of Jotan's own father. Jotan shuddered slightly. He could well imagine Jaltor's reaction upon learning that the daughter of his dead brother had been spurned in favor of a half-wild woman of the caves!

And then the lithe, softly curved body of Dylara came unbidden before his mind's eye ... and all else was forgotten. He rose stiffly from where he sat among his friends, conscious from their expressions that they knew he had arrived at a decision affecting them all.

"When the dawn comes," he said in a strangely toneless voice, "we break camp and continue on toward Ammad. Not all of us will go on, however. A few warriors shall accompany me in search of Dylara ... and I shall not return without her!"[Pg 64]

[Part   II]
[Pg 66]

Hers was the beauty famous across half a world

CHAPTER IV
THE SEEDS OF TREACHERY

OTAR, a warrior in the service of Vokal, a powerful and high-ranking nobleman of the city of Ammad, was violently unhappy this night. His sandaled feet beat an angry rhythm against the pavement in front of the arched opening in the high stone wall about his master's estate. Thirty paces one way, an about face executed with the military precision Vokal demanded of his guards, then thirty paces back again, spear held rigidly across his tunic-clad chest.

The velvety blackness of a moonless night weighted the street and matched his mood—a blackness only intensified by the feeble yellow rays of a lantern in a niche above the gate. Silently he cursed the captain of the guards who had demoted him to night sentry duty, then he cursed Vokal for his mad judgment in picking so heartless a captain to begin with.

There was a sound reason for Otar's unhappiness. Only the day before he had taken a mate—the incomparable Marua, daughter of one of Vokal's understewards—Marua, whose exquisite blonde beauty and matchless form had brought her a host of male admirers, many of them in high positions in Vokal's service. Among them was Ekbar, captain of the nobleman's guards; and therein, Otar knew, lay the reason why he was walking a midnight post outside Vokal's sprawling estate. The thought of his lovely new mate alone in his snug apartment in the guard's quarters while he paced away the hours brought a fresh flood of curses to his lips.

"Greetings," said a hoarse whispering voice behind him.

Otar, startled, whirled and leveled his spear in one rapid motion. "Who speaks?" he growled.

An indistinct figure, muffled to the chin in a black cloak, was standing in the street only a foot or two beyond reach of the questing spearhead.

"Fear not," said the harsh voice. "It is I—Heglar, nobleman of Ammad. I am here to hold an audience with the noble Vokal. At his own invitation. Here." He held out his hand from under the cloak and something gleamed from the center of his palm in the faint light. "Examine this by the rays from yonder lantern."

Cautiously, his heavy spear ready in his right hand, Otar took the object and backed away until he could see it clearly. His careful maneuvering was in line with orders, for attempts at assassination were fairly common among Ammad's nobles in their ceaseless efforts for power second only to Jaltor himself, king of all Ammad.

A single glance was all Otar needed. It was Vokal's personal talisman: a small square of gold bearing on one side a peculiar design cut in the soft metal. No humblest warrior in all [Pg 68]Vokal's vast retinue who did not know that design and his duties when faced with it.

He returned the talisman to the man who called himself Heglar and stepped back, bringing his spear sharply to a saluting position. "You may pass, noble Heglar. This path will bring you to a side door of Vokal's palace. The guard there will see to it that you are taken to him."

VOKAL stood on a small balcony of stone outside his private apartment on the fourth level of his huge, many-roomed palace. He was a tall slender graceful man in his early fifties, with a narrow face, small cameo-sharp features and a languid almost dreamy quality in his movements and expression. Prematurely gray hair waved back from a brow of classical perfection, and the hand he lifted to smooth that hair was narrow and long fingered and beautifully kept. He was wearing the knee-length tunic common to all men and women of Ammad, but his was of a better weave, its belt of the same material was a full two inches wider and trimmed with the purple of Ammadian royalty.

From this elevated position he was able to look out over the northern section of the city of Ammad—a vast orderly array of box-like stone buildings, some gray and some white, rising one to three floors above the streets. Fully five miles from where Vokal stood was the northern section of the great gray wall of stone encircling the city, and the buildings became smaller and simpler in design the nearer they were to that wall.

A man's position in Ammad was determined by how near the city's center his dwelling stood. At the metropolis' exact center was the mammoth palace of Jaltor, king of Ammad and supreme ruler of a vast country of jungle, plain and mountain extending a moon's march in all directions. Like Vokal's own palace, Jaltor's rose from the crest of one of the city's five hills; but the king's, in addition to being at the exact center of Ammad, stood on the highest of them all. It could be seen from the windows on the opposite side of Vokal's palace—the principal reason his personal quarters were here. Sight of that huge sprawling pile of white stone, its roof six levels above the ground, was a constant source of irritation to him.

A sound of soft knocking from behind him aroused Vokal from his reverie, and he turned unhurriedly and re-entered the room.

The knocking was repeated. Vokal sank gracefully into an easy chair covered with the soft pelt of Tarlok, the leopard, crossed his shapely bare legs and studied the effect with approval.

Again the sound of knocking, a shade louder this time. "Enter," called Vokal around a yawn which he covered with the tips of two fingers.

A door opened, revealing the rigidly erect figure and carefully expressionless visage of an officer of the palace guard.

Vokal concluded his yawn. "Yes, Bartan?"

"The noble Heglar is here, Most-High."

"Excellent! Permit him to enter immediately."

The guard executed a sharp quarter turn and stepped back, allowing a man swathed to the chin in the voluminous folds of a black cloak to push past him into the room.

"Greetings, noble Vokal." The words came out in a hoarse croak that grated against the host's sensitive ears.

"Greetings, noble Heglar." Vokal's smile seemed even dreamier than usual. "Remove your cloak, please, and be seated.... Bartan, tell a slave to bring us wine."

"At once, Most-High." The guard withdrew, closing the door softly.

Vokal's gray-blue eyes went to his [Pg 69]guest and he smiled blandly. "I trust all is well with you and the members of your family, noble Heglar."

STRIPPED of his cloak, Heglar was revealed as a man of extraordinary thinness and considerable age. The pronounced hollows in his cheeks and a thin nose the dimensions of an eagle's beak, together with the rocky ridge of an underslung jaw, gave him an emaciated look. But his body was straight as a young sapling, his shoulders for all their boniness were surprisingly broad, and his light blue eyes were alert and piercing.

He ignored his host's solicitous inquiry concerning his family and bent and unknotted the thongs of his heelless sandals. Kicking them off he leaned back in his chair and, sighing with relief, placed his bare feet on a low stool in front of him.

If he caught the faint wrinkle of disgust about Vokal's shapely lips he ignored it. "You'll forgive an old man for humoring his feet," he croaked. "I'm not accustomed to long walks these days."

"By all means give them comfort."

"I tried to learn from your messenger the reason behind your asking me here tonight. He would tell me nothing—simply gave me your message, handed me your emblem piece—" he dug a hand into a pocket of the tunic, took out the square of gold and handed it to Vokal—"and left without another word."

"You could hardly expect one of my men to do otherwise," Vokal said frostily.

"One never knows." The old man settled himself more comfortably in his chair. "I was curious and a little doubtful at the interest of the third most powerful man in all Ammad— especially when his interest concerns the most impoverished and least influential noble of that same country."

There was a soft knock at the door and a slave girl slipped in, placed a tray of wine and two goblets on a low table between the two men, and went out as silently as she had entered.

Heglar's eyes followed her trim figure until the gently closing door shut off his view. "Believe me," he said, watching Vokal fill the two goblets, "there was a day I had slaves like that one. Many slaves—and more warriors than any noble in all Ammad. Only old Rokkor himself, Jaltor's father, had more of them."

He sighed gustily. "But that's all in the past now. My only regret is that I must leave my young mate and our two children with little more than a roof above their heads when I die."

"Your love for the gracious and beautiful Rhoa is well known throughout all Ammad," Vokal murmured, handing his guest one of the filled goblets.

The old man gulped a third of its contents before taking the container from his lips. "And why shouldn't I love her?" he demanded harshly. "Thirty summers my junior, lovely enough to have her pick of men—and she chooses me. Forty summers I spent with my first woman—and what a sour-faced old hyena *she* was—and not a child to show for it. Now we have two, Rhoa and I—and I have nothing to leave them but a miserable hovel in place of the palace I once owned."

Vokal sipped daintily from his goblet and let the garrulous old man ramble on. Let him go on bemoaning his lowly position and living over his past glories. Every word of it would make the old one more agreeable to Vokal's proposition.

[Pg 70]

18

The nostalgic refrain went on until Heglar had emptied his first glass of wine and extended it for a second helping. This time he spilled a few drops on the floor as a voluntary offering to the God-Whose-Name-May-Not-Be-Spoken-Aloud—a tribute given usually only during formal dinners—gulped down several swallows of the alcoholic grape beverage, then turned those sharp eyes on Vokal.

"But," he said hoarsely, "you didn't ask me here to talk of the old days. What do you want of me, noble Vokal?"

THERE was a short period of silence during which Vokal appeared to be making up his mind. Wavering light from candles set in wall brackets about the long, richly furnished room gave a lean, almost vulpine cast to his calm face and a glittering sparkle to his cold eyes. Finally he said:

"I want to make you a wealthy man again, Heglar."

The hand holding the wine goblet jerked involuntarily and some of the wrinkles in the aged face seemed to deepen. "... Why me?"

Vokal smiled dreamily. "Right to the point, eh, Heglar? It is one of my reasons for selecting you."

"Hmm." The old one looked down into his half-empty goblet to hide the sudden gleam in his eyes. "Tell me more of these reasons for wishing to make me rich."

"The list is long," Vokal said graciously, "so I shall give only the principal ones. First, it is well known throughout all Ammad that you are a man of your word—that once you give a pledge nothing in this world or the next could force you to go back on your word."

Heglar scowled. "One of the reasons I am a poor man today!"

"Secondly," Vokal went on, "it is reported that you are a walking dead man, that you have only a few moons left to live because of the sickness in your throat." At the other's startled expression he waved a languid hand. "It is common knowledge, noble Heglar; your physician is a talkative man."

"Thirdly," he continued, his voice calm, almost indifferent, "your long and honorable career as a mighty warrior proves you a man of great physical courage, and you are still strong and active enough for a dangerous task."

A wry smile touched the old man's lips. "Then I am expected to earn this wealth you are offering me?"

"Of course. I am not noted for being a charitable man, noble Heglar."

"... Are there other reasons?"

"Lastly," Vokal said imperturbably, "as a nobleman you have the freedom of Jaltor's court and may come and go there as you please."

He looked sharply at the older man as he finished speaking and for a long moment they stared into each other's eyes in silence.

Heglar was the first to speak. "Now that you have listed my qualifications, what use do you expect to put them to?"

Vokal bent forward and fixed him with his penetrating gaze. "I must call upon the first of them before this conversation can go any further. Will you give me your solemn pledge that not one word of this will go beyond the two of us?"

"... Yes."

"Good. I want you to forfeit the few remaining moons of life left to you."

Heglar blinked. It was the sole sign of emotion aroused by that startling declaration. "Those few moons are priceless to me, noble Vokal," he said, a faint smile hovering about his lips.

"I am prepared to pay heavily for them."

"You would have to.... What do you want me to do?"

Vokal leaned back in his chair and placed the tips of his fingers lightly together, looking over them at the old man. His eyes had gone back to being dreamy again. He said:

"I want you to *attempt* the assassination of Jaltor, king of Ammad!"

The breath left Heglar's lungs in an explosive gasp. "What madness is this!" he cried hoarsely. "Why do you want Jaltor dead? Certainly his death would not better your position as a noble in the court. His son would take the throne; and even if something happened to *him*, his sister would be [Pg 71]next in line. Are you planning to do away with the entire royal family, noble Vokal?"

Vokal was shaking his head. "I'm afraid you did not understand me, my friend. I said that I wanted you to *attempt* Jaltor's assassination—not to kill him."

"This makes no sense to me!"

"It is very simple. I want you to attend one of Jaltor's morning audiences within the next day or two. Work your way close to him, draw a knife and make a clumsy attempt to stab him.

19

But be sure you fail. The guards will overpower you instantly; and when Jaltor demands to know why you tried to kill him, refuse to answer other than to hint that you were not alone in the plot."

"Knowing Jaltor as we both do, he will order you put to torture in an effort to learn the facts. Endure that torture as long as you possibly can. Then blurt out the name of the man who hired you."

Heglar was watching him through narrowed eyes. "I'm beginning to see the light," he said dourly. "The name I give him will be that of the man you are really after."

"Exactly."

"Whereupon I will be put to death."

"Jaltor has never been famed for his leniency, noble Heglar."

THE old man drained his goblet of wine and put it on the table with a steady hand. "At least he is a just man. He would punish only those he believed implicated in the plot; my family would not be persecuted." He seemed to be speaking to himself. "Rhoa would be a wealthy woman and my children would never know want or hardship...."

His eyes came slowly up to Vokal. "My price will be one thousand tals!"

It was a staggering amount—the equivalent of twelve thousand young male slaves—but Vokal never hesitated. "I will pay it, noble Heglar," he said quietly.

"In advance."

"As you wish. I need no assurance beyond your word that you will carry out the exact terms of the arrangement."

Heglar sighed. "You have my word.... What name will Jaltor's torture wring from my reluctant lips?"

"That of the noble Garlud."

"Oho!" Heglar nodded in tribute. "That clears up the picture. Garlud is second only to Jaltor as the most powerful man in all Ammad. With him out of the way, you, as the next in line among Ammad's noblemen, will take Garlud's place and all the benefits that go with it. I congratulate you, noble Vokal, on your shrewdness."

They filled their earthen goblets and drank. After a moment Heglar said, "There is one drawback to your plan, my friend. I hesitate to mention it, for a man as thorough as you has doubtless anticipated that flaw and taken steps to overcome it."

"No man is perfect," Vokal said equably. "To what do you refer?"

"Garlud has a son. As is our custom he will inherit his father's position and estate even though Garlud is executed for treason."

"And if the son is dead also?" Vokal said silkily.

"So you *have* thought of it! I might have known. In that case, since Garlud's mate died over a moon ago, his wealth returns to the State, except for the palace which is given to the next nobleman in line."

"Precisely."

"Uh-hunh. Do you know for sure that Garlud's son—let's see: his name is ... ah—"

"Jotan."

"Of course. A fine young man too—as I remember him. You're sure he's dead?"

"If not, he soon will be."

"But he is not in Ammad, I understand. Didn't he make a trip to Sep[Pg 72]har, Vokal?"

"He is due back within half a moon at the earliest."

"How will you handle the matter when he arrives at Ammad's gates?"

Vokal smiled his dreamy smile. "He will not arrive at Ammad's gates, O Heglar! The day you attempt Jaltor's assassination a party of my most trusted guards will leave Ammad to intercept Jotan and his men. Their orders will be to leave not one of them alive."

"It is clear that you have thought of everything!" The old man gulped down his wine and stood up. "It is late, and at my age I need a great deal of sleep—especially if I am to be tortured by Jaltor's experts in that line! So, if you will pay me my thousand tals, noble Vokal, I shall leave you."

"Of course." Vokal rose smoothly to his feet, went to the door and summoned a guard outside. "Arouse Yodak and instruct him to bring a thousand tals to me here."

"At once, Most-High." The guard saluted and went quickly down the hall.

Heglar was shaking his head admiringly. "You take some long chances, Vokal!"

The gray-haired nobleman glanced sharply at him. "What do you mean?"

"This matter of your guards calling you 'Most-High'. That is a mark of respect given only to kings, you know. I doubt if Jaltor would approve of your appropriating it to your own use."

THE other's blue-gray eyes seemed to film over. "Kings have been known to die, noble Heglar—and at times the ranking nobleman takes his place. One must prepare for every possibility."

"Even to having one's guards form the habit of saying Most-High, eh?"

The arrival of a small frail-bodied old man in hastily donned tunic ended the conversation. He was bearing a small cloth bag which gave off the sounds of clinking metal.

"The thousand tals, Most-High," he quavered, holding out the bag.

Vokal took it and dismissed the man. "... Would you care to count them?" he said upon placing the bag in Heglar's hands.

"It is not necessary," the old man said, then smiling, added: "You need my specialized services too badly to cheat me!"

Vokal summoned a guard and instructed him to appoint several warriors to escort the old man safely to his home, as robbery under cover of night was far from unusual on Ammad's numerous streets.

When the door had closed and Vokal was alone once more, he returned to his chair and filled his wine cup. "A thousand tals," he mused. "Heglar's assistance comes high indeed. But let him fondle them for a little while before they come back to me—along with the lovely Rhoa. I wonder what the old man would say if he knew his mate has been my mistress these past three moons!"

CHAPTER V
BEYOND THE HEIGHTS

AS Tharn felt those fingers close about his ankle he dropped instantly to his other knee to keep from being upset and swung his free hand in a sweeping blow at the point where reason told him the face of his attacker would be.

So quickly had he acted that his knuckles thudded home on an unseen jaw before its owner was able to shout an alarm. There followed a convulsive twist of a body in front of him and the clutching fingers loosed their hold.

His unconscious prize still hanging from his shoulders, Tharn regained his feet and raced cat-like for the mouth of the cave. Behind him he caught the sound of a startled grunt, followed by a wild yell that roused [Pg 73]every occupant of the cave while Tharn was still a good thirty feet short of his goal.

A huge form shot up in front of him, a raised knife silhouetted against the star light beyond. Behind him naked feet whispered against rock as several enemy warriors rushed to close with the foolhardy intruder.

Tharn was trapped! Burdened as he was by the limp weight of his captive, he knew his chances of leaving Gerdak's cave were almost nonexistant.

But not once did the thought come to him of abandoning his catch—his only means of locating the route of those who held Dylara. With a single bound he was upon the man in his path; a supple twist of his body allowed the descending knife to slip harmlessly past. At the same instant he drove a hip into his attacker, who, off balance, was knocked headlong into two other warriors.

The way was clear now to the cave's mouth and Tharn was congratulating himself that he would at least reach open air when two more warriors dropped from above onto the narrow ledge of Gerdak's cave. Evidently they had been aroused by the chorus of yells and had come down from their caves to investigate.

At sight of their leveled spears Tharn skidded to a halt. Behind him he could hear at least two of Gerdak's personal guards moving cautiously forward to take him from the rear. With no avenue for retreat, with a pair of trained fighting men cutting off his advance, his chances for escape were thinned indeed.

Yet not for an instant did his confidence waver. He had weathered worse situations, and the muscles and cunning developed by a thousand jungle battles were weapons superior to the flint-headed spears hemming him in.

Even as he came to a halt, his sharp eyes caught a glimpse of that stack of spears he had passed when first entering the cave. One bronzed arm shot out, circled the lot of those keen-pointed sticks and lifted and flung them in one continuous motion.

The warriors outside were engulfed by the minor avalanche of flint and wood. They stepped back precipitantly, and one of the men was tripped up as a shaft slipped between his legs. With a shrill cry of terror he tottered momentarily on the brink of the ledge, then went over backwards, his despairing scream rising thinly on the night air.

Tharn had not waited to learn the outcome of his ruse. While the remaining warrior was attempting to sidestep the shower of spears the cave lord was upon him. Avoiding the flint point licking out at his naked chest, he ducked and swung his free fist in a savage arc that ended wrist deep in an unprotected belly.

Bent nearly double by the blow, the enemy Cro-Magnard was lifted completely from his feet and propelled into space, his already unconscious body tracing a perfect parabola to death on the ground sixty feet below.

ALTHOUGH no enemy stood before him, Tharn was a long way from safety. A spear thrown from the cave behind him passed scant inches from his head signifying Gardak's personal guards had recovered their wits and were after him once more. Below him a score of cave mouths were disgorging armed fighting men and flaming torches dotted the cliffside. To attempt to descend by the path that had brought him here was worse than foolhardy.

As in most Cro-Magnon settlements, the chief's own cave was nearest the cliff's top. A glance upward revealed to Tharn the escarpment's top not more than twenty feet distant. To swarm up that almost vertical slope while burdened with a body would have taxed the agility of little [Pg 74]Nobar, the monkey. But there was no other avenue of escape except to battle an entire community—and no time to compute chances for scaling those heights.

Already two warriors, each armed with a stone knife, had gained the ledge on either side of him, grins of triumph curling their lips, while a faint scuffling sound against the cave floor behind him told Tharn others were slinking toward him from the rear.

With a muffled snarl Tharn wheeled and began to climb. His groping fingers and toes found outcroppings of rock to serve as almost invisible rungs of a perilous ladder. A lifetime of climbing, plus utter self-confidence, sent him up that sheer surface with incredible speed.

So completely unexpected was their quarry's route that Gerdak's men were thrown into momentary confusion. By the time the first shower of spears rose toward the climbing cave man he was three-quarters of the way to freedom. As a result most of the weapons fell short of their mark, while the others, because of the uncertain light and the swiftness of their target's progress, missed completely. Immediately a second flight of spears were launched—but time had run out. Tharn was already over the lip of the precipice as they were rising in his direction.

He found himself on rolling, grass-covered ground. A hundred yards ahead was a jungle-cloaked forest, its towering trees close-knit to the point of impenetrability.

With long, loping strides Tharn crossed the ribbon of grassland, melting into the shadows of the overhanging branches as the first of Gerdak's warriors appeared at the cliff's top.

The ground was too choked with verdure for more than snail-like progress, and Tharn, his unconscious burden still draped across one broad shoulder, took to the trees. With a celerity that long ago had become second nature to him he raced through the branches, moving parallel to the strip of grassland he had crossed a few moments earlier. The shouts of his bewildered pursuers faded, swallowed up finally by the noises peculiar to a nocturnal jungle.

Half an hour later altered his course and returned to the ribbon of open ground. By this time his captive was showing signs of returning consciousness and Tharn tightened his grip on the youth's arm to prevent him from attempting to get away. He could feel tremors of fear course through the flesh pressing against his shoulder and he smiled grimly. A terrified prisoner was usually a tractable one.

At this point the cliffside was neither as steep nor as high as that housing Gerdak's tribe. Tharn went over its edge without hesitation, slipping groundward with the reckless abandon of a falling stone, yet landing there without an appreciable jar.

The forest at this point came almost to the base of the cliff. Tharn entered, swung lightly up to the middle terraces and set out on the return journey to that point opposite Gerdak's caves where he had left Trakor.

While he had still a goodly distance to go he heard the sounds of shouting voices and caught an occasional glimpse of a flaming torch through rifts in the foliage ahead. Evidently Gerdak was not lightly giving up hope of getting his hands on the man who had made fools of him and his warriors.

An unerring instinct developed through years of travel through uncharted terrains brought Tharn to the very tree where he had left his new found friend. But even as he entered its branches his nose told him what his eyes verified.

"Trakor," he called out, keeping his voice down lest some nearby enemy warrior hear it. "Trakor, where are [Pg 75]you?"

There was no answer. Trakor was gone.

EVEN as Sadu left the ground in a final leap aimed at crushing Dylara's fleeing figure to earth, the girl sprang for a low-hanging branch of a jungle giant. As her fingers closed about its rough bark she flung her body to one side, Sadu's cruel talons raking the air scant inches away.

Before the beast could turn and leap a second time she was twenty feet above it and climbing with the speed of desperation.

She heard the sound of tearing foliage as the lion sprang blindly into the lower branches, a thump as it toppled back to earth, then an angry roar of protest at being cheated of its prey. She stopped her climb then and leaned her head weakly against the bole, panting and shivering from strain and utter relief.

Below her, Sadu stalked back and forth a time or two, voicing his displeasure. This lasted for no more than a moment or two, however; Sadu was too much of a realist to waste time in bewailing his ill luck. The rumblings of satisfaction from his fellows as they bore their kills into the forest, the screams of dying men, told him there was food aplenty back among the fires.

Dylara caught a glimpse of the brute as it slunk swiftly toward the terrified encampment. She crouched there, watching the awful scenes of carnage while gradually her heart stopped its mad pounding and the trembling left her legs and arms. She knew regret that many of the men she had learned to know and respect were dying so horribly, but the sight of what went on did not affect her beyond that. Except for these last few moons all of her eighteen years had been spent practically cheek by jowl with the jungle and its denizens, the only life she had known. The fiercest animals had stalked her at times, just as the warriors of her father's tribe had stalked them. She knew first-hand the stinging insects, the loathsome snakes whose bite or coils could bring a lingering death or a quick one. She knew the chill nights of the rainy season, the unbearable heat and humidity at other times. As a result death and suffering were able to touch her deeply only when they affected some one close to her.

It was a kind of life that had its compensations. She was far more self-reliant and much better equipped for survival under her present circumstances than the average Ammadian would have been. Her eyes and ears were more sharply attuned to impending danger, she could climb far better, she knew how to find water where her recent companions would perish of thirst, she could distinguish between poisonous and non-poisonous fruits and roots.

Yet for all of that she was still a girl, young and, by jungle standards, weak. She caught herself wishing Tharn were with her—and even as the thought came she knew a fleeting doubt.

Did she love him? It was a question she was not yet able to answer. The memory of his handsome face and splendid body rose to torment her with doubt. She recalled him as he appeared in Sephar's arena facing insurmountable odds with a laugh and a careless toss of his black-thatched head, remembered his blazing eyes and rippling muscles as he plummeted to earth between her and charging Sadu, appearing just in time to stave in the lion's skull with one terrible blow. In all the jungle, in all the world, there was no man a tenth his equal in cunning, strength and courage! Even among his own kind he was unique; for no man in Cro-Magnon history could use his nose the way the beasts used theirs, no man who could travel among the trees with the rock[Pg 76]eting agility of little Nobar, the monkey.

If only he had met and wooed and won her instead of seizing her by force and carrying her away like some bit of jungle loot! Pride and the awareness of her position as daughter of a tribal chief could not permit her to surrender to a man who would do such a thing. It was the way the Hairy Men* won their mates, and Dylara, daughter of Majok, must give her heart, not have it taken!

* The Hairy Men was the Cro-Magnards' name for Neanderthal Man. The Neanderthalers appeared in Earth's prehistory roughly 100,000 years before the birth of Christ and centered in Southern France and Spain of today. At the time of the Cro-Magnards' arrival, perhaps 80,000 years later, Neanderthal Man was nearly extinct, possibly because of climatic changes due to the recession of the last Ice Age. Cro-Magnon Man, the first of *Homo Sapiens* (true men), regarded these ape-like subhumans as little more than beasts and eventually exterminated them.—Ed.]

EVEN as she told herself this for the hundredth time, she realized such thoughts were probably empty. The chances were overwhelming that Tharn had not survived the rigors of the Sepharian Games: battles between men and between men and beasts for the entertainment of Sephar's populace and held in honor of the God-Whose-Name-May-Not-Be-Spoken-Aloud. Jotan and the others had told her many times that no man in all Sephar's history had ever come through those Games alive.

And even if he should! Would he undertake to follow her across the almost limitless stretch of plains, mountains and jungles to the country of Ammad? Even if he should accomplish such a feat—how could he hope to wrest her from the depths of a stronghold as impenetrable as she understood Ammad to be?

No, it was unthinkable. She had best wait until the lions were driven from the encampment below, then slip from her tree and go back to Jotan. Since the day he had won her from Sephar's high priest he had treated her with unfailing courtesy and kindness, declaring over and over his love for her but not once attempting to force his attentions upon her. After a little while she might allow herself to be won over into accepting him as her mate. It would be an honored, sheltered life and in time she might know complete happiness.

Dylara was shaking her head even as these last thoughts were crowding in. No. Her place was with her own kind, with Majok and the others. It was a long, long way back to them and in the attempt she might leave her bones to bleach on some mountain top or disappear down the maw of one of the great cats. But there was no other acceptable choice—and no time like the present to get started.

Carefully she began to work her way into the jungle, moving cautiously far out on a strong limb until she was able to clamber into the branches of the next tree. The curtain of greenery was too thick for the light of moon or stars to penetrate, leaving her to grope her way in utter darkness. Each vine she scraped against was pictured in her mind as the sinuous coils of Sleeza, the snake; each fluttering of a disturbed bird was an aroused panther or leopard.

She was not going on this way much farther; her nerves, steady as they were, could not take much of such suspense. Only deep enough into the jungle to keep the inexperienced Ammadians from following her trail; with the coming of Dyta, the sun, she would locate a game trail pointing in the direction she wished to go, then descend to the ground and follow it.

An hour later her trembling limbs refused to continue this inch-by-inch progress. And so Dylara made her way toward the high flung branches of a forest patriarch to where Jalok, the panther, and Tarlok, the leopard,[Pg 77]dare not go. Here the foliage was less compact and Uda's pale beams displayed to her rapt eyes an endless sea of tree tops everywhere about her.

Finding a comfortable fork fully a hundred feet above the jungle floor, Dylara composed herself to wait the coming of dawn. Finally she drifted off to sleep, while far below a lion roared that he had made his kill and filled his belly for the night.

And not long after, a jungle dweller, swinging swiftly through the trees, came to a sudden halt on a swaying branch as a vagrant breeze brought the scent of her to its quivering nostrils. For a full minute it remained motionless as if carved from stone, then it turned sharply aside and went on, fairly flying along the dizzy pathway of swaying boughs, following that scent spoor to its source.

WHILE Tharn was puzzling over the strange disappearance of Trakor, his keen ears caught a sudden yell of surprise from the direction of Gerdak's caves, followed by a chorus of exultant exclamations that told him the Cro-Magnards had flushed some sort of game and had succeeded in bringing it down.

Quickly he lowered his captive to a broad branch, stuffed a handful of leaves into its mouth, bound them there with a short length of vine, then lashed the wrists to the tree bole. This done he was on the point of swinging off to investigate what lay behind those sounds when he caught a glimpse of a familiar object swinging from a neighboring branch.

His blackwood bow and quiver of arrows left earlier with Trakor! With them in their accustomed places along his back and shoulder, Tharn swung the short distance between tree and clearing. From a wide branch he gazed down at the scene below.

A knot of enemy warriors was moving slowly toward the caves of Gerdak, among them the still struggling figure of Trakor. Wavering flames of resin-wood torches lighted up his features and Tharn saw there was only rage in his expression and nothing of fear. Already shouts from the group had aroused others of the tribe and a score of them were running forward to meet it.

With quick, certain movements of his powerful hands Tharn unshipped his bow and withdrew several arrows from his quiver. Steadying himself on the swaying branch, he notched an arrow, drew back the stubborn wood, steel muscles moving under his naked back, took careful aim....

"Twang!"

Like a plucked violin the bow sang his single note, polished wood flickered in the light of torches and one of Trakor's captors threw wide his arms and sank into a briefly twitching heap. Before his fellows could grasp the significance of what was taking place three more of their number were down, each with a thin-bodied arrow protruding from his chest or back.

There was a general scrambling as those holding Trakor released him and threw themselves headlong to escape the rain of death. The advancing wave of warriors halted with breathtaking abruptness, those behind the front rank crashing into it. Momentarily freed, Trakor looked wildly about him, as confused as the others.

"Run!" shouted Tharn. "Into the jungle, Trakor!"

The youth heard—and obeyed. As he broke into a run, one of Gerdak's fighting men, either more courageous than his companions or angered beyond reason at losing their prize, scrambled to his feet and lifted his spear for a cast at the flying figure.

Again Tharn's bow twanged and a tufted arrow appeared magically embedded in the spearman's chest. Voicing a piercing shriek he toppled back, spear rolling from his fingers.

Tharn was already among the low[Pg 78]er branches of a tree when Trakor came crashing into the jungle. As the boy plowed past, the cave lord reached down with one arm and caught him under the arms, lifting him to the branch beside him before the youngster was fully aware of what was happening.

"Tharn!" It was a gasp of such utter relief that the giant Cro-Magnard smiled.

"I thought I left you safe in a tree," he said.

"I meant to stay there, Tharn," Trakor admitted sheepishly, "but I heard one of them shout to the others that you had been captured and was being held in Gerdak's cave. I thought that because of the darkness I might pass among them without being recognized, reach the chief's cave and in some way set you free."

"You could never have done it." Tharn's voice was stern, revealing nothing of his inner feelings. He was more deeply touched by this evidence of loyalty than he cared to admit. For this untrained boy to pit his relatively puny muscles against an entire community in an effort to rescue his benefactor was proof enough that here was material for the shaping of a great warrior; and with this thought Tharn's last remaining reluctance to be saddled with Trakor during the search for Dylara disappeared.

THE warriors of Gerdak appeared to have recovered their courage; already several of them were entering the jungle in search of Trakor and the mysterious bowman. Two of them passed cautiously beneath the very tree in which their quarry was seated. Tharn touched his own lips in warning, pointed up at the branches overhead, then lifted the youth to his back and climbed in perfect silence to where he had left the captive Roban.

In the dim light Tharn could see the whites of rolling, fear-filled eyes and beads of perspiration dotting the receding forehead. A muffled chattering pushed through the wad of leaves and the prisoner shrank away as far as the vines binding his wrists to the tree would permit.

The cave lord was undecided as to his next step. He dared not remove the gag from Roban's lips and question him here. A single shout would bring Gerdak's men to the scene; and while this would mean little if any danger to Tharn and his new-found companion, it could mean he might lose the services of Roban as involuntary guide.

The alternative was to carry Roban deeper into the jungle where he might be questioned without interruption, but Tharn knew that Trakor could not hope to follow through the tree tops.

There was but one answer: he must carry both of them. Quickly he loosened Roban's bonds and swung him lightly across one shoulder, then turned to Trakor.

"Lock your arms about my neck," he said.

There was wonder and doubt in Trakor's expression as understanding came to him. But such was his faith and confidence that he did not hesitate to comply with the order.

And once more Trakor, heart in his mouth, rode the skyway. Where before the awful depths had sent cold fear to his core, he was now confident and unafraid; yet actually the danger of plunging earthward was far greater this time. Bough after bough bent perilously beneath their triple burden as Tharn threaded his way, like a tightrope artist, along them, held erect only by his uncanny sense of balance. Constantly he was forced to search out branches of sufficient strength, stepping out and onto them without the additional safety of a steadying hand hold.

Fifteen minutes of this was enough to satisfy him he was beyond any territory Gerdak's warriors would reach before dawn. The search would go on, [Pg 79]of course, until Roban, dead or alive, was found; for he was son of a chief and not lightly to be abandoned.

Near the pinnacle of a towering tree Tharn lowered his two passengers to adjoining branches. While Trakor watched, he removed Roban's gag, after warning him to utter no outcry on pain of instant death. The youth nodded violently in agreement, and for a moment he was unable to speak so cramped were his jaws.

Tharn glanced to where Trakor sat, an interested spectator to Roban's discomfiture. "This is the chief's son?"

Trakor nodded. "He is Roban."

Tharn turned his sharp eyes to the captive, who was glowering at him in mingled fear and hatred, and said:

"A few suns ago you saw a party of Ammadians scaling the cliffs near your caves. Exactly where was this?"

Roban scowled unpleasantly. "I don't know what you are talking about."

"You know well enough. Answer me or die!"

"You would not dare kill me," Roban blustered. "I am Gerdak's son. Unless you let me go at once he will come with many warriors and hunt you down. He will kill you, but not quickly. First he will take his knife and...."

He broke off suddenly, gasping as Tharn's fingers bit into his skinny shoulder. "I, too, can use a knife! Answer my questions quickly or I will prove it to you!"

Roban licked dry lips. "What do you want to know?" he mumbled.

"The exact spot where the Ammadians climbed those cliffs."

"What are Ammadians?"

THARN described them in a few words and Roban nodded grudgingly. "Yes, I saw them. There is a place in the cliffs, a sun's march to the west of my father's caves, where a river tumbles over the edge. It was there they climbed the cliffs."

"He is lying!" Trakor exclaimed. "At the cooking fires he said it was east of our caves."

Roban's small eyes, evil and ratlike, swung toward him. "Your mother was a hyena! Wait till my father gets his hands——"

Tharn shook him until his teeth rattled. "Where?" he growled. "The truth this time or I throw you to a lion!"

The words tumbled out. "Half a march to the west. There is a low point in the cliff there, making it easy to climb. They are not good climbers; it took them a long time to——"

"Were there shes with them?"

"Shes?" The youth's beady eyes flickered. "I—I cannot say. I did not see——"

Tharn shook him again. "Enough of your lies!" he thundered. "How many shes were with them?"

"T-t-two." Roban was thoroughly frightened now. "I saw no others, although there may have——"

"Describe them."

"One had black hair; the other's hair was the color of Dyta, the sun, as he seeks his lair for the night. Both were very beautiful, although the black-haired she was less beautiful."

Tharn's chest swelled with elation. At last he had found the trail of Dylara and those who held her. He was eager to be on his way, flying through the trees to wrest her from the Ammadians. They were only five suns ahead—a distance he could cover in a quarter that time....

His gray eyes went to where Trakor sat watching him. As those eyes met his, the youth smiled. "The golden-haired one must be Dylara," he said. "Your search is nearly ended, Tharn. Hurry on to her."

The cave lord caught the faint note of sadness in the young man's voice and his admiration for the lad went still higher. Even as he was urging Tharn to go on without him it was [Pg 80]with the knowledge that were the cave lord to do so it would mean Trakor's doom. Trakor could not now return to the caves of Gerdak without being slain on sight; yet to remain alone in the jungle would mean certain death.

Tharn rose to his feet on a swaying branch, light from the moon picking out his slow smile. "Come, Trakor," he said. "We must reach that point at the cliff before dawn."

Trakor offered a protest. "But I will only slow——"

In reply Tharn picked him bodily from the branch and placed him across his shoulder, hearing the young man's sigh of relief as he did so.

"But what about me?" cried Roban. "You can not leave me here!"

Tharn looked at him in simulated surprise. "Have you forgotten? Your father is coming with many warriors to hunt me down. You, yourself, have said so. Wait for them here."

"But Tarlok may find and eat me!"

"Even Tarlok does not stoop to carrion," Tharn pointed out. Before Gerdak's son could reply, Tharn and Trakor were gone into the inky depths below.

CHAPTER VI
JALTOR'S DECISION

KNUCKLES pounding heavily against his door awakened Garlud, nobleman of Ammad. There was an urgency in the sound that brought him bolt upright from his pillow in alarm.

"Who's there?" he called out.

"Open!" thundered a heavy voice. "Open in the name of Jaltor of Ammad!"

26

Hardly able to believe his ears Garlud left his bed and groped for the brazier of coals kept in one corner of the room. Igniting a tallow-soaked bit of cloth from it, he lighted two of the room's candles, crossed to the door and unbarred it.

Four stalwart warriors wearing the tunics of Jaltor's personal guard pushed into the room, leaving Garlud's major-domo, who had brought them there, hovering anxiously outside. At sight of the latter's worried face Garlud smiled a reassurance he was far from feeling and said, "Return to your bed, Bokut. I will see my visitors to the door when they are ready to leave."

He closed the door on Bokut's unrelieved expression and turned to Jaltor's men. One of them he recognized immediately as Curzad, captain of the king's guard, whose strong intelligent face was set in grim lines.

"Well, Curzad," Garlud said lightly, "your expression is forboding enough to put fear in the bravest of men. What errand brings you here?"

"My master's respects, noble Garlud," the captain replied woodenly, "and he bids me escort you to the palace at once."

"Does it require four of you to help me find my way to Jaltor's palace?" Garlud demanded, his voice suddenly sharp.

The captain's face seemed even bleaker. "I obey my orders, noble Garlud. I must ask you to don clothing at once and come with us."

For a moment it seemed that Garlud was about to refuse ... then a slight smile crooked the corners of his mouth and he turned to take up his tunic. He slipped into the garment without haste, drew the strings of his sandals tight about his ankles, then straightened.

"I am ready," he said.

IT was a cold, forbidding room, its walls, ceiling and floor of bare roughened gray stone, and located deep beneath the palace of Jaltor, supreme ruler of all Ammad. Against the far wall was a narrow bed occupied by the naked body of an elderly man. It was a body thin to the point of emaciation, the ribs standing out [Pg 81]sharp and distinct beneath yellowing skin. Two middle-aged men, their expressions grave, were gingerly applying liquid-soaked cloths against scorched blotches covering the naked man's chest. The man himself appeared to be in a comatose state, although from time to time he groaned and stirred feverishly under the attempts to soothe his suffering.

There was another man in the room—a man of such appearance that he dominated it through his physical dimensions alone. In height he was a full seven inches beyond six feet, yet built proportionately so that he did not seem that tall. His wide shoulders seemed to fill the room, his body sloping to narrow hips and long powerful legs. His face was almost startlingly handsome, with a fierce regal cast to its large, sharp-lined features. Chill black eyes of exceptional brilliance burned from beneath heavy black brows that matched the thick, slightly curling growth above a high rounded forehead. It was the face of a man of strength and intelligence, a man ruthless and proud and yet who could be given to quixotic acts of kindness, a man dictatorial but usually just, a man incapable of brooking interference.

He was pacing the room now with quick restless strides, badly restrained anger riding his expression. Once a quick turn caused him to brush against one of four stools grouped about a wooden table set on four crossed timbers, and he kicked the stool viciously aside causing it to shatter against the wall.

At the sound of splintering wood the man on the bed cried out in such utter fear that his two attendants fell back. He did not appear fully conscious however and they resumed their attempts to ease his pain.

That cry of fear had altered the pacing of the tall man momentarily and he turned his burning eyes on the men at the bedside. "Is he awake?" he asked sharply, his deep voice beating against the walls like surf against a rocky shore.

One of the attendants shook his head nervously. "Not yet, Most-High. But soon now, I think. He is old and weak and the burns are grievous."

"Time is short and he must not die—yet."

"Yes, noble Jaltor."

Again there was silence within the room, broken only by the mutterings of the half-conscious man and the heavy tread of feet as Jaltor resumed his pacing....

A brief knock at the room's only door brought Jaltor around sharply. "Enter!" he thundered.

The door opened and four guards came in. With them was a trim figured man a few years short of middle-age, his strong regular features impassive. As his escort halted he continued on into the room, pausing only when he stood facing Ammad's monarch.

"Greetings, noble Jaltor," he said quietly. "You sent for me?"

27

Anger and bewildered sorrow seemed to be fighting for dominance in the ruler's expression. "I thought you my friend, Garlud!" he burst out suddenly. "How could a senseless ambition so drive you that you would turn against your king?"

The blood seemed to drain from Garlud's cheeks and his eyes went wide in shocked wonder. "Turn against you?" he repeated, aghast. "What madness is this?"

Jaltor's eyes narrowed and a sneer curled his upper lip. "Before you add lies upon lies, Garlud, give greetings to a friend of yours."

With these words the king stepped aside, for the first time permitting Garlud to see the man on the bed.

The nobleman's jaw dropped. "Why, it's old Heglar!" he exclaimed. "What in the God's name has happened to him?"

"What usually happens to enemies [Pg 82]of Jaltor?"

GARLUD took a deep breath and let it out slowly. "You have spoken in riddles from the moment I came in here. For almost forty summers—since we were boys together—we have been more like brothers than friends. For that reason, if no other, I believe I am entitled to an explanation instead of badgering and half-veiled threats."

Jaltor's face darkened. "I'm the one who demands an explanation! Why did you set Heglar to attempt my life this afternoon?"

"I—set...."

"Do you deny," thundered the king, "that this very morning you held a long and carefully guarded conversation with Heglar in an ante-room outside my audience hall?"

"It is true that I spoke with him this morning," Garlud said slowly. "We did not talk for long, nor were we 'guarded' about it."

"I see!" Jaltor's tone was triumphant. "And what did the two of you talk about?"

"He sought me out as I entered the room on my way to the audience chamber. He drew me into a corner and asked if I had had word from Jotan, my son, recently. I told him I had not, but that I expected him to return within half a moon, perhaps even sooner."

Understanding dawned suddenly in Garlud's face and he added: "I wondered then why he drew me aside to ask the question, but at the time I thought little about it."

"And now?" Jaltor urged mockingly.

"I am beginning to see he had a reason of his own."

"You deny any part in the plot to kill me?"

"I do."

"But you knew there was such an attempt made this afternoon?"

"I heard some such rumor."

"But," persisted Jaltor, "you did not think it necessary that you learn if your friend—your *brother*, as you said a moment ago—had been injured in that attempt?"

"I was assured you were not even scratched," Garlud replied quietly.

"Humph!" Jaltor paced up and down a time or two, his face working, the great hands opening and closing spasmodically. Abruptly he stopped in front of the other and bent until his face almost touched Garlud's.

"Before you walked into this room, if anyone had asked for your opinion of Heglar what would you have said?"

"That I knew him well and liked and respected him."

"Would you have said he was an honorable man?"

"Certainly."

"Have you ever known him to tell a lie?"

"Not to my knowledge."

"Does he have any reason to hate you?"

"None that I know of."

"Have you any idea why he tried to kill me?"

"None. I am completely surprised that he tried to do so."

"Then why," Jaltor thundered suddenly, "did he say his attempt to kill me was engineered by *you*?"

Garlud met his angry glare without visible emotion. "I can hardly be expected to answer that question, Most-High, since this is the first I have heard of such a charge."

"Then Heglar lied in so naming you?"

"He—is mistaken."

Jaltor snorted. "Don't bandy words with me! When one man says he talked with another about killing a third, he cannot be *mistaken*. He is either telling the truth or lying. Which is it, in this case?"

28

"If Heglar's mind was clear at the time he so accused me, then he lied!"

"But my good Garlud," cried Jaltor, his reasoning tone a mockery, "you[Pg 83]told me only a moment ago that to your knowledge Heglar is an honorable man and does not tell lies."

"Then it must be," Garlud said, openly serene, "that he has started to tell them now. Either that or his mind has become affected by his disease. It is common knowledge that there is a sickness in his throat and he has only a few moons of life remaining."

JALTOR turned on his heel and began his pacing anew. The four guards remained stiffly at attention near the door, their eyes fixed unseeingly on the opposite wall, their ears obviously hearing none of this. Against the far wall the two attendants continued their unceasing efforts to bring consciousness and comfort to the old man on the bed.

Without pausing in his pacing, Jaltor said, his voice more subdued now: "It is useless to throw doubt on Heglar's sanity, noble Garlud. After his bungling attempt on my life I questioned him. He told me it was his own idea to take my life, that no one else had anything to do with it. Over and over he said that, even when my questions called for no such answer, until I began to suspect he was trying to shield an accomplice. When I charged him with this he became so upset I was sure he lied. So I had my guards torture him into telling the truth. That is when he named you."

"A man will say anything to escape torture, Most-High," Garlud pointed out calmly.

"Do you think I'm not aware of that?" growled the monarch. "It was not until he endured torture I doubt I could have stood up under that he gave your name."

"Naturally, in view of our long friendship, I thought he was lying. I ordered further torture to bring out the truth. Again and again he lost consciousness under the white-hot iron, and each time we revived him he gave your name. Finally I was convinced despite my reluctance. I then sent for you to hear the charge from Heglar's own lips."

Garlud shook his head. "I cannot believe that you would so easily turn against me, my friend. One man's unsupported word—and you believe the worst of me."

Jaltor's expression did not soften. "A word wrung from a man after long torture, noble Garlud, carries beyond ordinary denial."

"Would you wish to put me to the same test?" Garlud asked grimly.

"No. You are comparatively young and a brave man. Should you will yourself to deny Heglar's charge, no amount of physical suffering would wring a confession from you."

"Your pardon, Most-High." It was one of the men at the bedside who spoke. "The man is conscious now, but I fear he is dying."

"Good." Jaltor motioned to his erstwhile friend. "Come, Garlud, hear these things from the man's own lips."

They approached the bed, the two attendants falling back respectfully. From the narrow surface Heglar looked up at them, his faded blue eyes glazed with pain, his rib-ridged chest rising and falling with shallow, uneven breathing. The smell of burned flesh came from his body in sickening emanations and his lips were torn where he had bitten them in agony.

Jaltor said stonily, "I have brought the noble Garlud here to listen to your charges, Heglar. Now accuse him or clear his name!"

The faded blue eyes flickered to the erect figure of the other man. It was not until the third effort that he was able to speak.

"I failed, Garlud." The words were barely audible. "Forgive me, my friend. They ... made me tell. I am ... old. Once they would not ... have been able...."

Compassion came into Garlud's expression. "Heglar, Heglar," he said softly. "You know I had nothing to [Pg 84]do with your attempt to kill Jaltor. What have I done to you that makes you say this awful thing about me?"

Was there a flicker of remorse in those faded blue eyes? If so, it was gone before Garlud could be sure. "It ... is useless, Garlud," the feeble voice whispered. "I had to ... tell him."

"You are dying, Heglar." Sweat stood out on Garlud's forehead. "Would you face the God-Whose-Name-May-Not-Be-Spoken-Aloud with a lie upon your lips?"

"I ... I——"

The noble's hand closed on the old man's shoulder. "The truth, Heglar! Who is the real one behind this?"

The aged eyes closed and Heglar's face began to work. "No! No! I have ... no——"

"You must tell us, Heglar! Speak, man!"

Once more the lips opened. "I—I ... Rhoa!"

Abruptly Heglar's head rolled to one side, his body went limp and with his mate's name on his lips he died.

FOR a long moment there was silence within the room. Garlud stood as though turned to stone, his eyes fastened unbelievably on the lifeless face of the old man. It was a tortured face; death had brought peace to it. What terrible compulsion, Garlud wondered dully, had forced an honorable man to die with a lie upon his lips?

"You have heard, noble Garlud?"

It was Jaltor's deep voice—stern, unflinching, empty of feeling. Garlud looked up into those piercing black eyes and despite himself he felt a tiny chill move along his spine.

"I heard, Most-High."

Jaltor passed a hand over his own face—a slow pressing gesture that momentarily left the skin white beneath its tan. "For the sake of our long friendship," he said thickly, "I am prepared to temper justice with mercy. Admit your part in the plot and I will spare your life. Although," he added, "I will leave you nothing else. Your wealth is confiscate, your palace will go to the noble next in line, as is our custom, and you shall be turned from Ammad. Your king has spoken!"

"And if I persist in my claim of innocence?" Garlud said evenly.

"The evidence is plain. You will be put to death."

"Very well." Garlud did not hesitate. "Order your guards to kill me then, my friend! I shall die as honorably as I lived during the years when we were friends."

Jaltor's jaw hardened. "And what of Jotan?" he said coldly.

Something akin to fear darkened Garlud's eyes. "My son? What of him? Surely your sense of justice has not so rotted that you would harm him!"

Sudden rage twisted Jaltor's countenance. "No man speaks so to Jaltor of Ammad and lives!"

Garlud's smile was undismayed. "Have you forgotten, Most-High. I have already been sentenced to death!"

"And by your attitude," Jaltor shouted, "you have sentenced your son to the same fate."

"On what grounds?"

"I need no grounds! I know your son, noble Garlud. When he hears that you are dead and that it was my order, he will attempt to avenge you. I know the love he holds for you, and it will be that mistaken loyalty which will lead him into an attempt to assassinate me. Your power is great in Ammad, Garlud; I helped you gain that power because you were my friend. Because you have won the affection and respect of many warriors they would rise to his leadership against me. All Ammad might be torn by civil war. For that reason Jotan must die!"

Garlud's face was livid with rage [Pg 85]and his hands were trembling. "Then kill us both, you son of Gubo. You have become a fearful, evil old man who hides from shadows and who fears all men—even his friends! Kill us both that we may not pollute our lungs with the air you breathe!"

WITH an almost casual sweep of his mighty arm Jaltor hurled the raging nobleman into the grasp of the guards. "Confine him to the lowest pit beneath the palace!" he thundered. "Let the rats chew him a few suns before I have him torn to bits!"

Without a backward glance the king strode from the room. He made his way up flight after flight of steps, through room after room of the sleeping palace, until he reached his own wing. Through several long, winding corridors he moved, oblivious to the salutes of startled guards on night duty, until he entered his private apartment. He went directly to his sleeping quarters, curtly ordered his two personal slaves into the next room, then undressed quickly and got into bed.

But not to sleep. For over an hour he tossed on the huge bed wooing sleep that would not come. Finally he rose, drew a richly woven robe about his shoulders and stepped out onto a small balcony overlooking one entire half of the vast city six floors below.

The rays of a full moon bathed the impressive scene. Because of the lateness of the hour no lights gleamed from windows of the box-like buildings and the broad streets were deserted.

Slowly reason was beginning to take hold of him as anger faded. Was Garlud correct in saying that he was becoming an old man fleeing from shadows, suspicious of all men? He went back over the golden days when he and Garlud were young warriors taking their first taste of battle against the then scattered states that today made up the country of Ammad. He recalled the day Garlud had saved his life by leaping in front of him and taking the tearing impact of a thrown spear. Garlud had very nearly died of that wound and he—Jaltor—had remained day and night at his bedside until the crisis passed.

And that was the man he had sentenced to death! The man whose friendship had meant more to him than all his kingdom. Surely personal ambition alone could not have driven him into plotting the assassination of his best friend!

30

There was something behind all this that did not meet the eye. Had the would-be assassin been anyone other than old Heglar he would have dismissed his involvement of Garlud as a trumped up lie and executed the man on the spot.

Had Heglar lied? Was there some motivation so strong that the old man had been forced into bearing false witness against one of the most loved noblemen in all Ammad? Was all this some intricate plot, with Garlud instead of Jaltor as the real victim?

Jaltor, stern, ruthless and high-handed though he was, was a man with ideals and a strong sense of honor. Also, he was extremely intelligent and a veteran of the machinations of intrigue. The more he thought about this whole business the more certain he was that all the facts were not yet revealed.

For a long time he stood there on the small balcony, staring out over Ammad with unseeing eyes. After a while a slow smile came to his strong lips and he nodded his head a time or two in satisfaction. There was a way....

Leaving the balcony he strode quickly to the room's single door and threw it wide. "Quick!" he snapped to one of the startled slaves, "tell Curzad I want him here at once!"

When the captain of the guards, as [Pg 86]alert and bright-eyed as though he had not been dragged from a sound sleep by Jaltor's summons, appeared in the doorway the king bade him enter and close the door.

"Curzad," he said, "you have known the noble Garlud almost as long as I have. Does it seem likely to you that he would be mixed up in a plot to kill me?"

The iron-faced warrior shook his head impassively. "No, Most-High. His love and respect for you are beyond doubt."

"You think I acted unwisely in finding him guilty?"

"That is not for me to say, Most-High."

"I *know* that! But you are not made of stone; you must have formed some opinion."

"It is not wise to hold an opinion which differs from that of Ammad's king."

JALTOR gestured with sharp impatience. "This is man to man, Curzad. Give me your honest impressions of this affair."

"If you command it, Most-High. I do not believe the noble Garlud had anything to do with old Heglar's attempt to knife you. I think the old one hated Garlud for some reason and named him because of that hatred."

"But you knew Heglar's reputation as a completely truthful man?"

"I do not say he would lie for another's purpose. But for his own ... that is a different matter."

"But he did not give Garlud's name willingly, Curzad. Only after prolonged torture could we wrest the name from his lips."

The captain shrugged. "Would you for even a moment have believed him otherwise. Old Heglar was no fool, Most-High. Were his motive strong enough for bringing ruin to Garlud he would have planned it exactly that way. An accusation lightly given is usually lightly taken."

Jaltor smote a fist into his palm. "By the God, Curzad, I believe you've hit it! Only my thought is that the plan was not his. When a man hates another both are usually aware of that hatred—and Garlud was at a complete loss to understand why he was accused."

"That is true, Most-High."

"Very well, here's what must be done." Jaltor began to pace the floor, speaking the while. "I want you to speak with the guards who were with you when I questioned Garlud tonight. Swear them to complete secrecy on the entire matter on pain of death. The same goes for the two attendants who were working over Heglar at the time."

"It shall be done, Most-High."

"Good! Now who in Garlud's household knows you brought him here?"

"We encountered only Bokut, his chief steward, and two guards—one at an outer gate and one stationed at his palace entrance."

"Very well, take those three into custody. Question them as to whom they told of the incident and place *those* under arrest as well. Leave no one who can spread word that Garlud was brought to the palace at my orders."

"You see what I'm getting at, Curzad? Let us say there is someone whose identity we do not know at the bottom of this plot against Garlud. Heglar makes his clumsy attempt at killing me and fails according to plan. I order him tortured to learn the names of others involved. He gives me Garlud's name."

"Now, if I believe the charge, Garlud is arrested and executed, and the mysterious someone is satisfied. But if I do not believe the charge Garlud remains free, and this unknown person must try again or give up and the matter is never solved."

"But say Garlud simply disappears without anyone knowing what's become of him. Has he learned of what [Pg 87]was in store for him and gone into hiding, trying the while to learn who is responsible for his plight? Or have I executed him secretly? Is Heglar still alive and in a position to eventually expose the true culprit?"

"The man we want is going to have to get answers to those questions, Curzad. He'll use great care at first; but when each effort meets a blank wall he'll become increasingly desperate. Desperate men make false moves, Curzad—then is when we'll have him!"

The captain nodded expressionlessly but there was a gleam of admiration in his deep-set eyes. "And what of Garlud himself, Most-High? Shall I have him removed from the pits and placed in more comfortable quarters?"

Jaltor pulled thoughtfully at his lower lip. "N-no, I think not. Let him stew there awhile. I am not giving up my suspicions of him entirely, Curzad; old Heglar's dying statement can not be utterly disregarded until we have proof he was lying."

"And should Jotan, his son, return from Sephar while his father languishes in the pits?"

The king nodded. "I have thought of that. It may be necessary to take him and his men into custody before they reach the city itself. It would defeat my purpose were he allowed to enter Ammad and start hunting for his father. On the other hand I cannot arrest him openly; it would tell our mysterious enemy more than I want him to know."

"Let us wait a few suns to decide that, Curzad. We have the time; Jotan and his men are not due for half a moon yet. If our real quarry has not revealed himself in, say, seven suns, I shall send you and a detachment of guards out to intercept Jotan."

CHAPTER VII
THE SPIDER MEN

DYLARA awakened with a convulsive start as the lofty branch upon which she had been sleeping swayed and bent beneath suddenly added weight.

As she started up, a scream rising to her lips, hands reached out of the night's impenetrable curtain and tore her roughly from where she sat. Instinctively she attempted to struggle free, only to receive a buffet alongside the head that left her limp and only half conscious.

Her first impression was that one of the great apes, occasionally glimpsed among the more impenetrable reaches of jungle, had seized her; for she could feel coarse long hair matting its chest and arms. Even as the thought sent her heart sinking with fear and loathing, she knew she was mistaken, since the creature's body was much too slender, its arms too thin and frail to belong to one of the bulky anthropoids.

That she was in deadly peril Dylara did not doubt, but not to know the form such peril took was inconceivably worse. It was this, fear of the unknown that crystallized her determination to break from this stifling embrace or die in the attempt; and she was gathering her strength for the effort when her captor suddenly whirled about on the narrow branch and, with her across his back, dived headlong into space!

The shock was too much for human nerves. Dylara voiced a single scream and her senses fled under the lash of pure panic.

She came back to reality to find she was being borne through the trees with incredible speed. Now and then a vine flicked against her shivering body or leaves brushed against her face, and several times the thing carrying her leaped outward through space that seemed boundless, only to[Pg 88]land lightly upon a swaying branch in another tree.

Even Tharn, she realized, could not have matched the creature's amazing agility, for it was using both hand and feet with equal dexterity after the manner of little Nobar, the monkey.

Gradually, as the likelihood of being dashed to earth seemed more and more remote, Dylara began to think once more of escape. The time was not now, of course; she could only cling desperately to her captor's thin shoulders and wait for this breathless journey to end. Eventually those wiry muscles must tire and the creature stop—then she would make her bid for freedom.

Abruptly and without slackening its pace the hairy thing uttered a piercing shriek like nothing Dylara had ever heard before. Twice more the awful sound rang out; and then, far ahead, came an answering cry faint and wavering.

Instantly the creature put on an added burst of speed, rocketing through the branches in dizzying bounds that threatened to tear away Dylara's none too certain hold. So swift was the pace now that within a few minutes a wide clearing loomed ahead and her captor began to slip groundward.

Suddenly the hairy creature halted on a wide limb bordering the clearing as a host of shadowy forms rose around him. There was not enough light for Dylara to make use of her eyes but she sensed these were the figures of creatures similar to the one which held her.

They chattered shrilly among themselves in a completely unfamiliar tongue for several moments, then all of them moved ahead a short distance until the clearing itself was reached.

Dylara was expecting the entire party to descend to the ground. But instead they began to climb higher and higher. At last the one carrying her came to a halt well within the embrace of a jungle patriarch; and at that moment Uda, the moon, appeared from behind a cloud and poured her silver rays into the clearing.

FOR the first time since her capture she was able to see well enough to distinguish objects. She was surrounded by a group of some ten or twelve man-like beings—but beings like nothing she had ever dreamed of!

All were well over six feet in height, but so thin in body they seemed much taller. All were naked except for girdles of grass about their hips, the rest of their bodies being covered with monkey-like hair. Their arms and legs were incredibly long and thin, their toes long and prehensile. Each face was hairless and almost perfectly round, containing small beady eyes, a brief blob of nose, a tiny lipless mouth and almost no chin at all. It was more the face of some particularly repellent insect—a comparison that leaped to Dylara's mind at sight of the long hairy limbs, the thin torsos pinched in deeply at the waist and the quick, jerky way in which they moved restlessly about her.

The one holding her let her slide from its back and the others moved closer, reaching out to pluck at her tunic with abnormally long nailless fingers, their voices like the rising skirl of an insect swarm.

Angrily she pushed away the exploring fingers. "Who are you?" she cried, "and what do you want of me?"

One of the things, evidently angered at being repulsed, snaked out a long arm and caught her roughly about the waist, dragging her to him. Instantly the one that had brought her here leaped upon the intruder, nearly sweeping Dylara from her precarious footing on the branch. For an instant the pair clawed frantically at each other, but their companions [Pg 89]pushed between them and broke up the battle.

The incident seemed to touch off a long and heated discussion, during which Dylara was apparently forgotten. They stood in a tight knot among the branches, their ridiculous faces pushed together in almost a solid lump, while their keening voices went on and on with a monotonous kind of intensity.

A slow-moving cloud stole across Uda's shining face, plunging the scene into heavy darkness. Dylara felt sudden hope leap in her breast. Surely they were too intent with their arguing to notice her if she slipped away! Besides, how could even the keenest eye pierce the blackness of a jungle night?

She took a slow step away from them, balancing herself lightly on the broad bough. Another—and still another. The high-pitched debate went on in full volume.

Cautiously she lowered herself to a branch immediately below, then waited with pounding heart to learn if her move had been detected.

Nothing had changed! She bent again ... and from nowhere a sinuous arm slithered out of the blackness, caught her about the middle and jerked her back and into the group.

The discussion appeared to be ended. One of the creatures swept the cave girl into his embrace and continued to climb toward the stars, leaving his companions where they were.

A solid mass of foliage loomed suddenly in front of Dylara—and in that moment Uda came into the open sky once more. In the few seconds left for Dylara to drink in the scene she saw a sight she was never to forget.

SUSPENDED among branches of the trees about her were conical huts of twigs and grasses. Their floors evidently did not rest on the boughs themselves but each separate structure bobbed lightly up and down from the end of a thick grass rope tied to a branch overhead. In the base of each was an opening only large enough to permit entry on only hands and knees.

Dylara's breath went out of her in a sudden gasp. Now she knew why her first impression of these creatures had likened them to insects. There was a species of spider that built nests above the ground—nests conical in shape and swung from twigs!

The hair-covered arms, legs and bodies, the pinched-in abdomens, the round heads set flush with the shoulders. These were spider men!

A wave of unbearable nausea overwhelmed her, robbing her of all strength. Dazed, she felt herself being thrust through an opening in one of the swaying huts, felt the spider-man follow her in—then once more she was lifted by a pair of long thin arms.

Weakly she lifted her hands to strike out at the loathsome thing holding her—then blackness poured into her brain and she knew no more.

FOR the better part of two weeks Tharn and Trakor made little progress along the trail taken by those Ammadians who held Dylara. With the patient stoicism of all creatures of the wild he accepted the unavoidable delay in his plans brought on by his acquisition of the untrained Trakor; and as the best way of lightening his burden, set out to school the boy in the lore of the jungle.

Most of that first week was spent in acquiring the knack of using the tree tops as a highway. Trakor, like most Cro-Magnards, was accustomed to climbing in search of fruit and birds' nests. But when it came to hurtling from bough to bough and tree to [Pg 90]tree in a dizzying pathway high above ground, he was both hesitant and doubtful.

Patiently Tharn strove to build up the youth's confidence. At first he spent hours in developing within him that sense of balance which is the basis for forest-top travel. Once Trakor could thread his way along a swaying branch a hundred feet in the air without reaching wildly for a hand-hold, Tharn undertook to teach him the grasp, swing and release used in plunging through space from one jungle giant to the next.

At first the boy fell many times and his body was a mass of painful bruises. But he endured the pain without complaint, returning to the branches for more with unabated enthusiasm. Hour after hour, day after day he strove for something approaching Tharn's expertness at the craft, and while he knew he would never succeed in reaching the high standards of his teacher, he was gaining confidence that eventually he would near that mark.

Within a week he was bounding about the trees with a sure-footedness and celerity that brought praise from his companion. He took the utmost pleasure in challenging the jungle lord to arboreal races, and while he never won them he came close on several occasions. Soon his confidence passed into a cocksure attitude and he began to take long chances—leaping twenty feet across a treeless gap to catch some narrow limb waving in a strong breeze, or hurtling through space at the end of a trailing vine in imminent danger of being dashed to death on the ground below.

Nor did Tharn protest these activities or urge him to greater caution. The youth must learn from experience what could and could not be done. He gloried in Trakor's small triumphs and comforted him in his failures, and always he was careful not to say or do anything that would weaken the boy's mounting confidence.

WHEN Tharn was satisfied the boy was reasonably at home among the trees, by night or by day, the second phase of his education was undertaken. He taught him to follow an animal's spoor along the dust of a game trail, he showed him how not only to classify each into its proper category but schooled him in such fine distinctions as judging an animal's height, weight and age from imprints left by its feet. Luckily Trakor was endowed with eyes and ears beyond the normal in keenness, and it was not long until he was able to give an excellent account of himself in woodcraft.

And daily his strength was increasing under the unaccustomed tasks imposed on his muscles. Swinging by the hands through mile after mile of branches molded biceps and back muscles into bands of steel and endowed his fingers with a vise-like grip. His body, already deeply tanned, became burned to a dusky hue and he began to fill out into a specimen of perfect manhood.

If Tharn chafed at the delay in his reunion with Dylara he did not display it and he continued the boy's education as though he had a lifetime to put into doing so. But Trakor knew what all this was costing the other, and while he never mentioned it, the determination grew to make it up to the cave lord. There was a bond between them now, based on mutual respect and admiration, plus a hero-worshiping desire on Trakor's part to become exactly like Tharn himself.

Exactly half a moon from the day Tharn had snatched Trakor from under the noses of Gerdak's warriors, the boy made his first kill—a fat buck that had come down to a water hole to drink. He had dropped upon its back from the lower branches of [Pg 91]a tree, as Tharn had taught him, and a knife thrust into its heart had brought it down.

They sat side by side among the branches of a tree, gorging themselves on strips of raw flesh hacked from the side of Trakor's kill, while below them a pack of jackals quarreled over the buck's remains. Sunset was only minutes away and already dusk was seeping into the forest aisles.

Trakor was full of plans for the morrow. "When Dyta comes again," he was saying, "let us hunt out the lair of one of the great cats. I need a new loin cloth and I will cut one from the hide of Jalok or Tarlok—after I have slain him."

Tharn hid his smile by sinking his gleaming teeth into the meat in his hands. "And how will you go about killing Tarlok?" he said casually.

Trakor was surprised at the question. "The same way you slew Sadu the day we met. I will spring upon him from a tree and drive my knife into his heart."

"You will spring into his teeth!" Tharn said grimly. "Let this be your most important lesson: Seek no fight with the great cats. A life time in the jungle is not training enough to pick a quarrel with any of them. There will be times when one of them will stalk you down and trap you; then, if you are lucky, you instead of Tarlok or Jalok or Sadu will come out alive."

"But you have slain them!" Trakor argued.

"True. But never have I sought them out for that purpose. Each time we fought it was because I had no choice, and always the margin between victor and vanquished was so narrow it easily might have gone the other way."

"I am not afraid!"

"Fear has nothing to do with it. A true warrior does not doubt his bravery; only a coward feels he must prove to himself that he is brave. Survival in the jungle depends on knowing and respecting its denizens; he who struts along the trails looking for trouble finds himself filling trouble's belly!"

And so Trakor changed the subject and they talked of other matters. But deep within the boy burned the determination to hunt down one of the great cats at the first opportunity. Tharn, knowing this—his own development had gone through the same stage—said no more on the subject.

WHILE they talked Tharn watched his companion, marveling at the change these past two weeks had made in him. Trakor was every inch a true jungle dweller. He sat with his back comfortably against the tree bole, his shock of black hair falling almost to his shoulders in back and rudely hacked off above his eyes. His swelling chest and broad shoulders were burned almost black by the sun, the skin as clear and unblemished as a woman's. The thin waist, narrow supple hips and long straight legs were the hallmarks of a true warrior, and his sharp alert eyes and handsome clean-cut features were evidence of nobility and intelligence. Fate had placed worthy clay into Tharn's hands for molding and he looked upon his work and found it good.

With this realization came a decision. "Tomorrow," he said, "I must take up the trail of those who hold Dylara. Already she may be within the city of Ammad and I dare not wait longer."

Trakor flushed. "It is my fault. Had you not met me she might be with you at this moment."

"And had I not met you," Tharn said lightly, "I might still be looking for the trail I lost a moon earlier. Or Sadu might have caught and eaten me had I gone on instead of lingering here."

"A score of Sadus could not catch you!"[Pg 92]

Tharn did not reply and his smile was hidden by the handful of leaves with which he wiped the blood of his meal from his lips. "Let us sleep now," he said quietly. "We have many suns of traveling ahead of us."

OTAR was utterly miserable. Fresh blisters had broken on his feet for the fourth day in a row and each step was agony. Life as a guard in Vokal's palace had not been strenuous enough to prepare him for a long journey into the jungle, and as he limped along in the company of his fifty companions he heaped silent curses upon the head of Ekbar, captain of Vokal's guards, who had selected him to take part in this mysterious excursion into the jungles surrounding Ammad.

Otar knew full well why he had been one of those so selected. The lovely Marua had chosen him as her mate instead of Ekbar, and the captain was allowing to pass no opportunity to keep them apart. True, Ekbar was leading the expedition and therefore was unable to take advantage of Otar's absence from the side of his lovely mate. But in view of his aching feet and terror of the grim jungle hemming him in night and day, this was small consolation.

This was the eighth day since Ammad's walls had faded into the south and still no word from Ekbar as to how much farther they must go. Night was not far distant; at any moment now the several advance scouts Ekbar sent on ahead each day would be straggling back to make their reports to the captain. That would be the signal to make camp for the night—something others of the party besides Otar were looking forward to.

In a column two abreast the fifty shuffled along, war spears ready in their hands, bows and arrow-filled quivers at their backs, a stone knife in the belt of each tunic. Over them hung the brooding humid jungle on either side of the elephant path, while in their ears rose and fell the now familiar pattern of sound formed by buzzing insects, chattering monkeys and raucous-voiced birds. Except for the clouds of insects that had a way of working down inside a tunic this was not so bad. It was when night came and the challenging cries of Sadu and Tarlok and Jalok made hideous the darkness beyond the camp's circle of fires, that Otar knew the depths of fear. Then was when heavy paws padded against the earth nearby and yellow eyes gleamed out of the night.

"Here comes one of the scouts!" said the man next to Otar, pointing. "Look how excited he is!"

A stocky built man in a once white tunic was running swiftly along the path toward the column's head, waving his arms. Instantly Ekbar lifted his spear in a horizontal position and the column ground to a halt.

Otar could see the two of them, Ekbar and the scout, carrying on a heated discussion, but he was too far back to make out the words. While they talked, the remaining three scouts arrived and joined in the conversation.

It lasted for several minutes; then Ekbar, tall and square-shouldered, gave the signal to resume the march. Several of the troops groaned openly; but the groans changed to elated murmurs of satisfaction almost immediately when the winding trail debouched into a small circular clearing divided by a small jungle stream.

The order was given to make camp and prepare food. Those whose nightly duty it was to gather branches for a fiery circle to keep the cats at bay were called back when they started into the jungle—a matter that caused considerable discussion among the others.[Pg 93]

THEY were not long left in doubt. Ekbar gathered the warriors in a tight circle and, standing in its center, gave them their first explanation since leaving Ammad.

"An enemy force lies encamped an hour's march ahead of us," he said in his high-pitched, almost querulous voice. "For that reason we must forgo our nightly fires lest the glow be seen and the enemy warned. Instead, once you have eaten, you are to spend the night in the trees. A few of us will go on ahead under cover of darkness and learn the number of enemies we must face. Early on the morrow we attack!"

His chill eyes went around the circle, then he lifted one arm and began to point out individuals, calling their names and ordering each to step forward.

Otar, anger stiffening his jaw, was among the first to be summoned. When the new group reached six, Ekbar dismissed the others and bade them follow him.

Half an hour after leaving the main body darkness came down upon the seven Ammadian warriors, blacking out their immediate surroundings. Unconsciously they moved closer together and their voices stilled. The jungle was unfamiliar territory to most of them and a place where death might lay behind each bush along the way.

Presently they detected a wavering glow filtering through the trees ahead, and Ekbar warned them in a low voice to proceed with added caution. A little later he motioned them to a halt and went on ahead, his body crouched, his spear and knife ready for action.

He reappeared almost immediately. "They have made a dry camp in a small clearing just around a bend of the trail," he whispered. "Follow me and let not so much as a blade of grass bend under your feet!"

Like disembodied wraiths the seven members of Vokal's palace guard crept among the towering trees to one side of the trail. With slow stealth they worked their way forward until they lay, side by side among the thick undergrowth at the clearing's edge. Trained ears would have marked their passage long before they reached that position, but the ears of the five sentries on duty were no keener than those of the average Ammadian.

Most of the camp lay sleeping behind barricades of burning branches, their huddled shapes beneath sleeping furs visible by light of flickering flames. The sentries were pacing to and fro, stopping occasionally to pass a remark or two among themselves. The only sounds came from the crackling wood of the fires and, very distant, the hunting squall of a leopard.

Ekbar's eyes, a bit keener than those of his companions, noticed something. "Look!" he whispered. "Several in a row of sleepers nearest us have bandages on their heads. Yes, and one of the sentries is carrying his arm in a sling. They've come through a fight of some kind recently."

Otar, who had been peering intently at the five sentries, voiced a muffled explanation.

"Your scouts were wrong, Ekbar!" he said, his voice rising to its normal volume. "These men are——"

A savage hand about his neck choked off his words. "Quiet, you fool!" whispered Ekbar, his fingers tightening their hold.

One of the watch had lifted his head and was staring intently in their direction. After a long moment he shrugged slightly and busied himself with adding branches to the fire. Only then did Ekbar release his hold.

OTAR, anger and bewilderment plain in his expression, massaged his aching neck. "I tell you," he whispered, "those are not enemies. They are warriors of the palace of the noble Garud of Ammad. One of those sen[Pg 94]tries is Dretox, an acquaintance of mine who went with Jotan, Garud's son, to Sephar several moons ago. It is plain that they are returning to Ammad and we should go out and welcome them instead of skulking here in the bushes."

"And I say these men are enemies!" hissed Ekbar heatedly. "Listen and judge for yourself."

"The morning of the day we left Ammad an attempt was made on the life of Jaltor, our king. The news swept the city; I know that some of you, at least, must have heard it. Vokal, our master, as one of Ammad's noblemen, learned Garlud was behind the attempted assassination. On the direct and secret orders of Jaltor himself, Vokal has sent us to intercept and kill Jotan, who once he learns Garlud is dead after plotting to have the king slain, may attempt to even the score by leading a revolt that could plunge all Ammad into civil war."

"That is why we are here and that is why these men are enemies. And on the morrow we shall attack them and put them all to instant death!"

It was reason enough and they were satisfied. Such intrigues were common in Ammad; several of the six had served more than one nobleman during their lifetimes.

"One thing bothers me," Ekbar was whispering. "It was believed Jotan took fifty men with him to Sephar, also two friends who are sons of noblemen. These last two must be overcome and spirited away without learning our identity. When Jotan and the rest are dead, we will release the pair of them and let them find their way to Ammad. I want a suggestion on how that can be done."

No one spoke for a while. The sentries continued to move among the fires a few feet away, and the sounds of a nocturnal jungle rose and fell about them.

It was Ekbar himself who hit on a plan, as befitted one of a captain's rank.

"We shall need one of those sleeping men," he said. "I will take two of you and circle the camp to the opposite side. After we have time enough to reach that point, the rest of you will make a noise of some kind to attract the guards' attention. Be careful not to make them too suspicious lest they rouse the camp. While they are looking in your direction, we will creep up and grab the first man we come to."

The men signified that they understood, and Ekbar, Otar and a warrior named Kopan set out to take up their arranged positions. Hardly were they ready when a low moaning sound rose from among the bushes across the clearing and the foliage there began to shake violently.

Instantly the five guards grouped behind that section of the burning circle nearest the disturbance. They raised their spears ready for casting and one of the five hurled a burning branch across the narrow ribbon of open ground.

"Now!" Ekbar grated.

STOOPING, the three men raced for the encampment. They cleared the burning barrier at a bound, snatched up the nearest of the sleeping figures, muffling his face with his own sleeping furs before he could awaken, then turned and vanished into the jungle. So quickly had they acted, so swift and sure their motions, that none of the other sleepers so much as stirred and the guards never noticed.

The instant the abductors had disappeared the moans stopped and the shaking foliage stilled. For a long time the guards continued to stand there waiting, but when no other disturbance materialized they sighed with relief and went back to the restless patrolling.

Meanwhile Ekbar and his men were returning to their own camp, their[Pg 95]captive with them. They drew him into a sheltered place under the trees, lighted a small fire that his expression might tell them if he answered their questions with lies and went to work on him.

He was a young man, clear-eyed, intelligent and not at all frightened. He stared at his captors without recognition, obviously puzzled to find they were men of his own nationality.

"What is your name?" rasped Ekbar, scowling menacingly.

"Tykol—if that helps you any! What is the meaning of this? Who are you?"

"I will ask the questions here!" Ekbar snapped. "And you will answer them if you wish to see Dyta, the sun, again! Do you understand?"

"I understand well enough, but that does not mean I will tell you anything!"

Without the slightest change of expression Ekbar whipped out the knife at his belt and sank three inches of the cold flint into one of the man's thighs. Tykol cried out involuntarily and struggled to free his arms from the vines binding them to his sides.

Ekbar waited until his struggles ceased. A small stream of blood welled from the knife wound and began to drip against the leaves beneath.

"What," said Ekbar, "are the names of the two young noblemen accompanying Jotan?"

Tykol, his active mind racing, did not at once reply. It was clear these men meant no good to any of Jotan's followers. His cue was to simulate a certain amount of fear to satisfy them his answers were the truth until he could discover exactly what was afoot.

Ekbar leaned forward and lifted his knife again. "Shall I give you a second taste of this?" he growled.

Tykol appeared to flinch. "No," he mumbled. "I will tell you. Their names are Javan and Tamar."

"How many men are with them?"

"Thirty-seven."

"You lie!" Ekbar snarled. "Fifty were in the party when it left Ammad."

The young captive digested this information quickly. It proved these men were Ammadians like himself; how else could they have known that?

"I am not lying," he said sullenly. "Three nights ago lions attacked our camp and killed and ate the others, wounding many of the rest of us."

EKBAR, remembering the bandages he had glimpsed while spying on the camp, nodded to himself. It would make his task of wiping out the balance of them that much easier.

"What positions do these two men hold in the line of march during the day?" he demanded.

"Javan now marches at the head of the column."

The captain's head jerked up sharply. "Don't lie to me, you son of Gubo! Jotan marches there; he is in charge of his men. There is no need for you to attempt to shield him—he will be dead in a few hours!"

It was all Tykol needed. He knew now that he himself would not live to see tomorrow's sun; and while the thought was sobering enough it did not dim his determination to save the life of his beloved master.

And so Tykol threw back his head and laughed—laughed until a heavy blow from the fist of Ekbar sent him sprawling. The captain gestured angrily to the others to drag the youth upright again, then said:

"You laugh, fool. Does the thought of Jotan's death mean so little to you?"

"That is not why I laugh," Tykol told him, grinning. "I laugh because no act of yours can take his life—for he no longer has a life to take!"

Strong fingers twisted into the front of his tunic and jerked him forward. "What do you mean? The truth, jackal, or I cut you in bits!"[Pg 96]

Tykol appeared properly cowed. "The lions got him—as they got the noble Tamar. It was terrible, I tell you! For hours they crouched just outside the circle of fires while their roars filled the night. We tried to drive——"

"Enough!" growled the captain. "We shall soon find out if you are lying. If our scouts learn Jotan is still with his men I promise you a slow and horrible death."

"And when you find I am telling the truth," Tykol said, feigning eagerness, "will you then let me go?"

Ekbar sat there fingering his knife, thinking. If this man spoke true words there would be no need for massacring Jotan's warriors. It would be far better to permit them to reach Ammad and tell of his death under Sadu's rending fangs. Thus the last threat to Vokal's plans would have been accomplished without an air of mystery behind it that some one, becoming curious, might dig into.

But he would need more than this man's word. On the morrow he would send scouts who could recognize Jotan, back to spy on the column. If Jotan was not there, then Tykol's story would be proved true; Ekbar would withdraw his men and return to Ammad, leaving the remnants of Jotan's troops to straggle back unmolested by him.

Either way he no longer had use of Tykol. His attention came back to the bound man in front of him. "Yes," he said, replying to the young man's last question, "you shall have your freedom. In fact I shall give it to you now."

With those words he lunged forward and drove his knife into Tykol's heart!

Thus died a true warrior—loyal unto death to the man he served, knowing his heroism would lie with his bones unknown, yet making his supreme sacrifice without hesitation and without self-pity.

38

Ekbar wiped clean his stone blade on the dead man's tunic and rose to his feet. "Haul this carrion deeper within the jungle," he told his sober-faced men, "and rouse the camp. We start back to Ammad at once."

CHAPTER VIII
A PRIZE FOR VOKAL

"I TELL you it is useless, Jotan," Tamar said. "For three suns now we have beat the jungle searching for some sign of her. How long do you expect to keep up this useless hunt?"

There were five of them in the group: Jotan, Tamar and three of the former's best fighting men. They were seated on a fallen log at the edge of a narrow stream, having finished washing away the stains of jungle travel only minutes before. Directly overhead hung the midday sun, flooding them with humid heat, and hemming them in on all sides stood towering giants of the forest.

Jotan shook his head and said nothing. The strain and hopelessness of the last three days had aged him visibly: there were new lines in his face and his eyes were haggard. He recognized his injustice in subjecting his friends to the dangers of jungle travel, especially when their number was so small; but Dylara meant everything to him and he could not give her up without a struggle.

"I beg of you," Tamar persisted; "give up the search that we may turn about and rejoin the others. We are not equipped to follow this trail all the way back to Sephar. Already we have lost two of our men—one of them the only man among us who was qualified to track her down. For all we know she may be dead—the victim of one of the numerous cats infesting this section of the country."

"You may return if you like," snapped Jotan, stung by that last remark. "I am going on—alone if necessary! [Pg 97]Oh, I know why you want to call it off," he went on, scowling. "You never had any use for her because she is a girl of the caves instead of a nobleman's daughter. But whether you like it or not, Dylara is the only woman I shall ever love and I am going to find her—or give my life in the attempt."

Tamar, hearing, knew his friend meant exactly what he said. It was useless to plead with him on the basis of not being able to pick up her trail. But there was another way—and he bored into it, playing it up for all it was worth.

"Your life is your own, Jotan," he said stiffly. "But do you have the right to sacrifice the lives of the rest of us in a quest that is completely hopeless? If we had found anything to indicate we were on the right trail I would not for an instant try to dissuade you. It is true I do not think the girl worthy of your love—but that is not important. You do love her and I would fight against the world in defense of your choice."

"But to go on this way without a single lead to show us we have even the faintest chance for success, to throw away the lives of these three men—and our own—is rank folly! Perhaps you regard it as some sort of admirable determination; in truth it is sheer stubbornness."

For a long time Jotan sat there staring with unseeing eyes at the sluggishly moving waters of the tiny river. There was no denying the truth in Tamar's words. He knew his best friend meant every word of his statement that he would back Jotan's choice of a mate against a world; he had proved that back in Sephar by saving Dylara's life by a bit of quick thinking, when he might as easily have let a plot against her go on to its inevitable end. Equally as undeniable was his statement that it was sheer injustice to sacrifice needlessly the lives of loyal men on what could only be classified as a fool's errand.

Impulsively he turned to one of the three warriors sitting in a stolid row beside him. "Tell me, Itak," he said, "what is your greatest desire at this moment?"

"To serve you, noble Jotan," the man replied promptly and with complete honesty.

"And after that?"

Itak's dark face split in a wide smile. "When we left for Ammad, my mate was heavy with child. I would like to learn if I have a son or a daughter."

Slowly Jotan rose from the log and stretched his long, powerful arms. "We have rested long enough," he said, his face empty of all emotion. "Let us be on our way—back to join our companions!"

Open relief showed in the three warriors' faces. Only Tamar fully understood what those words had cost his friend and he stood up and laid a comforting hand on his shoulder. For only a second he left it there and neither spoke.

Then packs were swung to stalwart backs and the five men disappeared among the trees along the narrow game trail leading into the south—and Ammad.

CONSCIOUSNESS returned to Dylara at the moment the spider man was placing her roughly on a heap of foul-smelling grasses. In the almost impenetrable darkness she was aware that his hands were moving lingeringly along the contours of her body and in sudden terror she struck out at his face, guided by the sound of hoarse rapid breathing.

Her nails struck home and she raked them fiercely across an unseen cheek, bringing forth a startled cry of pain and anger. An open hand caught her heavily above the ear and once more her senses swam, leaving her weak and defenseless.[Pg 98]

Dimly she was aware that the awful creature was dropping to its knees beside her and once more long slender hair-covered fingers tugged at her tunic.

And then there was a startled grunt, a flurry of motion—and she was alone. Even as she started up wonderingly the floor of the swinging hut vibrated sharply under a heavy impact, followed by the sounds of furious struggle.

What it all meant, Dylara did not know. Perhaps one of the other spider-men, jealous of her captor's prize, had come to take her for himself. Or perhaps the spider-man's mate had arrived to protect the sanctity of her home.

Whatever the reason, it was Dylara's chance—and she took it without hesitation. Hugging the walls to keep free of the two battling figures rolling about the floor, she edged her way swiftly toward the small aperture that served as a door, then dropped to her knees and crawled through. At any moment she expected one of those slender hands to close about one of her ankles; but that did not happen and she gained one of the branches outside.

Never in all her life before had the daughter of Majok descended from a tree with such reckless abandon—but never before had she so strong a motive for haste. In fact she slipped and fell the last ten feet, her heart bounding into her throat as she toppled into Stygian blackness.

She was on her feet like a cat, not stopping to learn if the fall had injured her, and ran blindly into the tangled fastness of brush, vine, creeper and tree. Thorns tore at her skin and tunic, brambles tugged painfully at her hair, the stems of bushes tripped her up, trees loomed up too late for her to avoid slamming into them.

But Dylara was impervious to pain and heedless of obstacles. On and on she went, stumbling, running, crawling—fighting to put distance between her and the ugly monstrosities in those conical, tree-top huts.

How long this mad flight endured or how far it took her Dylara was never to know. But at last overtaxed muscles rebelled, her laboring lungs refused their task, and the cave girl collapsed in a pitiful heap among a tangled maze of head-high bushes.

Twice she sought to rise and go on. But each time her legs turned to water beneath her and she sank back to earth. Tears of utter helplessness flooded her eyes; she put her head down against one arm—and in that instant she fell sound asleep.

When she awakened night had fled and sunlight, pale and without warmth after filtering through layer upon layer of foliage, made visible her immediate surroundings.

SHE got shakily to her feet and stood there swaying a little as outraged muscles reminded her painfully of last night's mad flight. Little lines of dried blood on her arms and legs marked where thorns had raked her and she realized her body was one aching mass of bruises. Added to this was an inflexible stiffness brought on by sleeping on damp earth.

But all this was relatively unimportant. She was free once more—free to begin her long journey back to the cave of her father. She must hasten back to the trail which Jotan and his men had followed from Ammad and retrace her way southward toward home.

And at that moment the full impact of her predicament came home with stunning force.

She was utterly and completely lost! Whether the trail to Sephar was to the east or west of where she now stood was as unknown to her as the opposite side of Uda, the moon. True her goal lay to the north; but unless she could locate the original path Jotan had followed, she might spend [Pg 99]the rest of her life picking a way through the towering mountains and endless plains between.

Surging panic cut her legs from under her and she dropped into a sitting position on a fallen log and buried her face in her hands. For a long time she sat thus, fighting back her tears, trying to think logically. But what use was logic in this tangled wilderness of growing things?

Still, she told herself, she could not sit there forever, an unresisting morsel for the first meat-eater to come along. She stood up, brushed away an accumulation of leaves, thorns and dirt from her tunic, and struck resolutely out toward the east, pushing her way slowly through the walls of plant life everywhere about her.

Monkeys raced and chattered among the branches overhead and disturbed rodents and the crawling things that infest the rotting jungle floor fled from her path. After a dozen yards she was bathed in perspiration and her skin seemed to crawl with the dampness.

40

If only she could find some sort of pathway that would allow her to make progress without battling this ocean of pulpy, slimy vegetation—a footing solid enough to prevent sinking to her ankles with every step. Three different times she narrowly avoided treading on snakes—small, brightly colored reptiles whose bite would have meant a lingering death; and once she nearly collapsed with fright when a looping vine caught her about the neck unexpectedly and she thought it the folds of a python.

And then, after an hour of this, she stumbled unexpectedly into an elephant path, its powdery surface marked by the passage of numerous other animals. Unfortunately for her purpose it ran almost due east and west instead of north and after following it into the east for the better part of two hours, it began gradually to veer southward, taking her further and further from the caves of her father.

Her only hope was that sooner or later she would come upon an intersecting trail that would lead northward. The thought of leaving the narrow strip of open ground and plunging back into that green maze was more than she could endure. And so she went on, staggering now and then under the lashes of heat and weariness, finding an occasional waterhole to quench her thirst and stripping fruit from trees and bushes to satisfy hunger.

Near nightfall she came upon a large clearing through which flowed a wide shallow stream. It had been several hours since last water had passed her lips and sight of the river lifted her spirits. She pushed her way through a heavy growth of reeds on the near bank, knelt and drank thirstily, then slipped out of her tunic and submerged her entire body in the brackish liquid.

Emerging at last, she dried her body with handfuls of grasses, her lithe, sweetly rounded figure gleaming like an image molded of pure gold in the fading sunlight. Her spirits were soaring again, for when first leaving the water she had glimpsed the beginnings of a second trail into the forest—a trail pointing straight as a spear shaft toward the north.

Already her plans were made. She would spend the night among the high-flung branches of that tree at the trail's entrance, when dawn came again she would start out once more—this time toward home.

Donning her tunic she ran lightly toward the tree, its base buried among a heavy growth of bushes.

While from the depths of tangled undergrowth near the bole of that tree, a pair of glowing yellow eyes were fixed in an unblinking stare upon the swiftly approaching girl!

A STORM was blowing up. Tharn, belly flat against a broad branch [Pg 100]while he gnawed the sweet pulpy interior of a hard-shelled fruit, caught the signs of it in the scent of the air, in the uneasy pattern of a shifting breeze, in the faintly yellowish cast of the sky overhead. He mentioned the possibility to Trakor, who, wedged into a fork nearby, was dozing in the heat of day.

"A nice dry cave would come in handy if the rain comes," the youth observed. "I know how Gerdak's warriors hated being caught in a storm. They say the jungle is never more dangerous, with winds blowing branches through the air with the speed of flying spears, great trees being uprooted to crash down and crush the unlucky, while Rora, the lightning, flickers angrily about their heads."

"It is a part of jungle living," Tharn said philosophically. "This one will not come for half a sun yet—if it comes at all. Or it may be only a little storm."

"And if it is a bad one?" Trakor asked.

"Then we find a very big tree that is not too old and stand under it until it passes."

"But sometimes storms last for many suns!"

"Not at this season. The rain may fall for suns on end but then the wind is not too strong and there is no danger in moving about."

This was the sixth day since he and Trakor had set out in sustained pursuit of those Ammadians who were holding Dylara. They traveled mostly during the morning and afternoon hours, laying up during the heat of day. To Trakor every hour brought new confidence, increasing dexterity in tree-top travel and his store of jungle lore, under the expert tutelage of Tharn, increased by leaps and bounds. He could stalk Neela, the zebra, or Bana, the deer, across wide stretches of grasslands and, more often than not, get close enough to this wariest of all prey to bring one down with a single spear cast. Tharn had spent all of one sun making him a bow, and with it and a handful of arrows from Tharn's own quiver the boy had learned to handle the weapon with some degree of success. No member of the cat family had faced him and his new-found abilities thus far, but the time must eventually come and he looked forward to it with ill-concealed impatience.

But it was in the trees where Trakor excelled. Already he could keep pace with Tharn for short periods, although he was far from being able to match his friend's over-all agility and stamina. Only when it came to racing swiftly through the trees in the blackness of night was he hopelessly outclassed; for here success depended on an uncanny kind of sixth sense that Tharn had managed to develop only by constant practice and use since almost the day he was able to walk.

Nor was Trakor capable of such quick thinking as that displayed by his hero. A sudden development would freeze Trakor momentarily, while Tharn, because of both environment and heredity possessed reflexes that would have put Rora, the lightning, to shame, would already have the situation in hand.

And as the days passed the bond between the two of them increased in strength and permanence. To Trakor, Tharn was even more a god than on that day he had dropped from the skies to save the youth from the fangs of Sadu. He sought to emulate everything about him—his expression, his walk, his way of speaking—even his way of thinking. Almost every word the mighty Cro-Magnard uttered was stored deep within the mind of his worshiping companion, to be secretly mulled over and absorbed. As for Tharn, he admired the boy's boundless enthusiasm, his unflagging desire to master the lore of the jungle, his uncomplaining accept[Pg 101]ance of hardship and his quiet courage.

To Tharn the jungles and plains of his world made up all he wanted from life. To range far and wide in search of adventure, to match his wits and prowess against its savage denizens, animal and human, had made that life complete. With the advent of Dylara, and love, fresh horizons had opened before his eyes, but not once had he pictured life with her as his mate as closing the door on his previous existence. He would have her, he reasoned, and the jungle too.

BUT with the admission of Trakor still another phase presented itself. Self-sufficient as he had always been, even unto childhood, loneliness was no more than a puzzling word. But now he caught himself thinking of ranging those jungles and plains with a companion—one nearly his own age—and the thought pleased him more than he permitted to show. As the days passed the resolve grew to bring Trakor with him and Dylara back to his own people. Always there would be the three of them—Dylara, Trakor, Tharn, inseparable.

The eddying gusts of wind suddenly brought a strangely familiar scent to Tharn's sensitive nostrils, dispelling his mood of reverie and bringing him instantly upright on the swaying branch.

Trakor, startled by the abrupt move, looked up at him sharply. Tharn was standing with head thrown slightly back, his nostrils quivering, his entire body as motionless as though cut from stone.

"What is it, Tharn?"

Tharn's eyes went to the boy and in them was something that brought Trakor beside him instantly.

"Come," the cave lord said.

Side by side they set off through the trees, following the winding path far below. Tharn was moving swiftly, and when he elected to do so few in all the jungle could match his pace. Trakor, to his consternation, began to fall steadily behind and he put on a fresh burst of speed, taking chances he ordinarily would never have dreamed of. Despite this, Tharn continued to widen the gap and within minutes the youth lost sight of him altogether.

The passage of both was practically soundless, for that is important for survival in the wild. As a result Trakor was unable to make use of his ears in trailing the other, but as Tharn had continued on above the pathway, it would seem logical that he would continue to do so. He hesitated to call out, for to do so, he thought, would be to confess his lesser ability; besides a cry might serve to warn whatever had excited Tharn's interest.

While far ahead of him now, Tharn raced onward, his face an expressionless mask, his heart thudding with desperate hope.

FIVE dust-covered, disheveled men moved steadily along a winding game trail, the rays of a noon-day sun pouring down on their tunic-clad backs through rifts in the arching branches overhead. They moved in single file without speaking, almost without thinking, their every energy intent only on cutting down the distance between them and the major portion of their party.

Jotan was at the rear of the column, Tamar and he alternating at holding down this exposed position. The back of the warrior ahead of him was ten or twelve feet distant—a space Jotan almost automatically maintained.

The trail underfoot swerved abruptly to by-pass an especially heavy growth of trees and momentarily Jotan was out of sight of his companions. A dozen more strides and he too would make the turn and rejoin them.

A sudden rustling among the bran[Pg 102]ches directly overhead caused him to look up in alarm, just as a crushing weight struck full upon his shoulders and drove him to his knees. Steel fingers sought and instantly found a hold on his neck, choking back an instinctive cry for help.

Jotan was a powerful, fully trained warrior, with muscles superior to most of his kind. Yet in the first few seconds of struggle he realized with sinking heart that his strength was as a child's when compared to that of the unseen and silent creature on his back.

A film began to form before his protruding eyes, his senses reeled, his laboring lungs fought for air—then blackness poured into his brain.

... Slowly the fog of unconsciousness left Jotan of Ammad and at last he opened his eyes. At sight of the half-naked man crouched over him instant recognition dawned in his expression. "You!" he gasped.

"I," said Tharn impassively, "Where is she?"

"I do not know."

"You lie!" The cave lord's hand shot out and sank incredibly powerful fingers into the Ammadian's bare arm. "Tell me where she is or I will kill you!"

Jotan raised a shaking hand and massaged the aching muscles of his throat where those mighty fingers had left their mark. He saw now that he was high in the branches of a tree, that sitting on a branch behind his captor was another cave man—a youth, rather—who was watching him from inscrutable eyes.

"She never really believed you were dead," the Ammadian said slowly, almost as though thinking aloud. "I tried to tell her no man comes through the Games of the God alive. Even now I can hardly believe that you are actually here."

Tharn was not to be side-tracked. "Where is she?" he growled. "For the last time—or do I choke the information from you?"

"That will not be necessary, my friend," Jotan said sadly. "For all I know Dylara may be dead."

Nothing changed in Tharn's expression but his fingers bit sharply into Jotan's arm bringing an involuntary cry to the Ammadian's lips. "What do you mean?"

Whereupon the young nobleman of Ammad recounted the events of that terrible night when the lions had fallen upon his followers and sent Dylara racing for the safety of the trees. Tharn heard him out, his face as empty of emotion as though carved from granite.

"For three suns," Jotan said in closing, "we searched the jungle for a sign of her. But to no avail. Either the lions got her or she is somewhere to the north, making her way back to the caves of her people. Two suns ago my men and I gave up and we were on our way back to rejoin the rest of our party when you found me."

"Where is this place from which Dylara fled Sadu?"

"A sun's march to the south."

Tharn nodded. "You may return to your friends," he said. "If she is still alive I will find her. If she is dead, or if I find her alive and learn that you have harmed her, I will come back and kill you!"

Jotan shrugged. Not for an instant did he doubt that the young giant meant exactly what he said. Somehow his own life seemed unimportant with Dylara gone. He knew that, alive or dead, Dylara was lost to him and that he would never see her again.

He shook off his thoughts. "Then I am free to go?"

"Yes."

"Where will I find my friends?"

"The trail where I found you is directly below. They have discovered your absence and have backtracked in search of you."[Pg 103]

Without another word Jotan rose to his feet and began the long descent groundward.

Once the intervening foliage hid the Ammadian from view, Tharn said to Trakor, "A sun's march to the south," he said. "We should make it in half that time—perhaps less. Come."

Side by side the two Cro-Magnards set off through the leafy reaches of the trees.

DYLARA, only a few yards from the trail's mouth, came to a sudden halt. Years of elbow rubbing with the jungle and its inhabitants reminded her that trail mouths a short distance from water were where Sadu and Tarlok were most likely to be lying in wait for game. And this was the time of day the meat-eaters began their search for food.

Standing there near the clearing's edge, she peered intently at the waist-high grasses shrouding the boles of trees on both sides of the trail. A light breeze stirred them softly, and at one spot directly beneath a jungle patriarch's broad boughs, a trailing vine swayed in unison with the wind.

43

But wait! That vine was quivering unsteadily, then moving *against* the breeze! Instantly Dylara's eyes were fixed on that spot. Little by little her searching gaze made out the outlines of some amorphous shape crouching motionless behind a curtain of grasses.

Imagination? Perhaps, she told herself. But the jungle dweller without it soon left his bones to bleach along the trails. Cautiously she took a backward step ... another, and yet a third.

The long grasses at that point were very still now as the breeze died. Was she being overly careful—running from shadows? A tree stump, a fallen log—any of several explanations would cover that motionless bulk lying there.

Suddenly the brooding silence was torn apart by a thunderous roar and Sadu, the lion, aware that his prey was on the point of escape, sprang from the depths of foliage and bore down upon her with express-train speed, snarling and growling as he came.

Even as Dylara turned to flee, she knew her life was finished, that nothing could save her now. Any hope that she would reach safety among the trees was futile; the nearest was long yards away and Sadu would have buried his talons and fangs in her defenseless flesh while she was still far short of escape.

Yet so strong was the urge of self-preservation that she was racing like the wind for sanctuary despite the uselessness of flight; while behind her Sadu was cutting down the gap between them as though the Cro-Magnard princess were standing still.

The knowledge that his prey was inescapably doomed did not cause Sadu to loiter along the way or grow over-confident. He judged the intervening space with a practiced eye; and, at precisely the right moment, he launched his great, heavy-maned body in the final Gargantuan leap that would end full in the center of that smoothly tanned back.

It was then that Dylara caught a foot in a tangle of grasses and plunged headlong!

Sadu, soaring in a majestic parabola, overshot his mark and landed a full two yards beyond. Instantly he wheeled to pounce on his dazed prey—and in that instant twelve heavy warspears tore into his exposed flank!

The combined impact of those dozen flint heads knocked him to the ground. Fountains of blood darkened his shimmering hide; his legs scrambled madly to bring him upright—then he slumped back and moved no more.

Dylara, wide-eyed and shivering, was rising to her feet when a horde of white-tunicked Ammadians hem[Pg 104]med her in. One of them, a tall, square-shouldered warrior of middle-age, caught one of her arms and helped her up.

Still dazed by her narrow escape from death, Dylara looked about the circle of curious faces. None of these men was familiar, although their dress and appearance told her into whose hands she had fallen.

"Who are you, woman?" demanded the square-shouldered one roughly, "and what are you doing thus far from Ammad?"

She met his stern gaze unflinchingly. "I am Dylara, daughter of Majok, and I do not belong in Ammad. Let me go at once!"

THE man's eyes narrowed speculatively. "What have we here?" he said, an appraising gleam in his eyes. "Your bearing and appearance is that of a nobleman's daughter; your words have the sound of the cave-dwellers. Which are you, anyway?"

Briefly, Dylara weighed her chances of deluding this sharp-eyed man into believing her the daughter of some Ammadian. Even as the thought came to her she realized such a story would never stand up. Either way he would take her to Ammad; and from the expressions of some of those warriors crowding about her and feasting their eyes on her face and figure, she would be better off telling the truth. The mere mention of Jotan's name, while expunging her last hope of being released, would at least save her from possible molestation....

"I am the noble Jotan's," she said, thankful that the earnest young man was not around to hear that declaration. "I was accompanying him from Sephar to Ammad when an attack by lions separated us."

The Ammadian leader's expression was one she could not analyze. He said, almost humbly, "Perhaps you are the daughter of some Sepharian noble?"

It might have been wise for her to make such a claim. But strong within this lovely girl was pride of race and a faint contempt for these comparatively frail and dull-witted people.

"No," she said, head held high, "I am not a Sepharian. I am the daughter of Majok, chief of a tribe. I was captured by the Sepharians and I was given to Jotan."

The man's bow was a travesty on humbleness. "It is an honor to meet a slave of the noble Jotan. I am Ekbar, captain of the guard of the noble Vokal. You will find my master one who can properly appreciate such beauty and charm as yours. Come, let us hasten on that you may the quicker become known to him!"

44

Dylara felt the blood drain from her face. "You fool! Do you think the noble Jotan would allow such to happen? Were your master to lay so much as a hand on me, Jotan would kill him!"

"You think Jotan's slaves mean so much to him?" Ekbar said mockingly.

"I am no slave," Dylara blazed. "I am to be Jotan's mate."

The other's smile broadened. "I'm afraid Jotan is past needing a mate. You see, Jotan is dead!"

CHAPTER IX
TRAKOR'S MISTAKE

IT was close to nightfall when Tharn and Trakor reached the clearing where Jotan's party had been attacked by lions several nights before. Ashes from the long-dead fires still showed their outlines, tracked now by the hoofs and paws of jungle beasts. An air of desolation seemed to hang above the scene like the miasmic vapors from some foul swamp.

The two Cro-Magnards knelt at the stream and quenched their thirst. For nearly an hour the two young warriors sat side by side on the bank without speaking, while gradually [Pg 105]shadows from the encircling wall of trees stretched farther and farther across the glade. And then with the suddenness peculiar to tropical climes night filled the forest and the voices of hunters and hunted rose and fell about the clearing.

Trakor stirred uneasily as the roar of Sadu, monarch of the jungle night, rolled across the forest aisles from nearby. His ears, far sharper now from constant use, caught a faint stirring among the river reeds a dozen yards from where Tharn and he were seated; and an instant later those rustling stalks parted and Tarlok, the leopard, slunk into the open.

The young man from Gerdak's caves sat very still, hardly daring to breathe, as the lithe, powerfully muscled feline stood clearly revealed in the light of stars. For a long moment the cat stood as motionless as some beautifully carved statue, then gracefully bent its neck to dip the soft furry muzzle into the water.

Trakor felt a cool breeze against his face and knew why Tarlok failed to sense the presence of Tharn and him. What, he wondered, would happen if Siha, the wind, should suddenly reverse its course and bring their scent to Tarlok's sensitive nostril's? Would that terrible engine of destruction spring instantly upon them, rending and tearing before they could give effective battle? It was an interesting problem to weigh, although Trakor felt he could do it far more justice from a seat on some lofty branch.

Tarlok finished slaking his thirst and without an instant's hesitation turned and vanished among the reeds. Trakor listened to the almost inaudible sounds of the cat's passage and felt a little glow of pride. A moon ago he would have mistaken those rustlings as the passage of Siha—if he had heard them at all.

Tharn stirred. "I am hungry!"

"And I!" agreed Trakor, abruptly aware that he had not eaten since mid-morning.

"Let us find a comfortable branch for the night, then I will hunt food while you wait there."

"Why can't I go with you?" Trakor demanded. "I am a good hunter. Did I not, a sun ago, track down and slay Neela, the zebra, with my own knife?"

"That was while Dyta was high in the sky," Tharn reminded him. "Hunting Neela or Bana at night requires long practice and many disappointments. Tonight I am too hungry to wait."

A towering forest giant offered a secure and comfortable haven for the night; and while Trakor sat there fuming at being left out of things, Tharn swung off into the darkness in search of their dinner.

Less than an hour later he was back, a haunch of venison across one shoulder. Together they squatted on a broad branch and cut strips of the still dripping flesh from Bana's flank. They ate quickly and in silence, Trakor already having adopted the almost taciturn air common among jungle dwellers; and when they were finished, a handful of leaves served each as a napkin.

Not long thereafter both were sleeping soundly on their swaying couch, as indifferent to the cacophony of roars, shrieks and screams making hideous the jungle night as though such sounds did not exist.

THEY dined on the remainder of Bana's haunch shortly after sunrise the following morning. After descending to drink from the stream in the clearing, Tharn set out to explore the former site of Jotan's camp in an effort to pick up Dylara's trail.

Trakor squatted on his haunches and watched the cave lord with wide, wondering eyes. For several minutes Tharn moved slowly about the cleared ground, his powerful body bent low, his unbelievably keen eyes searching every inch of earth. Gradually his [Pg 106]companion began to understand there was nothing aimless in his movements: he was circling in a gradually narrowing spiral toward the exact center of the camp site.

After a while Trakor tired of watching and went back to the river to drink. He was on his way back when a sharp exclamation from his friend caught his attention.

He was amazed to find Tharn on his hands and knees sniffing at the ground. Those nostrils appeared to quiver, to expand and contract, like an animal's when it picks up a fresh spoor.

A prickling sensation tugged at Trakor's scalp. Was it possible that this god-like human could actually scent, and *recognize* that scent, where a man or woman had stood days before? No human nose had any business being that efficient!

Tharn looked up to find him standing there. "She slept here for several hours," he said. On hands and knees he began to move in a straight line across the ground, swerved to one side near the former location of the fires, then on again across the wide ribbon of open ground between the heaps of ashes and the forest's edge. At the base of a large tree, he stood up and beckoned to Trakor.

"Sadu chased her to this tree," he explained, his voice as confident as though he had witnessed the entire proceedings instead of reconstructing them through the mediums of sight and smell. "He did not get her. Come."

Lightly Tharn swung himself into the branches, Trakor close behind him. To the cave lord this was an engaging sport—a sport made more interesting because happiness for him depended on his ability to follow a cold trail.

Here a bit of lint from Dylara's tunic had caught beneath a segment of bark; there a newly budded shoot had been crushed by a naked foot. A speck of green moisture on an adjoining branch marked where that same foot had come to rest a little later; and further on a scuffed section of bark, almost too small to be detected, showed where a foot had slipped slightly.

To Tharn, guided by uncanny powers of perception and a woodlore second not even to the beasts themselves, all these marks were as evident and recognizable as words on a printed page to a scholar.

Dylara's progress had been snail-like that night as she worked her way through impenetrable darkness; Tharn moved along her pathway speedily and without faltering, Trakor following.

In ten minutes the cave lord covered the distance Dylara had required an hour to travel. Abruptly he altered his course upward toward the forest top, until, high among the smaller branches, he stopped and looked to his nose for information.

Almost at once Trakor noticed a troubled expression carve itself on Tharn's handsome face. "What is it, Tharn?"

His companion's lips set in a narrow line. "I do not know. Some strange manlike creature with long hairy arms and legs surprised her here and carried her away."

Moving slowly now, with many pauses, Tharn set out on the arboreal pathway accompanied by the bewildered Trakor.

FOR nearly three full hours Tharn continued on through the middle terraces. It took him a good part of that time to get some sort of accurate picture of how that strange, hairy creature had regulated its progress. The distance between marks left by its hands and grasping feet seemed far too great for anything other than the most agile of monkeys.

So intent was Tharn on following the spoor, and so intent on Tharn was his companion, that the first indica[Pg 107]tion either had of danger was when fully a score of spider-like forms engulfed them from the depths of as many hiding places among the foliage.

The first wave swept the still inexperienced Trakor completely from his branch, and he would have fallen headlong through space toward the ground below had not one of the ambushers caught him by an ankle and jerked him roughly back to a different type of danger. In a mad fury that was half rage and half fear the youth struck out blindly with his knife, killing three of his attackers and wounding several more before he went down beneath the sheer weight of numbers.

It was Tharn who took the subduing! With the first rustle of foliage his knife was in his hand and he met the onslaught of twisting, shrieking spider-men like a rocky crag meets a storm-swept sea. Enemy after enemy toppled into the void, their bodies torn by his keen blade of flint; others went to join them with skulls crushed by superhuman blows or with spines snapped like twigs. Early in the battle Tharn learned it was useless merely to push them from the limb: they would fall a few feet until some long sinuous limb would catch a lower branch and back they would come to the fight.

But the odds were far too unequal, and very slowly they pulled him down, as a pack of dogs will pull down a wide-antlered elk. Thick vines lashed his arms to his sides until he was trussed and helpless.

Then both captives were lifted by the loudly exultant spider-men and borne to a conical shaped hut of grasses hanging by means of a thick rope of that same material from a pair of stout branches above its roof. Here they were thrown roughly to the swaying, bobbing floor on opposite sides of the structure, then left to themselves as the long-limbed spider-men departed.

Trakor waited until he was certain the last of them was gone, then despite his bonds he managed to roll over until he was facing his friend three or four yards away. The cave lord was lying motionless on his side, swathed with strand upon strand of stout vines, his eyes open, his expression as calm and untroubled as though he were comfortably ensconced in his own cave.

"What will they do with us, Tharn?" whispered the youth.

Those broad shoulders moved in a faint shrug. "Who knows?"

It was far from being a satisfactory answer. Trakor was silent for a little while, thinking unhappy thoughts. Through the hut's thin walls came the shrill, unfamiliar chattering of many voices. Evidently the spider-men were holding some kind of a meeting—a meeting, Trakor was sure, concerning the eventual fate of their captives.

"Tharn...."

"Yes?"

"Can't we *do* something? Must we lie here like two helpless old men until they get around to k-killing us?"

Tharn caught the slight break in the youth's words and his slow smile disclosed flashing teeth. "They will not kill us for a while—otherwise we would have been dead before this. Perhaps they intend to torture us first—either to enjoy our suffering or to honor their tribal god."

"But now we can do nothing. Four of them are watching our every move through chinks in these walls; our first move toward escape would bring them upon us."

Trakor's eyes roved about the hut's sides. He could see no signs of gleaming eyes peering in on them, but long ago he had learned never to doubt Tharn's ability to know things beyond the evident.

His voice went down. "Can they hear us?"

"Of course," Tharn said. "But that does not mean they can understand [Pg 108]us. We do not speak their tongue, so we need not worry of being overheard."

"But what can we *do?*" Trakor demanded for the second time.

"At present, nothing. There is a way for us to escape but it depends on them leaving us here until Dyta finds his lair for the night."

"And if they don't leave us here until dark?"

Tharn's smile appeared again. "Would you cheat them of their pleasure by worrying yourself to death?"

TRAKOR digested that in silence, seeing the wisdom in his friend's quiet words. He found his fear lessening fast; there was something in Tharn's calm acceptance of their present difficulty that inspired confidence in their eventual escape.

With the waning of his own fear he found room for concern about someone else. "Tharn!" he gasped. "Are these the ones who captured Dylara?"

A somber expression crept into the cave lord's eyes. "I am sure of it."

"Do you think that they have ... that they...." He could not finish.

"After we get away," Tharn said grimly, "I will learn the answer to that. She may be held in another hut at this moment; but if they have slain her...."

The rest of the morning and the long afternoon which followed wore on. None of their captors entered the hut to learn how they were faring, although not once were they unobserved from without. During the heat of midday the sound of shrill voices stilled; but along toward evening it started up again.

Tharn's position was such that he could see through the small aperture which served at the hut's doorway. As a result he was able to see a horde of the spider-men begin the construction of a good sized platform of small branches in a neighboring tree. At first their purpose was not clear to him; but when, shortly before darkness set in, he saw two tall straight branches denuded of vegetation thrust upright, side by side, into the platform, he understood something of what they had in mind. This understanding became certainty a little later when he noticed a score of the female members of the tribe busy at the task of putting sharp points on many long straight sticks, using flint knives for that purpose.

He and Trakor would be bound to those stakes and slowly prodded to death! The all-important question was, would that take place this night or would the spider-men wait until dawn? It hardly seemed logical they would be so tortured without sufficient light for the spider-men to observe their sufferings; and to use fire among the inflammable tree tops would be sheer folly—if indeed these creatures were fire users at all.

Darkness came and still none of the spider-men entered the hut. Both men were suffering the pangs of thirst, but hunger had not yet become a problem. Evidently their hosts had no intentions of pampering them.

Sometime later three of the spider-men crawled into the hut and immediately set about examining the prisoners' thongs. So intense was the darkness now that they had to depend solely on the sense of touch. Satisfied the bonds were intact, the three found places on the floor and presently the sounds of even breathing told all were asleep.

Tharn lay there unmoving while the minutes slipped by and became hours. With the inexhaustible patience of all wild creatures he bided his time, waiting until the sleep of those guards was sound. Several times he heard Trakor stir impatiently and he smiled a little under cover of darkness. Trakor was waiting for a miracle.

The position of the three spider-men[Pg 109] was such that leaving by the door was impossible, even were the prisoners able to gain use of legs and arms. Even if they were able to loose their bonds, a simultaneous attack could account only for two—leaving the third free to raise an alarm.

Slowly, with many pauses lest the jiggling of the flooring arouse those guards, Tharn began to roll himself to Trakor's side. So carefully did he move that almost a full hour had passed before he reached his objective.

He felt the animal heat of the youth's body, and a barely audible word reached his ears. "Tharn?"

"Shhh!"

And then Tharn began to gnaw at Trakor's bonds. His strong sharp teeth bit into those tough green vines, filling his mouth with an unpleasant taste. It was slow, jaw-tiring work and the vines were many, stringy and reluctant to part. But the cave lord's indomitable patience and perseverance were not to be denied.

AT long last Trakor was able to free his hands. He winced as blood began to move again in his veins and minutes passed before he was able to control his hands. His questing fingers found the knots holding Tharn helpless and very soon both men were free to act.

Still lying side by side, Tharn began to whisper instructions. Twice one of the sleeping spider-men stirred and the two Cro-Magnards held their breaths until he had quieted.

When Trakor nodded to indicate Tharn's plan was clear to him, the cave lord rose to his feet and, like a shadowy wraith, moved to the nearest wall. This was a tense moment in the execution of his plan; its entire success depended on how substantial that wall would prove to be.

A brief examination by the means of touch alone told him the hut was constructed by first forming a cage-like skeleton of fairly thick but pliable boughs, then interlacing the openings with grass. The horizontal "beams" were roughly three feet apart; the roof, as Tharn had earlier been careful to gauge, was something like fifteen feet above the floor at its highest point.

Tharn's original plan had been to force an opening in one of these walls large enough for Trakor and him to wriggle through into the open air. But his ears and nose told him that this hut was practically ringed with patrolling sentries, several of which were perched among branches directly above the hut itself. The minute he and Trakor appeared outside they would be buried under an avalanche of spider-men.

But there was another way—a way daring and imaginative and infinitely dangerous. But in its daring lay the very chances for its success—while danger was so common a phenomenon in jungle life as to rouse little more than indifference among its dwellers.

Using the relatively sturdy skeletal branches foot—and hand—holds Tharn began to climb up that rounded wall. After some eight feet of this the inner side of the conical roof began and the cave lord was hard pressed to cling to the inward sloping surface.

But his steel thews served their purpose, and a moment or two later he had gained the single heavy section of branch at the very point of the roof. Here the thick grass rope which held the entire hut in the air entered from above, its ends tied securely about the cross piece on which Tharn was now perched.

From a hidden pouch in the folds of his loin cloth Tharn took a bit of keen-edged flint: the primitive razor with which he painstakingly scraped each second day his sprouting beard. With this he began to saw through the taut rope holding the hut aloft!

Gradually the straining rope began to part. Once it gave, the entire struc[Pg 110]ture, weighted by its five occupants, would plummet toward the ground nearly a hundred feet below. There were enough intervening branches to break the fall sufficiently to keep them from being dashed to instant death; but for those three sleeping spider-men it would be a mad, whirling journey that, once it ended, would daze them long enough for Tharn and Trakor to break for freedom.

Three strands remained, then two. The entire hut lurched sickeningly, the final strand parted with an audible snap as Tharn caught frantically at the cross piece, and down went the hut!

It was a mad mixture of crashing sounds, of breaking branches, of shrill screams, of falling and bouncing bodies, of clawing hands and feet. Slithering, scrambling shapes sought to stabilize themselves by attaching themselves to walls, ceiling or roof, but to no avail. Only Trakor, digging his fingers and bare toes desperately into the yielding flooring, and Tharn, wrapped tightly about that crosspiece, were able to hold their positions; while back and forth between them shuffled the three spider-men.

HALFWAY down, one entire wall broke loose, spilling the guards into the void. As the mazes of foliage grew denser nearer the ground, the remains of the hut began to slow its fall, grinding to a complete stop some twenty feet above ground.

Instantly Tharn and Trakor were out of the ruins and racing away through the branches. Behind them they could hear a wild chorus of angry screams, but apparently the spider-men were still too dazed and bewildered to set up a planned pursuit.

An hour later Tharn called a halt. They stood silently on a high branch for a little while, listening for some sign that their late captors had taken up the chase.

"We have thrown them off," Tharn said finally. "I'll give them a few hours to get over their shock and return to sleep—then I'm going back."

"Going back!" echoed Trakor, aghast, "Why?"

"I must learn what they have done with Dylara. Too, my knife, rope and bow and arrows are somewhere within the wreckage of that hut."

"But even you, Tharn, would be helpless against so many," protested Trakor.

Tharn shrugged. "It is the only way," he said, and there was that in his tone which ended further discussion.

They stretched their bodies out on adjoining branches and after a while Trakor fell into a troubled sleep. He awakened with a start, to find the first flush of dawn across the eastern sky and an empty branch where Tharn had been during the night.

He had little time to worry about his companion's absence; for barely had he opened his eyes than a rustling among the foliage of a neighboring tree brought him hastily to his feet in time to see Tharn emerge into view.

Across the caveman's back was his quiver of arrows, his bow and his rope; thrust within the folds of his loin cloth was his flint knife, and across one shoulder was the meaty foreleg of Neela, the zebra. This last he thrust into Trakor's dazed hands.

"Fill your belly," he said, grinning at the youth's slack-jawed expression. "We have work to do."

"But—But——"

"It was easy," Tharn said, "but only because I was very fortunate. When I got there they were not sleeping; for the commotion I doubt that they will sleep for a long time. While waiting for an opportunity to climb among their huts to hunt for Dylara, I set out to get back my weapons. The knife and rope were still in the broken hut and I found them at once. But I was forced to hunt about under the [Pg 111]trees for my arrows and bow—and a good thing it was!"

"Why do you say that?"

"I came across Dylara's trail. It seem——"

"In the *dark*? How could you *see*?"

Tharn tapped his nose and smiled as understanding dawned in his young friend's eyes. "It seems," he continued, "that she managed to get away from them just a little while ago, for her scent spoor was still fresh. I followed it far enough to learn that she found a game trail leading into the east which she followed. It is not far from here; feed, and we will set out to overtake her."

EARLY that afternoon Tharn and Trakor were swinging lightly through the trees above a winding elephant path cutting almost due south through the jungle. Even from his elevated position Tharn was able to make out an occasional print of a sandal in the powdery dust below. Dylara had left those marks—left them so recently that the passing feet of animals had not yet obliterated them.

The thought of her nearness brought an almost painful sensation of swelling deep within his chest and a strange ache at his wrists. The realization that he might soon be holding her within the circle of his arms, that his lips would be pressed against hers before another sun or two, made him eager to race madly ahead, outdistancing his slower companion.

But would she be as moved at sight of him? He recalled words spoken by her on those two brief occasions they had been together—first when he had wrested her from the caves of her father and taken her deep within the jungle. How her eyes had blazed with loathing! How her voice had rung out with hatred and disdain. "I hate you!" she had said; nor did she retract those words days later when, at the last possible instant, he had slain Sadu to save her life.[*]

[*] "Warrior of the Dawn," December, 1942-January, 1943, *Amazing Stories.*—Ed.

True, when Sadu sank lifeless to the ground between them, she had thrown herself into his arms, and the warm promise of her lips had crystallized forever within him his love for her. But that impulsive act might have been born of gratitude alone; he had been given no opportunity to find out one way or the other; for Jotan and seven of his men had arrived at that moment to take her from him.

Love, Tharn had long before decided, was a wonderful and annoying thing, bringing, as it did, both pleasure and torture, peace and unrest. All his wondering, all his doubts were for nothing until he could come face to face again with Dylara. And even then he might not know her answer; she would welcome him, of course, for in him alone was her sole hope of returning to her people.

But he did not want her to return to her own caves! She must go with him to his tribe— and go she must, with or without her own consent!

The winding trail below ended suddenly at the edge of an extensive clearing, through which ran a wide shallow sluggish river. From deep among a thick growth of reeds on the latter's opposite shore came a spine-tingling chorus of snarls and growls and the sounds of jaws grinding against bones.

Tharn seemed literally to fall the fifty or sixty feet between his elevated position and the ground below. The density of that growth of reeds kept him from seeing what animals were feeding there and the wind at his back left his nose useless in obtaining that information. Yet he charged in that direction with all the silent ferocity of Sadu himself, a swelling fear within him that it was Dylara's soft flesh which was furnishing those un[Pg 112]seen beasts with their dinner.

KNIFE in hand, lips curled back in a savage snarl, the cave lord tore his way through the tangled growth. With the first sounds of his passage, that chorus of growls ceased, and Tharn knew those unseen jungle dwellers were prepared to defend their kill.

Without slackening his pace he burst full upon a pack of hyenas surrounding the half-devoured carcass of Sadu, the lion. Snarling and spitting their rage they held ground, evil teeth bared, the hair standing stiff along their spines, ready to give battle; for, in numbers, cowardly Gubo was a force to be reckoned with.

An instant later three of them lay dead and the rest fleeing wildly into the surrounding jungle, while Tharn restored his bloody knife to its place in the folds of his loin-cloth and knelt beside Sadu's remains.

Trakor arrived on the scene while Tharn was completing his examination. Wide-eyed he stared at the lion and then at the stern face of his companion. He said, "What happened to Sadu, Tharn? Surely Gubo did not kill him?"

The cave lord shook his head. "Sadu died under many Ammadian spears."

"Ammadian?" repeated Trakor, astonished. "Not those who were hunting for Dylara?"

"I am not sure—yet."

Tharn rose and began to circle slowly that section of the clearing adjacent to Sadu's remains. Trakor watched him, fascinated, as he scrutinized the trampled grasses in an effort to piece together details of what had taken place. Twice he knelt and placed his nostrils close to the ground, the last time remaining in that position for several minutes.

Finally he straightened and beckoned to Trakor. "They have her," he said tonelessly. "She was fleeing from Sadu. Their spears cut him down in time, then they took her with them. There are many of them—at least fifty—and they are none I have come across before. Evidently we are very near to Ammad."

"How far are they ahead of us?"

"A sun's march—if that."

"What do we do now, Tharn?"

"Overtake them, of course—and take Dylara from them."

He said this last with a crisp decisiveness that left no room for doubt. But Trakor was shaking his head.

"There are fifty of them, Tharn. How can two of us fight so many?"

50

"There are other ways than by fighting. First we must catch up with them; then we will work out a way to get her."

THE swift journey through the jungle that afternoon was something Trakor was never to forget. As though driven by some overpowering urge, Tharn raced southward through the middle terraces with astonishing speed. Trakor sought manfully to match his pace, but time and again the cave lord left him behind, only to hold up on some high flung branch until his younger companion could close the gap. Twice Tharn stopped for rest periods—not because his own iron physique needed them, but to prevent Trakor from collapsing entirely. The realization was galling to the youngster, and it brought home forcibly to him that, for all his rapid progress in jungle lore and jungle living since Tharn had adopted him, he was still as a new-born child compared to Tharn.

And while Tharn fretted at thus being forced to slow his pace, he kept his impatience from showing by expression or word. Paradoxically he had spent almost a moon in teaching his companion the ways of the forest and its inhabitants without progressing along the trail to Ammad, but Dylara was a comparatively long way ahead at that time. Now that she was[Pg 113]within a few hours of him, even an instant's delay galled him.

Night came with the abruptness peculiar to this part of the world, and still the winding elephant trail below showed no signs of the Ammadians. Lack of light slowed Trakor to a comparative crawl, and while from time to time he urged Tharn to go on without waiting for him, the cave lord only shook his head.

And then, two hours after Dyta had sought his lair for the night, a faint glow against the southern sky marked the location of fire. This could have meant the most dread of all jungle perils—a forest fire; but the glow seemed too small and much too localized for that.

"The Ammadian night fires," Tharn said in reply to his friend's question. "Doubtless they have camped in some clearing along the way and have made a circle of fire to keep Sadu and Jalok at bay."

Not long thereafter the two Cro-Magnon men came to a halt high in the branches of a great tree. Below and before them was a wide clearing, in the center of which a host of white-tunicked men squatted about small cooking fires. The savory odors of freshly grilled meat rose on the air and Trakor felt his mouth water. Food had not passed his lips since that morning and traveling, he realized, made for large appetites.

The entire encampment was girded by windrows of blazing branches and thorn bushes under constant attendance by several of the Ammadian warriors. Spears, knives, bows and arrows were much in evidence, and there was that atmosphere of relaxed competence about the entire scene that indicated beyond doubt these were seasoned veterans who knew the jungle and its ways.

But of it all nothing existed for Tharn beyond a slenderly rounded white-tunicked figure seated in the company of several warriors about a cooking fire almost exactly in the center of the camp. At sight of that wealth of reddish gold hair and the sweet curve of a tanned cheek, he knew his search was over, that the girl he loved was almost within his reach. A burning impulse bade him throw caution to the winds and charge among those hated Ammadians and wrest her from them.

[Part III]
[Pg 97]

Under the threat of the guard's sword he knelt in a humble way
[Pg 98]

THOSE who let emotion rule filled early graves, however. A dead Tharn was useless to himself and useless to Dylara—and any such wild charge would be completely suicidal. Dylara seemed in no immediate danger, although it was clear from her actions, as well as the actions of those about her, that she was not sharing that cooking fire as an honored guest.

He fingered the string of his bow at its place about his shoulder. How he would have liked to send her some message that help was near, that soon she would be taken from these men and restored to the arms of one of her own kind. An arrow from out of the darkness into the heart of one of those men near her!

No. To do that would rouse the camp, keep them all awake for the rest of the night. For Tharn's purpose those Ammadians must remain lulled by a sense of security provided by their circle of fires. The quieter the night, the smaller the number of sentries to be posted when the time came for seeking sleeping furs for the night.

Trakor, too, was making good use of his eyes. This was the first party of Ammadians he had ever seen and he was open-mouthed with interest. The strange white skins they wore, the pieces of beautifully shaped leather on their feet, fascinated him and he longed to own such wondrous things. He stared for a long time at Dylara, marveling at her beauty. Even Lanoa, whose beauty paled into nothingness that of every woman of Gerdak's tribe was just another she when compared to this vision of loveliness. The thought made him smile a little sadly. It was the first time he had thought of Lanoa in nearly a moon.

Tharn said, "Remain here, Trakor, while I hunt for food."

The younger man nodded and Tharn slipped silently away. After he was gone Trakor lay down on a branch so situated as to give him an unimpeded view of the scene below and continued to watch....

A slight movement of his support aroused him. Tharn, laden with meat from a fresh kill, came to squat beside him and they filled their bellies with the hot, succulent raw flesh.

The young man wiped his hands and lips free of blood and turned inquiring eyes on his companion. "Have you thought of a way to take her from them, Tharn?"

The cave lord shook his head. "It will depend on where she sleeps and on how many guards are posted. Nothing can be done until the camp is settled for the night. Now we shall sleep."

With Tharn wedged into a tree fork in a neighboring tree, Trakor was left to select his own couch. He made no move toward doing so, however, but continued to lay along that same branch watching the Ammadians. He wondered how Tharn was able to go so calmly to sleep when so much that was new and exciting was taking place. His own weariness was completely forgotten.

An hour passed. Most of the camp was sleeping now. Four guards were moving slowly about the circle of fires; these and a group of five or six warriors talking about the ashes of a cooking fire were the only exceptions. Dylara was sound asleep, wrapped in a bundle of borrowed furs and lying well away from the nearest Ammadian.

A PLAN was taking shape slowly in Trakor's active mind. Why couldn't *he* rescue Dylara? This was his big chance to show Tharn how well he had profited by the cave lord's teachings. How proud his friend would be when he awakened to find Dylara beside him safe and sound, rescued by the stealth and daring of his protege!

The longer Trakor thought about it, the better it looked. Impatiently [Pg 99]he glowered at the dawdling warriors about the last fire. Were they to sit there gossiping throughout the night? At any moment Tharn might awake and spoil the whole thing!

Good! That last group was breaking up. One of them went over to the side of the sleeping girl, bent and stared at her, then straightened and called something to his companions. There was a brief sound of coarse laughter, the warrior rejoined his fellows and all sought their sleeping furs.

Another hour inched by. It was an unusually quiet night. Only twice did Trakor hear the voices of the big cats and each time it was from a distance. The darkness was absolute except for the dying flames from the protecting circle of fire below. Heavy clouds, forerunners perhaps of the storm Tharn had forecast, obscured moon and stars.

Those four guards continued their casual pacing. Trakor, watching intently, observed something finally that served to crystallize his plans. At fairly regular intervals those four came together at a point well away from where Dylara lay. Each time they stood in a group for several moments while they exchanged pleasantries, breaking the monotony of standing guard.

With slow caution, lest he arouse Tharn, the young cave man slipped groundward. There he began a slow circling of the clearing, masked from the sentries by heavy foliage. When he reached a spot on a direct line from where Dylara lay, he gently lowered himself bellyflat in the ribbon of grasses between the forest and the protecting wall of fire and began to inch himself forward like a giant snake.

Luckily the grass was high enough to hide him. His greatest danger was that one of those experienced warriors might glimpse the manner in which the grass tops were swaying.

He was near enough now to feel the heat of flames. His heart was pounding mightily and his fingers seemed to be trembling as he dragged himself still closer. Did they tremble with fear, he asked himself? No; it was only excitement that caused him to react so—of this he was certain.

According to his calculations those four guards should be close to another of those brief meetings on the opposite side of the camp. Slowly he lifted his head until he could make out their, and his own, position.

He was a few seconds behind schedule: the four of them were already together and not quite as far away as he would have liked. But in his favor was the fact that he was much closer to where Dylara lay sleeping than he had expected to be.

There was no time for hesitation, no time to bolster his courage. Rising to his feet, his body bent into a deep crouch, Trakor sped with swift silence through a break in the fire wall.

52

Beyond this, five hurried strides brought him beside the sleeping cave princess. He wasted no time in glancing around to learn if his daring move had been witnessed. He could feel the skin crawl at his back as he bent, shoved a fold of the girl's sleeping furs across her face to drown out any involuntary cry, and swung her up into his arms.

He wheeled to flee ... then froze in his tracks at sight of three spears leveled at his naked chest.

CHAPTER X
BEYOND AMMAD'S WALLS

THE stifling folds of fur suddenly thrust forcibly against her face awakened Dylara from a sound sleep. So dazed was she by the sudden attack that her paralyzed muscles were unable to resist as she felt herself swung up into a crushing embrace.

Then her momentary inertia snapped and she was on the point of strug[Pg 100]gling to free herself when the strong arms about her abruptly relaxed their hold and she staggered free.

With her eyes uncovered once more she saw a young warrior of the caves—a youth no older than she—beside her. Straight and tall he stood, menaced by three spears in the hands of three Ammadian fighting men, his strong, handsome, intelligent face reflecting fierce pride and deep chagrin. About his shoulders were looped a heavy blackwood bow, a quiver of stone-tipped arrows and a long grass rope. A flint knife was thrust within the folds of a loin-cloth of panther skin.

He stood there, a barbaric figure, eyeing those three spearheads leveled at his broad chest—eyeing them with a kind of dignified contempt that so reminded Dylara of Tharn, greatest warrior of them all, that she felt quick tears spring to her eyes. How truly magnificent were the men of her own kind when compared with these underdeveloped, almost frail, Ammadians!

Now came Ekbar, captain of Vokal's guards, pushing his way roughly through the press of aroused warriors hemming in both captives. He shoved his tall, square-shouldered body in front of Trakor and took in the situation at a glance.

"Disarm him!" he barked.

Hands tore away bow, arrows, rope and knife. Ekbar moved closer, his deep-set gray eyes moved appraisingly over the youth's splendid frame, and the already surly cast to his countenance deepened under a scowl.

"So, barbarian," he thundered, "you sought to take your mate from us! Only a stupid cave beast would expect to outwit Ammad's warriors. By what name are you called?"

"Trakor," said the youth, his voice emotionless.

"Trakor, eh? Where lie the caves of your tribe?"

"I belong to no tribe."

Without warning, Ekbar brought up a calloused hand and struck the young Cro-Magnard across the face, staggering him. "Another of your lies," he snarled, "and I turn you over to my men as a spear target. Where are your caves?"

Trakor made no attempt to reply. An angry red welt marked his cheek where Ekbar's hand had landed. His eyes were gleaming like sun against ice, but nothing else in his face betrayed the fury and hatred boiling within him. Truly, Trakor had come a long way since that day when Tharn had saved him from Sadu.

"How many came here with you?" Ekbar demanded.

"I came alone."

"Is this girl your mate?"

"No. I have never seen her before."

"Do you expect us to believe you risked certain capture to steal from us a girl you never saw before?"

Trakor shrugged. "You asked me. I do not care whether you believe me."

Ekbar's scowl deepened as he turned to Dylara. "You said you were brought here by Jotan. Was this barbarian one of his slaves?"

Dylara shook her head. "No. Nor have I ever seen him before tonight."

The captain chewed his lip uncertainly. "It is very strange," he complained. "I think both of you are lying. Well, if there are others who hope to take you from us, they will get the same welcome!"

He motioned to two of his men. "Bind this cave beast's arms and legs. Put him and the girl together in the center of the camp and triple the guard. Vokal shall have two new slaves at least!"

AN hour later most of the Ammadian camp was asleep once more. A dozen guards now patrolled the site and the fires were high again with additional fuel.

Dylara lay on her side, covered with sleeping furs to keep out the chill of[Pg 101]damp earth and night air. Only a few feet away lay Trakor, bound and helpless, his broad back turned to her exactly as they had left him.

It was a good-looking back, she admitted—not yet fully developed since its owner was still quite young, but it was well-formed and muscular nonetheless.

What, she wondered, was the real reason behind his attempt to take her from the Ammadians? Was he a member of some neighboring tribe? Had he come to spy on the men of Ammad, caught sight of her and tried to take her for himself?

She flushed a little at the thought. Not given to false modesty, Dylara knew she was very beautiful. But beauty, it seemed, could be more curse than blessing. It was that beauty which had led Tharn to take her by force from her own people; that beauty which had brought Jotan to her feet and caused him to take her with him on his return to Ammad. And now it appeared this handsome young cave warrior had been drawn into a lifetime of slavery by a single glimpse of her!

Yet she was woman enough to feel a little glow of pride at this tribute to her loveliness. He was young and very attractive—in many ways like Tharn, although his physical development was far short of the latter's.

The thought of Tharn brought an image of his mighty steel-thewed body and god-like face before her mind's eye. Where was he this night? Were his bones dotting the sandy surface of Sephar's arena while Nada, his mother, mourned? Or had he won through against hopeless odds and escaped to return to the caves of his people. She did not know, of course; perhaps she would never know....

Trakor rolled over to face her.

For a long moment the man and the woman stared deep into each other's eyes. Then the youth's lips parted in a slow smile, his strong regular teeth gleaming in the distant light of the fires.

"I am Trakor," he whispered. "You are Dylara!"

Open astonishment showed on her face. "How could you know that?"

She had spoken in her natural voice and alarm flickered in Trakor's eyes as they shifted to look about the silent camp. "Shhh!" he hissed. "Keep your voice down, else they hear and separate us."

Obeying, she said, "But how do you know my name?"

"Tharn told me."

"*Tharn!*" In spite of Trakor's warning, the word burst from her throat in a single loud exhalation. "But that is im——"

"Shhh!"

A SLEEPER a yard or two away stirred and turned over, while Dylara and Trakor lay unmoving, hardly daring to breathe. Dylara felt her heart thumping wildly while a hundred mixed emotions seemed to be battling within her. Questions, many questions welled up and sought to force her lips apart. At last she could bear it no longer.

"He is alive?" she whispered. "Is he still in Sephar? When did you see him last? Did he send you to find me? How were you able to follow me here?"

Trakor was shaking his head, smiling. "Tharn did not send me. I came here with him. He is in one of the trees bordering this clearing!"

"Ohhh!" Dylara closed her eyes as a wave of weakness seemed to roll over her. Tharn is here! Tharn is here! Elation, thanksgiving and relief swelled her heart almost to the bursting point. No matter now that fifty Ammadians lay between her and the cave lord. Fifty times fifty of them could not prevail against the might and cunning of Tharn!

Suddenly a new thought cut sharply across the flood of elation. Why [Pg 102]was she so happy and thrilled to learn he had sought her out? Had not she, only a few suns ago, decided in favor of Jotan?

But Jotan was dead; the grinning Ekbar had told her so. Now, as then, she marveled at how little the news depressed her. Yet she had brooded many times over the thought that Tharn was dead....

She opened her eyes. "But why did he send you to take me? Has he been hurt?"

Trakor reddened. "It was my idea; I wanted to help him."

He told her the whole story then, how he had met Tharn, the debt he owed the cave lord, their hunt, together, for Dylara—everything. When he came to that part of his story detailing his ill-advised attempt to free Dylara, he stammered a little but got it all out.

Dylara was smiling as he finished. "It was very brave of you to try what you did. And although they caught you and have us both now, we need not worry. Tharn will take us from these people."

"I know that," Trakor said quietly. "It is only that he may think less of me for bungling things this way."

The girl shook her head. "You must know him better than that."

They fell silent as one of the guards sauntered in their direction during his routine inspection of the camp. Dylara, weary from her hours of jungle travel during the day before, fell asleep before the guard was at a safe distance for further conversation with Trakor.

When the youth saw she was sleeping, he lay there for a long time, staring at her loveliness and thinking bitter thoughts of his clumsiness in being taken captive. Tharn, he knew, would be unable to attempt a rescue with so many guards about; but tomorrow night the Ammadians, their suspicions lulled, would doubtless post no more than the usual number of sentries. To Tharn, four of the dull-witted Ammadians would be hardly any problem at all!

SHORTLY before dawn the men of Ammad were filling their bellies and preparing to break camp. When the line of march was being formed, Dylara and Trakor were separated—the girl being placed between two warriors midway along the column; while the young caveman, his arms bound firmly behind his back, was stationed well up toward the front. Ekbar strode back and forth along the line, making certain each man was in his appointed spot, inspecting Trakor's bonds, and cautioning those responsible for both prisoners.

Shortly before Dyta pulled his shining head above the eastern horizon of serrated tree tops, the Ammadian captain barked an order and the double line of warriors got under way.

By mid-morning both forest and jungle began to thin out as the path underfoot lost its level monotony and began to become a steep incline. The air seemed to grow steadily cooler and gradually all underbrush beneath the trees began to thin out, then disappear entirely, leaving an almost park-like appearance to the forest. Even the trees were further apart and more and more often there were stretches of grassland without any trees whatsoever.

Shortly after noon, Ekbar called a halt at the edge of a vast plain covered with a rich green species of grass which seemed to grow no higher than a man's ankles. Here and there on the gently undulating vista of grassland stood trees, usually no more than one or two together. To the south, nearly at the horizon, was a long dark line that Trakor at first took to be clouds but which, later, he was to learn was the beginning of another expanse of forest and jungle.

Food was distributed and eaten, an hour's rest period was announced, and[Pg 103]the Ammadians gathered their strength for the final stage of the journey. From remarks the two prisoners overheard they learned that Ammad lay half a day's march beyond that distant line of trees, and that every man in the group was anxious to put the city's strong walls between him and the hated jungle.

Trakor was beginning to worry. Crossing that vast plain during the heat of day was bound to be a trying experience, especially for the comparatively frail girl. But worse than that, Tharn was going to be placed at a disadvantage in following them. These Ammadians were not complete fools; they would keep a sharp lookout in all directions against possible attack from animals or men; for Tharn to attempt to follow them during daylight hours would mean certain detection. Still, even though the cave lord was forced to wait until darkness before venturing out into the open, he could easily overtake the Ammadians while they were camped for the night.

ALL during the long afternoon which followed, Trakor kept shooting brief glances over his shoulder toward the north, half-expecting to catch a glimpse of his friend. But other than a distant herd or two of grass-eaters, no sign of life appeared.

Night came while the column was still an hour's march from the last barrier of jungle between it and Ammad. At any moment Trakor expected to hear the captain call a halt.

That call never came. Instead the group pushed on until the trees were reached; a brief stop was made near the mouth of a wide trail at that point while gumwood branches were found and ignited, and once more the column took up the march.

After two hours of plodding along the winding game path, flames from the smoking torches casting eerie shadows among the thick foliage and heavy tree boles, Trakor could stand this uncertainty no longer.

"When," he said to the Ammadian warrior next to him, "are we to make camp for the night?"

The man gave him a sidelong glance and a crooked grimace of derision. "I thought you men of the caves were accustomed to walking long distances?"

55

"I can walk the best of you into the ground!" retorted Trakor. "But when night comes you usually stop and huddle behind fires lest the great cats get you."

The Ammadian scowled. "We are afraid of nothing! But only animals and uncivilized barbarians wander about the jungle at night. We are but a little way from Ammad; it would be senseless to spend a night in the open when the city is so close."

Trakor's heart sank. "Only a little way from Ammad!" The words beat against his mind like the voice of doom. Dylara and he were lost; Tharn could not save them now!

Yet hope did not leave him entirely. His boundless faith and admiration where the cave lord was concerned would not let it die. He caught himself glancing time and again at the low-swaying boughs overhead. Every flickering shadow from the torches was transformed into the lurking figure of his giant friend.

But as the hours passed and nothing happened those last faint glimmerings of hope began to fade and his spirits sank lower and lower.

Ahead of him, Dylara was going through much the same travail. She staggered often now from weariness; for she had been on her feet, except for that brief period at noon, since early morning and she lacked the strength and stamina of the others. She wondered, too, if Tharn would make an attempt at rescuing Trakor and her before Ammad was reached; but the memory of his fearless en[Pg 104]trance into Sephar in search of her brought the thought that he might do the same thing this time.

ABRUPTLY the forest and jungle ended at open ground. Beyond a mile of open ground, flooded by Uda's silver rays, stood the towering stone walls of Ammad.

To the dazed, unbelieving eyes of Trakor it was like a scene from another and wonderful world. In either direction, as far as he could see, rose that sheer, massive man-made wall of gray stone, broken at wide, regular intervals by massive gates of wood. Far beyond the wall he could see mammoth structures of stone at the crest of five small hills. The sides of those hills were lined with other, and smaller buildings of the same material. Lights twinkled from breaks in their walls, an indication that, unlike the cave men, Ammadians did not spend most of the night hours asleep.

Dylara, accustomed to city walls and buildings of stone from her long stay in Sephar, was not so overcome by the scene. Still Ammad's size, even from the small part visible at this point, brought a gasp to her lips. She had thought Sephar wonderful beyond compare, but next to Ammad, it was hardly more than a frontier outpost.

A challenging voice rang out from the shadowy recess shielding the nearest gate and Ekbar's column ground to a halt. Three Ammadian soldiers, their white tunics gleaming under the moon's rays, moved toward them and Vokal's captain advanced to meet them.

After a brief discussion, the three warriors returned to their posts, the twin gates swung wide, Ekbar's command sounded and the column of fifty Ammadians, accompanied by the two prisoners, filed briskly through the opening.

Trakor, looking back over his shoulder, saw the twin gates move slowly, grindingly together, saw the reaches of distant jungle narrow, then disappear as those two sections of heavy planking ground firmly into place.

And in the dull, sodden thud of their meeting, the last flicker of hope was extinguished in Trakor's heart.

IT was the hour of Jaltor's daily audience. The vast throne room was crowded with men and women from all walks of Ammadian life. Slaves, freedmen, merchants, traders, warriors and noblemen crowded that two-thirds of the room set aside for their use.

At the far end of the hall-like chamber, set off from the heavily crowded section by a line of stalwart guards armed with spears, stood a pyramid-shaped dais, its sides serrated into wide steps. At the flattened apex stood a richly carved, high-backed chair of dark wood. Here sat Jaltor, king of all Ammad, his tremendous, beautifully proportioned body seeming to dwarf not only the chair and its supporting dais but the entire room as well. He was bending forward slightly at the waist, his head turned slightly the better to hear the words a nobleman was droning into his ear. The shuffling of many feet, the buzz of many muted voices from beyond the line of guards formed a backdrop of sound against the message he was receiving.

Because of the ever-present possibility of assassination at the hand of some disgruntled commoner or a hired killer, only the noblemen of Ammad were allowed to pass that spear-bristling line of guards. As a result, the citizenry of the city was split into factions, each faction owing its allegiance to that nobleman situated in its district. The nobleman justified [Pg 105]the loyalty of his faction by protecting its members against criminals and vandals both within and without his district and by pleading their side of any dispute that could be settled only by Jaltor, head of the State.

Rivalry between noblemen was strong and usually bitter, although none of this ever appeared on the surface. A nobleman whose influence and power showed signs of weakening found his territory subjected to raids, his followers won away from him by threats and promises. With the loss of influence and power his wealth would dwindle, his guards and warriors would desert to other noblemen, until at last Jaltor must step in and elevate some favorite of his own, or some friend of another noble, into the victim's place.

Against a side wall of the teeming throne room, on this particular afternoon, stood Vokal, nobleman of Ammad. On his smooth, finely featured face was his accustomed air of dreamy disinterest in his surrounds, his soft gray hair was carefully arranged to point up its natural wave, his slender shapely arms were carelessly folded across the chest of his plain white tunic. There was no purple edging on that tunic now; in the palace of Jaltor only the king himself could display that color.

Beneath that serene exterior, however, was no serenity. Vokal was badly worried. Eleven suns had passed since the day word of Heglar's attempt to kill Jaltor had electrified all Ammad. Guards had hustled the old man roughly from the throne room—and from that moment on no one heard of him again.

But he should have been heard of! Four slaves of slaves—the lowest human element in Ammad—should have dragged his traitorous old body through Ammad's streets to be spat upon and reviled by loyal citizens.

And Garlud—what of Garlud? No one had seen him either since that day. Not that his absence caused much speculation—almost none in fact. It was not unusual for Ammad's noblemen to absent themselves from the city for days, even moons, on end. A hunting trip, a visit to friends in other of Ammad's cities—any of several explanations would have accounted for his disappearance.

THE true reason should have been his involvement in Heglar's plot to do away with Jaltor. But only Vokal of all Ammad's thousands could know that—and he had no business knowing it. Garlud's affairs were going on smoothly in his absence, in charge of the captain of his guards. By this time, if Vokal's plans had not miscarried, the silvery haired nobleman should have been summoned by Jaltor, told of Garlud's perfidy, and his holdings and position handed to him in view of Jotan's continued absence.

And then there was Rhoa—Heglar's young and beautiful wife ... and Vokal's mistress. He had not seen her since the day her husband had made the attempt on Jaltor's life. This was agreed upon between them for safety's sake; the understanding was that once Heglar's death was known, Vokal could court and win her in the usual manner.

But what had been foreseen as only two or three days of separation had lengthened into eleven and still no word of Heglar's fate. Long before this those thousand tals paid to Heglar should have come back into Vokal's hands, accompanied by Rhoa herself. Vokal was becoming increasingly uneasy about those missing tals; let enough time elapse before he could take Rhoa as mate and she might reconsider, refuse Vokal and keep the thousand tals for herself. There would be nothing he could do about it, either. To threaten her or use force could anger her into betraying him.... Vokal shuddered. Only this morning [Pg 106]she had sent word to him that she was tired of this uncertainty, that something must be done to learn what had happened to her husband.

Another thing: Ekbar and his men should have returned before this—returned with word that Jotan, Garlud's son, was dead and no longer in a position to step into his father's sandals as first ranking nobleman of Ammad. What was delaying the man?

Well, Vokal told himself doggedly, he could wait no longer. There were ways to get at the truth—ways that would not betray his interest in the matter. For instance, there was Sitab, an officer in Jaltor's own palace guard....

But first would come another plan at breaking that wall of silence. This same morning, Vokal had remembered a case involving a merchant whose shop was on the boundary line between Vokal's territory and the neighboring district belonging to Garlud. A moon or so before, one of Vokal's collectors had informed Ekbar that this merchant was claiming allegiance to Garlud, even though his shop was not in the latter's territory.

It was a minor matter and as a rule a nobleman did not complain to Jaltor about these single isolated cases. It was only when there was evidence of some systematic raid by a neighboring nobleman that a complaint was filed. Clearly Garlud had not ordered any such raid, but enough evidence was there at least to bring the matter to Jaltor's attention, thus making it necessary for Garlud to defend himself against the charge.

57

"Vokal—the noble Vokal." The cry of Jaltor's personal clerk rang out over the packed room. "Approach the Throne and present your plea."

With gentle courtesy Vokal pushed between the press of humanity, passed through the line of armed guards and mounted the steps of Jaltor's dais.

He bowed low before the giant ruler of Ammad. "Greetings, Most-High. Vokal, your loyal subject, begs permission to plead a grievance."

Jaltor gave him a warm and friendly smile. He had always liked Vokal; the nobleman's quiet manner and gentle courtliness were always welcome.

"It is unusual for the noble Vokal to *have* a grievance," he said. "That in itself is in your favor. What is troubling you?"

"A matter of a boundary dispute involving a merchant in my territory. It seems he has been 'influenced' into transferring allegiance to another nobleman."

Jaltor nodded his understanding. "Have you been bothered by many such cases involving the same nobleman?"

"No, Most-High," Vokal said. "And I am quite sure Garlud knows nothing of this one. Perhaps one of his collectors is a bit—over zealous. By bringing the matter to Garlud's attention at this time, further incidents can be averted."

NOTHING changed in Jaltor's expression at mention of Garlud's name; Vokal was sure of that. He said, neither too quickly nor too slowly:

"I agree, noble Vokal: this must have happened without Garlud's knowledge. Unfortunately the matter can not be brought to his attention just now, but I shall see to it that he hears about it at the earliest possible moment."

It was an opening Vokal could not resist. "The noble Garlud is not in Ammad at present?"

"I believe not." Jaltor's voice and manner remained unchanged, but something flickered in his eyes—something Vokal did not miss.

"My deepest thanks to you, Most-High," he said with that gracious and gentle air for which he was noted.

"It is always a pleasure to talk with you, Vokal."[Pg 107]

It was a dismissal and Vokal, bowing low, withdrew. As he crossed the huge throne-room toward the exit, his thoughts were sharp and incisive.

Something had happened to Garlud. Jaltor's eyes and the brevity of his answer to Vokal's question confirmed that. But what? And why was the nobleman's fate kept such a secret? Did Jaltor suspect Garlud of having accomplices other than old Heglar?

These were questions demanding quick and positive answers. First he must learn what had happened to the missing nobleman. If his death could be verified—and, of course, Heglar's as well—there was a way to make the information open to the public. That done, and Vokal would be free to move up in rank to a place second only to Jaltor himself—as well as being able to marry Rhoa and recover his thousand tals.

A great deal of careful thought must go into his next move. And so Vokal left the palace and returned to his home, where, in the quiet of his private apartment, he would be able to concentrate on these pressing problems.

WHEN the long hour of public audience was over, Jaltor returned to his quarters. His step was quick and purposeful and his dark eyes were alight with an inner excitement.

At the entrance to his apartment, the guard on duty there leaped to attention at his approach. To him Jaltor snapped, "Find Curzad at once and inform him I wish to see him immediately."

The guard saluted and went swiftly off along the corridor.

A clay jug of wine, cooling in a low basin of water on one of the tables of polished wood, caught the monarch's eye. Not bothering to use one of the several goblets standing nearby, Jaltor swung the jug to his lips and took a long, satisfying draught on the contents, wiped his lips on the back of a muscular forearm and began to pace the floor.

A light knock sounded at the door and Curzad, as iron-faced and reserved as ever, came into the room. He was in the act of closing the door behind him when Jaltor said, "Wait. Send the guard out there away. I don't want our conversation overheard, even by the most trustworthy of your men."

Curzad obeyed, then closed the door and came into the room, standing there stiff-backed, waiting further orders.

Jaltor jerked a thumb at a chair. "Sit down, my friend, and help yourself to the wine."

The captain of the palace guards let himself gingerly down into the luxurious depths of soft upholstery and reached for the wine jug and a goblet. Most of Ammad's noblemen would have lifted outraged eyebrows at such familiarity between the world's most powerful monarch and a mere warrior. But Curzad and Jaltor had fought side by side in many a battle and through many a campaign, and each honored and respected the other.

The tall broad-shouldered king dropped into a chair across from Curzad and took up jug and goblet. "Tell me, Curzad, how fares the noble Garlud?"

"As well as in the days he walked Ammad's streets a free man," the captain said in his deep calm voice. "As an old fighting-man, hardship affects him but little."

"Perhaps his cell is too comfortable," Jaltor said, his lips twitching slightly.

"There are no comfortable cells beneath your palace, Most-High. Garlud's least of all. He sits alone and in utter darkness, the only sounds the scurrying feet and squeaking voices of rats. Only the strong mind of a great warrior can endure such [Pg 108]for very long without cracking."

"Are you suggesting I am too harsh with him?" Jaltor was openly smiling now.

"I am suggesting nothing to Ammad's king."

"It has been eleven suns since I sent my closest friend to languish in those pits," Jaltor said, smiling no longer. "Nor has it been easy for me, Curzad. But I must learn who, if not Garlud, was behind old Heglar's attempt on my life."

He tossed off the wine and put his goblet down on the table top. "Something happened today," he said, "that may be the first crack in this eleven-sun wall of silence. One of Ammad's noblemen brought up Garlud's name to me during the afternoon audience."

SOME of the impassiveness in Curzad's expression slipped a little and his fingers whitened on the goblet's stem. He made a sound deep within his massive chest but said nothing.

"It may mean nothing, however," Jaltor went on, "for the way in which it came up was both necessary and natural. To make it even more likely to amount to nothing, the nobleman was Vokal—a man I have never hesitated to trust."

"Garlud once enjoyed a similar distinction," Curzad commented dryly.

Jaltor's eyes flashed. "Do you forget that Garlud was named by a man whose word had never been doubted?"

"I forget nothing, Most-High," was the quiet reply.

A moment's silence followed, then Jaltor said, "Well, a few more days, one way or the other, will not matter. If Vokal is the man we are looking for, he will make another attempt at learning Garlud's whereabouts. So far he is our only lead—other than old Heglar's beautiful mate, Rhoa. Twice she has come to me, asking what has happened to him, and both times I have refused to say. Oddly enough," he added thoughtfully, "she seemed more curious than worried."

"Perhaps it would be wise to have her watched."

The monarch gave a brief snort of laughter. "I am not completely a fool, my friend. Rhoa has been under constant surveillance since the day old Heglar died. Thus far her actions have been above suspicion."

Curzad's shoulders rose and fell in a shrug. "Meanwhile," he said, "Garlud's son, Jotan, draws closer to Ammad. Any sun now he and his men may approach its gates."

"Which is one of the reasons I sent for you. Shortly before Dyta brings his light tomorrow, send fifty of your most trusted warriors to intercept and take captive Jotan and his men. Return them to Ammad under cover of darkness and confine them all in the pits. It might be wise to place Jotan in the cell next his father and a trusted warrior in a neighboring cell to listen in on their conversations."

"You'll never trick Garlud so easily."

"No man is perfect, Curzad," observed Jaltor, smiling grimly. "I intend to overlook no possibility in getting to the bottom of this matter."

CHAPTER XI
CAME THARN

ONCE Tharn was satisfied that the column of fifty Ammadians, with Dylara and Trakor in its midst, meant to cut directly across that wide expanse of sun-baked grasses, he set out on a circuitous course to pass them that he might be the first to reach the distant forest beyond. It meant covering a quarter again as much ground, but the advantage made this extra effort worth while.

As he moved across the prairie at a tireless trot, bitter thoughts filled his mind. Last night Dylara had been [Pg 109]almost within arm's reach and it seemed his long search for her was on the point of ending. Caution, ever a strong attribute of jungle dwellers, had brought on his decision to wait until the camp was settled down for the night before he attempted to wrest her from the Ammadians who held her captive. Had the circumstances demanded it, Tharn would have unhesitatingly charged all fifty of those armed men; but only the inexperienced uses force where stealth will do.

And so Tharn had restrained his impatience, deciding to nap an hour or two while he waited. He had awakened to loud voices and had witnessed, in helpless rage, Ekbar's cross-examination of Trakor and Dylara. His first reaction was anger that Trakor had attempted a deed beyond his still limited prowess, but understanding came at once. It was in this fashion that the boy had sought to show his gratitude to Tharn, and in so doing had alerted the camp—and gotten himself captured in the bargain!

Thus by the impulsive act of a hero-worshiping boy had Tharn's original task become a double one—and doubly difficult to accomplish successfully.

At first he considered entering the camp after another hour or two, but with the trebling of the guard he gave up the idea—for the night at least. There would be other nights—nights when the number of guards would be normal and their behavior the same. Guards, it was well known, were apt to become heavy-eyed and less alert along toward dawn.

All during the following morning Tharn trailed the Ammadians. At first he did so from a position among the branches above them; but along toward mid-morning the trees began to thin out, as well as the undergrowth normally covering the ground between the giant boles, and he was forced to lag further and further behind. When the fifty men reached the prairie's edge and stopped to rest, he managed to work his way close enough to hear conversations among several of the men.

Their talk was filled with eagerness at being close to Ammad once more, and Tharn was aware of a feeling of sharp disappointment. Was it possible this group would reach the city before nightfall? If that were true, his chances of freeing Dylara and Trakor were small indeed.

An hour later Tharn was standing in the shelter of a large tree, his eyes regretfully watching as the entire party forged across that broad stretch of open ground where he might not follow.

Two hours before sunset Tharn reached the wall of jungle and trees. The column of Ammadians were still far out in the grasslands and would need another three hours to reach the game trail where Tharn was standing. The cave lord decided to spend that time in reconnoitering. There was the possibility that Ammad itself lay not too deep within the forest to make it worthwhile for the approaching column to continue its march even after darkness fell.

It was as he had feared. Less than an hour's swift progress through the forest's upper terraces brought him to the edge of a vast clearing, much like the one surrounding Sephar, beyond which rose sheer grey walls of stone. From his elevated position he could see beyond that barrier, and he saw that, except for its far greater size and magnificence, Ammad was not much different from Sephar. But in size alone did Ammad make Sephar seem a small jungle clearing by comparison. In diameter it was at least ten miles and there were five small hills grouped near its center, at the apex of each a magnificent structure. The general layout of streets was much the same as he had found in Sephar, but there were more people on them.[Pg 110]

FOR nearly an hour Tharn sat high among the concealing foliage of his tree and watched the scene below and before him. Hunting parties well laden with trophies of the hunt entered the clearing from the trail beneath him and the great gates of wood, guarded by Ammadian warriors, swung open to let them through the massive wall. It was a wall much higher and stronger than Sephar had boasted and getting past it was going to take some doing.

Tharn shrugged and turned back to pick up those who were holding Dylara and Trakor. Perhaps, he thought as he moved swiftly along the aerial highway, it would not be necessary for him to pass those walls. Even if those fifty Ammadians did not make camp for tonight, he might still find a way to rob them of their captives. Let them lower their guard for even a moment, let them become only a little careless—and their hands would be empty before their minds had caught up with their eyes!

He arrived at the prairie's edge only a few moments before Ekbar and his men reached the game trail's mouth. Tharn, narrow-eyed and alert, watched them halt and gather gumwood torches, saw these latter ignited and the march resumed. It was as he had feared: they intended to press on until Ammad's walls hemmed them safely in.

Even Tharn's iron-willed reserve broke a little at this last blow. Through the velvety darkness of a semi-tropical night he moved stealthily above them, his fangs bared slightly, his hand hovering often near his blackwood bow and the quiver of arrows.

Several times he saw Trakor's upturned face as the youth sought to pierce the wavering shadows cast by the flaming shadows. He knew well what was passing through Trakor's mind and, despite his own disappointment, he smiled a little. Let the headstrong cave youth worry a little; it would be small payment indeed for the trouble he had caused!

60

But most often Tharn's eyes went to Dylara. He saw her stagger now and then from sheer physical exhaustion and his heart went out to her. How he would have loved to wrest her from that spear-bristling line of warriors! There was no way to do that, however. A barrage of arrows could have cleared away those men directly around her, but a rope about her wrist had its other end bound about the arm of the man beside her; and even had Tharn leaped down on the heels of his arrows to slash away that rope spears might fell either or both of them.

No, for all his giant strength and agility he was as helpless to aid the girl of his choice as though miles lay between them.

Finally the time came when Tharn realized Ammad was only a short distance ahead. He must resign himself to the unescapable fact that Dylara and Trakor were going to be taken beyond those walls whether he liked the idea or not. This meant his energies and cunning must be diverted to a different channel; and with this in mind the cave lord halted on a broad leafy branch above the column, waiting while the twin lines moved ahead at a snail's pace.

A pair of tall husky Ammadian warriors were last in line. One of them carried a blazing torch, the other had a heavy pack about his shoulders. They plodded along, weariness evident in the lines of bent shoulders and dragging feet. The one with the pack seemed especially tired and every fifty or sixty feet he would pause momentarily to shift his burden to a new position. Each time this happened the distance between him and his companion became a matter of ten or fifteen feet until, pack adjusted, the man hurried forward to join his unheeding partner.[Pg 111]

A wry smile touched Tharn's firm lips. With uncanny ease he slipped to the ground and moved silently along behind the wall of undergrowth flanking the trail, his course parallel with the column's rear guard.

A BEND in the path was coming up. Already most of the column had made the turn and was out of sight. Quickly Tharn raced ahead until he was at a point no more than ten feet from the turn. Crouching here, concealed by a maze of creepers and brush, he picked up a short length of dead branch and waited.

As the last two Ammadians reached a position directly opposite to the crouching cave lord, Tharn thrust out the branch two or three inches above the path's surface and squarely between the legs of the pack bearer.

The man's swinging foot struck against the unyielding wood and, weighted by the heavy pack and weary from the long hours without rest, he stumbled and fell headlong.

His companion, aroused by the thump of a falling body and a string of curses rising on the night air, turned back and bent to help him up.

"What happened, Posak?"

"What does it look like? Do you think I decided to lie down and rest awhile?"

Still muttering under his breath Posak got shakily to his feet and turned his back on his companion to pick up the heavy pack. When he turned back again, his amazed eyes beheld his friend face down and motionless in the trail and the mightily muscled figure of an almost naked cave man standing over him and holding the torch.

Posak opened his mouth to yell a warning to the others of the column. The cry was never voiced. An iron fist swept from nowhere to crash full against the point of his chin. There was a sharp brittle sound like a branch breaking and Posak sank lifelessly to the ground, his neck snapped cleanly in two.

Quickly Tharn propped the torch of gumwood against a tree bole and dragged the two corpses into the brush. With rapid care he stripped tunic and sandals from one body and donned them. The tunic he found to be tight across his chest but still adequate; the sandals fitted him perfectly.

So quickly had the cave lord acted that by the time he caught up the torch and rounded the bend in the trail, the end of Ekbar's column was no more than a dozen yards away. No one seemed to be looking back of his shoulder in search of the missing pair, a fact probably explained by the sight of open ground directly ahead.

Blazing torch held high, thus leaving his face shadowed, Tharn moved easily along at the rear of the column of Ammadians, across the ribbon of open ground about Ammad's walls, and on through the city gates.

VOKAL awakened under the touch of gentle but insistent fingers against his shoulder. He opened his eyes to find one of his personal slaves, a lighted candle in one hand, bending over him.

"What do you want, Adgal?" he demanded, scowling.

"Ekbar has returned, Most-High," the slave replied, cringing. "I told him you were sleeping but he demanded that I arouse you at once."

61

The nobleman bounded from the bed and caught up his tunic. "Where is he?"

"In the outer chamber, Most-High."

"Good. Tell him I'll be out immediately."

When Vokal entered the wide living room he found the captain of his guards standing at rigid attention just inside the door. The nobleman, his tunic fresh and unwrinkled, his [Pg 112]thick grey hair as smoothly brushed as though this were midday instead of the dead of night, strolled to a nearby table, poured out a single glass of wine and sank into a chair. His thin shapely fingers lifted the goblet slowly to his lips, he sipped the liquid as slowly, savoring its bouquet. Finally he put down the goblet and swung his dreamy-eyed gaze to the uncomfortable and self-conscious captain of the guards.

"Well, Ekbar?" he said softly.

"He is dead, Most-High."

"Indeed? You took care of the matter yourself?"

"No, Most-High. He was killed many suns before my men and I came upon his men. Sadu, the lion, slew him."

Vokal stiffened slightly. "How do you know this?"

Ekbar retold, in detail, the story given him by Tykol. For several minutes after he finished Vokal sat there and thought it over while he sipped from his goblet of wine. "... You are sure he was not lying?"

"Yes, Most-High. There were but thirty-seven of them, where once there was fifty, and many wore strips of cloth over wounds left by Sadu's claws. Scouts who knew Jotan by sight reported he was not with the column." He hesitated. "One part of their report I did not understand, however, although it probably is not important."

"Tell it to me."

Ekbar shrugged. "There was a woman with them—a young and very beautiful girl. The scouts say she was very lovely—dark-haired, a pleasing figure and clearly the daughter of some nobleman."

"Why did you not ask this Tykol who she was?"

"I learned about her the following day. By that time Tykol was dead."

Vokal nodded. "The balance of Jotan's men were not aware of being watched?"

"No, Most-High. I took pains to keep that from them. Since Jotan's earlier death was something we had not foreseen, I acted as I thought you would order. Since Jotan is not with them it would be better that they reached Ammad and told of his death under the fangs and claws of Sadu."

"You have acted wisely, Ekbar, and I shall not forget it."

The captain flushed with pleasure. He said, "We did not return empty-handed, noble Vokal. Two cave people fell into our hands—one of them a beautiful young woman who told us some wild story about being Jotan's intended mate."

At Vokal's look of languid interest, Ekbar repeated the story Dylara had told him.

"And you say," Vokal said when the captain finished, "that this cave girl is very beautiful?"

"There is none in all Ammad who is more lovely," Ekbar said, his deep-set eyes glittering.

"How interesting!" Vokal leaned back in his chair, his long, well-kept fingers toying with the stem of his wine goblet. "Where is she now?"

"Both she and the cave man we captured a little later are under guard in the outer corridor, Most-High. I thought you might wish to look them over before they were placed with the other slaves."

"Bring them in, my good Ekbar," murmured Vokal.

THE captain saluted stiffly and withdrew. A moment later he was back again followed by the two captives and a second guard.

For several moments the nobleman let his eyes move slowly over the two cave people. The man, he saw, was, despite his youth, a remarkable physical specimen, extraordinarily handsome and evidently intelligent and keen-witted as so many of the cave dwellers were. With the proper attitude toward his new master it would [Pg 113]not be long before he rose to the status of a warrior and an end to his position as slave. Judging from the flashing eyes and his air of insolent contempt, it would take a few days of iron-fisted discipline, however, to make him amenable. Well, Ekbar was a past master of that art.

The girl, though, was another matter entirely. Ekbar had not exaggerated in naming her more beautiful than any of Ammad's women—including those of noble birth. Despite her travel-worn tunic and the weariness evident in every line of face and figure, her beauty shone through like Dyta's brilliant rays. A man could lose his heart in that red-gold wealth of softly curling hair falling to her shoulders; he could drown in the depths of those sparkling brown eyes. He smiled a little at these thoughts. What would Rhoa, dark-haired, olive-skinned, beautiful and passionate, think if she knew he was having such thoughts about a wild girl of the caves?

Well, Rhoa need not know. Most noblemen had beautiful slave girls and most noblemen's wives ignored the fact....

Dylara bore his steady gaze with calm indifference. The enforced association with the men of Ammad during the past several moons had taught her a great deal about them; that, plus a native shrewdness, told her she could expect little sympathy and no help from this silver-haired, languid-eyed man whose property she now appeared to be.

"Your name, cave girl?"

The soft, almost caressing voice repelled her. There was something ugly and evil behind it—a reflection of the man's true personality.

She met his gaze unflinching. "I am Dylara."

"What is this wild story you told the captain of my guards—the story that you were the noble Jotan's mate?"

"I was never his mate. I am no man's mate."

"But he wanted you. Why, then, did he not take you?"

"Because, in spite of his being an Ammadian, Jotan was a true nobleman. He sought to win me with kindness and consideration instead of taking me by force."

Deliberately Vokal let his eyes wander over the beautiful lines of her figure. "From your tone I judge that you do not believe all Ammadians would be so considerate. From looking at you I would say he was more stupid than anything else...."

"However, that is no longer important. Jotan is dead—and you now belong to me—to do with as I see fit. You may be sure I will not confuse consideration with stupidity!"

There was no mistaking his meaning. Dylara felt her cheeks burn, but before she could voice the angry retort trembling on her lips, Vokal turned his eyes to the silent and expressionless Ekbar.

"Confine the girl in one of the private rooms in the slave quarters," he said. "As for her companion, put him in with those slaves who work on the palace grounds. Keep me informed as to his general attitude. If he gives you any trouble, have him beaten until he becomes tractable."

ONCE past Ammad's walls. Tharn permitted the rest of Ekbar's column to draw gradually away from him until, to the eye of the casual passerby, he was not a part of that body but only a solitary warrior abroad on some affair of his own.

He would have liked nothing better than to continue on with the column until it passed through the walls of whatever estate they were headed for. But already his luck had held up far beyond what he had originally expected; to remain longer with Ekbar's warriors would have meant risking almost certain discovery that he was [Pg 114]not one of its original members.

He must keep the column in sight, however, until it reached its goal. Once he knew which of these stone walled estates was to swallow up Dylara and Trakor he would be free to enter in his own way and undertake their rescue.

At this late hour Ammad's streets were nearly deserted. An occasional solitary figure strode along with purposeful steps, and twice small groups of men, staggering and loud-mouthed from too much wine, blundered and weaved along the paved thoroughfares. On these latter occasions Tharn was careful to cross the street to avoid contact, for drunken men were notoriously unpredictable.

At last Ekbar's column ground to a halt outside a wide gate in a high wall of stone midway along one of the streets. Twin lanterns burned from a niche above those gates, their rays glinting on the spear points of four armed guards stationed there.

From the shadows of a wall across the street, Tharn watched as Ekbar held a brief conversation with those four sentries; then the gates swung wide and the column, Dylara and Trakor among its members, disappeared from view.

Tharn voiced a low grunt of approval and satisfaction. Somewhere within the huge sprawling building of four floors looming massively against the night sky was the girl he loved and the young man he had befriended. Within another hour the dwellers of that cliff-like dwelling would have finished welcoming the returning warriors and be back in their beds. Then would Tharn enter in search of their captives.

IN the interim a general reconnaissance seemed in order. The palace sat squarely atop one of Ammad's low hills amid wide grounds. Here and there behind the encircling wall a tree lifted its crested top, the night's gentle wind stirring its leaves and branches.

Making certain his bow, quiver of arrows, grass rope and flint knife were in their accustomed places, Tharn set out for a leisurely stroll. For several hundred yards the street he

63

followed lay unbroken by any intersecting avenue and in all that length the only life in sight was the group of four guards lounging outside that wide gateway which had swallowed up Dylara and Trakor.

When he reached a position directly opposite those four Tharn was aware that all of them were watching him from across the strip of paving that made up the street itself. At any moment he might be challenged and ordered to a halt.

But the challenge did not come and he passed casually on along the walk. They were behind him now and, unless he turned his head to look back, out of range of his eyes. His ears, however, were busy and soon they caught the sound of voices.

An intersection appeared ahead and unhesitatingly the cave lord cut diagonally across it and moved out of sight of the four sentries. If he expected to find this section of the wall unguarded, however, he was doomed to disappointment. Half way down the block a single lantern sent out feeble rays from a small niche directly above a single gate—a gate guarded by a patrolling sentry.

Because of the comparative narrowness of this street and the high walls on either side, heavy shadows left it in almost total darkness. Tharn, across the street and still a good hundred and fifty yards away, had not yet been observed by that lone sentry.

He might, Tharn realized, be able to pass the man once without arousing undue interest or suspicion. But should he attempt to retrace his steps later on the guard would be almost certain to take some sort of action. [Pg 115]It was not that Tharn would be unable to handle the matter if that should happen, but there was always the possibility that others might be aroused by a warning cry.

Stooping, Tharn removed his sandals and, hugging the wall where shadows lay deepest, began a slow, careful advance.

Thirty paces the guard took in each direction before executing a brisk about face and retracing his steps. The leather soles of his sandals made crisp clear rhythmical sounds against the stone underfoot. Each time his measured pacing brought him toward Tharn, the cave lord remained frozen, hugging the wall; when he wheeled and started back Tharn raced lightly ahead, even while he counted off each step the sentry took. On the twenty-ninth pace Tharn would freeze again, then repeat the maneuver.

Finally the man of the caves reached the point where he dared go no further. He was still fifty or sixty feet down the street and another fifteen feet to one side. Hardly daring to breathe, he stood as motionless as the wall at his back until the man finished the routine of thirty paces toward him; then, as he wheeled and started back, Tharn unslipped his bow with unthinkable swiftness, fitted an arrow to its string. Mighty muscles rippled smoothly across that bronzed back as a steady hand bent the stubborn wood, a single musical "twang" sounded against the still air and flint-tipped death flickered for an immeasurable instant between the two men.

True to its target flew Tharn's arrow, the sharp point striking squarely at the juncture of neck and the skull's base. Wide flew the sentry's arms and he fell soundlessly in a crumpled heap, the spear still tightly clutched in one dead hand.

Even while the body was still falling Tharn was bounding toward the now unguarded gate. Unbarring it, he drew the lifeless warrior out of sight beyond, then closed the gate with his back.

HERE at the wall's base was darkness, but a few steps beyond was a moonfilled clearing dotted with carefully spaced bushes and an occasional tree. A curving path of crushed rock led across cropped grass and ended at a wide door of the palace itself.

Although the hour Tharn had alloted himself before entering the palace was not up, there were no signs of life anywhere about the grounds, nor did man-made light gleam through any of the windows on this side of the building. Yet uppermost in Tharn's mind was that sense of caution when caution was possible, and he decided to wait for a while before entering the palace itself.

With a quick soundless rush he crossed the stretch of greensward between him and the nearest tree. A single agile leap took him among its branches and, finding a comfortable fork, he settled himself to wait.

Unexpectedly, it proved a wise move. Hardly was he at rest when a group of six guards, their spear-points and white tunics sharp and clear in the light of Uda, the moon, rounded a far corner of the building.

At first Tharn thought some one had sighted him entering the grounds and given an alarm. He abandoned the idea immediately, however, for the actions and general attitude of the six indicated this was no more than a routine patrol. Evidently Ammad's nobleman had many enemies....

In a way Tharn's choice of a point to break into this palace was an unfortunate one. He would have preferred to enter on the side where Uda's rays did not reach. But four guards instead of one were stationed at that gate and an attempt to pass them would have been foolhardy at best.[Pg 116]

Now, indeed, he must wait—wait until he could learn how much time would elapse between appearances of those six guards. He settled himself firmly into the branch's fork, using this period of enforced idleness by attempting to locate some means of ingress in that section of palace wall visible to him.

All windows of the first two floors appeared to be guarded by slender columns of stone. He had seen such forms of protection on some of Sephar's structures and he knew that even his own great strength would be unable to force them.

The windows of the top two floors were shielded only by drapes of soft material, with here and there a balcony dotting the white stone surface. Could he but reach one of the former, entry would be simple. But nowhere on the smooth sheer surface could he make out hand- and foot-holds for that purpose.

Half an hour dragged by. Nobody passed by, no light showed at any of the windows, no sound broke the tomb-like silence. He wondered at the failure of the six-man patrol to appear a second time.

Well, he could not remain in this leafy retreat forever. With a slight shrug of his giant shoulders, Tharn descended to the lower branches, took a long and cautious look around, his ears and nose alert for some sign of life. Nothing.

Dropping to the ground, the cave lord ran lightly toward that corner of the palace around which those six guards had disappeared more than half an hour before. He was within feet of his goal when a sudden chorus of shrill cries from behind him broke the silence.

A single glance over his shoulder told him the story. The ground patrol had chosen this particular moment to reappear!

ONCE Dylara had been thrust not ungently within a room off a fourth floor corridor and its door barred from the outside, Trakor was turned over to a single guard to be taken to one of the slave dormitories. From the cave youth's appearance of utter hopelessness, the dispirited droop of his shoulders, it was clear all fight had gone out of him since Ammad's gates had closed at his back. He shuffled wearily along the hall ahead of his yawning guard, down a flight of stairs to the third level and along a lengthy corridor, lined with doors and completely deserted at this hour.

At the corridor's far end loomed two massive doors, heavily barred. While Trakor stood passively by, head hanging listlessly, the Ammadian put down his spear and reached with both hands to lift free the broad bar. In so doing he momentarily turned his back to the cave youth— and that momentary lapse spelled his doom.

Steel fingers closed about his throat, a naked leg tripped him up and he was flat on his back before his lips opened to a cry that was never uttered. Blindly the guard sought to reach the knife at his belt; but Trakor, anticipating this, ground a knee into that wrist.

The man's heels hammered spasmodically against the stone in mute agony and fear and his by no means weak body thrashed and bucked. But those fingers only tightened their hold.

Trakor, his face only inches from that of the enemy, saw those fear-filled eyes start from their sockets, saw lips and cheeks turn dark with constricted blood, felt the broad chest beneath his rise and fall wildly as the lungs fought for air.

For several minutes after the Ammadian warrior lay limp and still beneath him Trakor kept his fingers buried in that lifeless throat. Finally he rose shakily to his feet and looked [Pg 117]down upon the body of his first kill. Exultation filled him, and pride—and a strange sense of sadness....

He shook his head briefly as if to clear away such thoughts. Guided by the dim light from candles in wall brackets set at wide intervals along the corridor, he bent and stripped the corpse of its tunic and drew it over his own shoulders. His late foe had been a tall man and the tunic came a bit higher on Trakor's legs than Ammadian fashion dictated, a grievous matter which he ignored. A keen-edged knife of stone went under the tunic's belt; the heavy spear he left where the warrior originally had placed it.

TRAKOR went back along that corridor with long swinging strides, his naked feet soundless against the stone, his head erect, his ears and eyes alert for the slightest sound or movement.

Ascending the same flight of stairs he had descended a few minutes earlier, he paused at the top and looked carefully at the twin lines of closed doors. The seventh on his left; he had counted them off carefully while on his way to the floor below.

For a full minute he stood motionless outside that barred portal, listening for some indication that others were up and about the palace. Then he turned back, lifted the bar and pushed open the door with slow care.

A flicker of motion from within the darkened room caused him to leap sharply back, just in time to keep a heavy wooden chair from caving in his head. Unchecked, the chair struck the floor with a resounding crash, the impact tearing it loose from Dylara's hands.

By the time she had bent to pick it up for a second try, Trakor was inside and the door closed. He threw out a hand to ward off Dylara's impromptu club, whispering, "No, Dylara! It is I—Trakor!"

A muffled sob of relief and thanksgiving was torn from her throat, then she was in his arms.

At the feel of her body against his, the heady scent of her hair in his nostrils, Trakor felt his heart leap within him and his arms tightened suddenly about the girl's smooth, softly rounded shoulders.

Then the moment was gone and they drew apart.

"I can't believe it, Trakor!" Dylara whispered. "How did you manage to get away?"

"There's no time for that now," he said. "We've got to get out of this place and back to the jungle where we belong. Tharn is out there somewhere and we must find him before he enters Ammad in search of us."

"But how...."

"I don't know—yet. If we can reach the streets without being seen...." He went to the door, pressed an ear against its planks for a moment, then very gently drew open the heavy section of wood and put his head cautiously out. The corridor, in either direction, was deserted.

"Come," he whispered, and hand in hand they stole silently toward the head of those stairs Trakor had recently climbed.

From somewhere below them a door slammed heavily and sandaled feet, several pairs of them judging from the sound, approached the base of that same flight of steps.

Without speaking Trakor and Dylara turned and, on tiptoe, raced in the opposite direction. As he ran, Trakor drew his knife in preparation for any enemy who might suddenly loom in their path.

A turn in the corridor brought them to a second flight of steps, down which they raced at full speed. Past landings at the third and second floors they fled, stopping at last in front of a closed door marking the main level of the palace.

"Wait!" Trakor breathed, placing [Pg 118]a restraining hand on the girl's arm.

SILENCE seemed to press down upon them, a silence so complete they could hear the breath rustling in their nostrils.

With almost exaggerated care Trakor drew back the door. Moonlight streaming in at several stone-barred windows revealed a large hall, its walls hung with rich tapestries and a long wide table, lined with chairs, running almost its entire length.

Dylara, familiar with such scenes from her days in Sephar, said, "The palace dining hall." She pointed to an open doorway in the opposite wall. "That should lead to the kitchens. No one will be there at this time of night."

"Good!"

They crossed quickly to the designated opening, along a short narrow hall, through a second doorway and on into a low-ceilinged room whose furnishings bore mute testimony that Dylara's guess had been right.

"Look!" whispered Dylara, pointing.

Thin lines of moonlight formed a rectangle on the far wall, marking a doorway leading to open air. Quickly Trakor was across the kitchen and straining to lift the heavy bar from its catches.

And in that moment a sudden chorus of deep-throated shouts of alarm from beyond that door reached their ears.

CHAPTER XII
NO DEEPER DUNGEON

JALTOR, king of all Ammad, rose from his chair as his four visitors entered the apartment. Straight and tall he stood, his magnificent body in its purple-edged tunic seeming to dwarf all else within the room.

No one spoke. Curzad, captain of the palace guards, closed the door softly and stood with his back against it, arms folded and his rugged features empty of all expression.

It was Jotan, son of Garlud, who was the first to speak. The anger that showed in his burning eyes and the thrust of his chin thickened his words until they were more nearly a growl.

"What means this, Jaltor? Why was my party intercepted outside Ammad's walls and dragged here in secrecy? Why are we thus treated like common criminals? I demand an explanation!"

"You may request an explanation, Jotan," Jaltor said calmly. "As Ammad's king I answer no man's demands."

In the strained silence following his words, Jaltor's gaze moved on to where Alurna, daughter of Urim and princess of Sephar, stood staring at him in wonder and uncertainty. His expression softened and when he spoke his voice had lost completely its former edge.

"Curzad has told me of your father's death. We have both suffered a great loss, for Urim was my brother—my only brother. Later I should like to know the details of his passing; but first I wish to explain my reasons for what has happened tonight."

There were mixed emotions evident in the expressions of his listeners. Tamar was clearly worried and puzzled, Javan appeared even more dazed and uncomprehending than usual, while Jotan was close to bursting with outright anger and injured pride.

Jaltor indicated chairs with a wave of his hand. "Be seated, please. This may take some time."

They obeyed in silence, and even though sitting none of them was relaxed. Jaltor remained on his feet, legs spread, his keen eyes somber.

"A little less than half a moon ago," Jaltor began, "an attempt was made to assassinate me. The reason it was not successful lay in the peculiar clumsiness of the assassin. He was [Pg 119]captured immediately and put to torture in an effort to learn the names of others, if any, involved in the plot. He was an old man, strangely enough, and before he died he told me who had hired him."

"I don't see," Jotan burst out, "what this has to do with any of us. Certainly we are not involved."

"The name he gave," Jaltor went on, as though there had been no interruption, "was Garlud!"

In the sudden, shocked silence that followed the measured tread of a guard in the corridor outside came clearly through the closed door.

"I don't believe it!" Jotan shouted. He leaped from his chair to face the monarch. "Ever since I can remember you and my father were the closest of friends!"

"And long before that Jotan," Jaltor said quietly.

"Yet because some common killer gave his name, you believe such an impossible story? My father could have no reason for wanting you dead. What have you done to him?"

JALTOR ignored the last question. He said in the same quiet voice: "Not a common killer, Jotan. It was old Heglar who so named your father."

The young Ammadian nobleman fell back a pace in complete amazement. "Old Heglar? Why, he wouldn't...." His voice trailed off.

"Exactly. Heglar would not lie."

Jotan lifted a shaking hand to rub his forehead in a kind of dazed helplessness that struck to the heart of every person in the room. "No," he said, his voice suddenly loud, "I do not believe it. Where is my father? Let me talk to him."

"Where," Jaltor said coldly, "would apt to be any man who plotted the death of Ammad's king?"

Slowly Jotan's hand fell from before his eyes as the meaning of those chill words came home to him. "You—you *killed* him? Garlud? My father? Your friend?"

Nothing altered in Jaltor's sober expression—and in that Jotan read his answer. With a strangely inarticulate snarl he launched himself at the king, seeking to lock his fingers in that deeply tanned neck.

Curzad leaped from his place at the door, brushing past the paralyzed onlookers, and reached out to engulf the crazed young nobleman in his strong arms. Jotan, helpless in that iron grip was borne back, tears of rage and frustration streaming from his eyes.

Jaltor raised a steady hand to his bruised throat, his expression unchanged. "Confine him in the pits, Curzad. Later I shall decide what is to be done with him."

Tamar started up from his chair in angry protest. "What kind of justice is this?" he cried. "Will you send a man to his death because grief causes him to——" He stopped there, stricken into abrupt silence by what he saw in the ruler's eyes.

It took the combined efforts of Curzad and two of the corridor guards to subdue Jotan sufficiently to get him out of the room and on his way to the pits. When the room was quiet again, Jaltor dropped into an empty chair across from Alurna and the two young noblemen.

"Now," he said, "I can tell you the whole story."

And tell them he did, from start to finish. "So you see," he summed up, "why Jotan must be kept captive. Had I told him the truth nothing would have satisfied him until his father was freed and another method used to force the real accomplice into the open. When this unknown conspirator learns that Jotan's party has returned from Sephar, apparently without Jotan himself, he is going to be more puzzled than ever. A puzzled man makes mistakes—which is what we want him to do."[Pg 120]

Alurna shuddered. "But the pits! If they are like the ones beneath Sephar, you are punishing terribly two men who are innocent of wrongdoing."

"You must understand," Jaltor reminded her, "that the possibility exists that Garlud is guilty. I have lived long enough to know that ambition can drive the noblest of men to ignoble acts. Old Heglar's dying words cannot be lightly dismissed."

"You," he continued, nodding to Tamar and Javan, "are free to return to your homes. Should anyone ask what has happened to the leader of your party, tell him that—well, that the lions got him. That will fit in with what happened during the night that you were attacked by Sadu."

The two young noblemen rose to leave, greatly relieved by Jaltor's explanation, but still concerned. After they were gone, the monarch said to Alurna:

"I know you must be worn out from your long journey from Sephar. But sit there a little longer, if you will, and tell me the circumstances of my brother's death."

IT required the better part of an hour for the dark-haired princess to relate what had taken place in Sephar nearly three moons before. She spoke often of Jotan during the account, and the tenderness in her eyes at mention of his name told Ammad's king more than she realized. And when she told of Dylara's disappearance and the possibility that Sadu had devoured her, Jaltor caught the unconscious satisfaction in her tone.

For a little while after she had finished, Jaltor sat staring thoughtfully into his wine goblet. Then: "Urim's mistake was to coddle that rascally high priest. In Ammad the priesthood is no problem at all; we keep them few in numbers and with no power to create unrest. Long ago I put a stop to the Games honoring the God-Whose-Name-May-Not-Be-Spoken-Aloud.... Perhaps some day I shall find a means of avenging the cowardly assassination of Urim, your father and my brother."

He smiled gravely into her eyes. "Do not worry about Jotan, my princess. Soon, I hope, he will be free again and you shall have your chance to win him."

Alurna's gray-green eyes flashed momentarily ... and then she too smiled. "Ammad's king is a wise and understanding man," she murmured.

Jaltor straightened and put down his goblet. "And now I shall show you to the suite of rooms which I ordered made ready for your use. Come."

FOR a long time after the slave woman detailed to serve her had gone, Alurna lay wide-eyed on the soft bed. Moonlight through the room's wide window formed a solid square on the floor, and in its ghostly radiance the furnishings seemed shadowy and unreal.

It was the first bed she had been in for a long, long time and sleep should have come to her the moment she touched the pillow. But too many thoughts raced through her mind to permit sleep—thoughts jumbled and confused.

Ever since Jotan had rejoined the main body of his men after his unsuccessful search for Dylara, he had been moody and distraught. Those warriors who had accompanied him and Tamar on the hunt seemed confident—out of Jotan's hearing!—that the jungle had gotten her, just as it had claimed the lives of countless others.

And now that the way was clear to win him, Alurna slipped easily into a new role—a role of silent understanding and ready sympathy. Slowly and unconsciously Jotan had begun to respond to treatment. It might take several moons, she realized, before he would begin to look upon her as a de[Pg 121]sirable woman in addition to a warmhearted and friendly companion. But she could wait—for many moons if necessary.

Now the intrigue of some unknown enemy of Jotan's father had given the young nobleman new worries. If only there was some way to help him—some method by which she might earn his gratitude. Gratitude, she knew, was an excellent base on which to build romance.

Somewhere in the bowels of this very building Jotan and his father lay in dark, damp cells, put there on the orders of her own uncle. As king of Ammad and brother of her father he was entitled to her loyalty and respect. But when it came to the point of choosing between Jaltor and Jotan ... there was no doubt in her mind as to her ultimate decision!

As she lay there on her back, her eyes fixed unseeingly on the ceiling beams, a plan began to shape itself in her mind—a plan which, as details took concrete form, brought a faint smile to her lips.

And still smiling, Alurna fell asleep....

AS the Ammadian patrol bore down upon him with leveled spears, Tharn's blackwood bow seemed to leap into his hands and two arrows flashed across the intervening space. Two of the warriors toppled and died under those flint arrow heads, but before the cave lord could release a third he was forced to leap hastily aside to prevent impalement by three thrown spears. So narrow the distance now that his bow was useless, and so he tore his knife from its place at its belt and, with the silent ferocity of a charging lion, hurled himself upon the remaining four guards.

Two more of the Ammadians collapsed in death, their heads almost severed as polished flint tore into their throats. The remaining pair, upon seeing that and hearing the bestial snarls issuing from that broad chest, drew back sharply, wavering on the verge of outright flight.

Tharn, sensing their indecision, tensed to renew his charge and put them to rout.

A cacophony of loud shouts from behind him told of the arrival of reinforcements. There were eight of them this time, still a good thirty yards away but fast approaching.

Instantly Tharn, his knife sweeping high for a thrust, lunged at the remaining two warriors who turned and fled a short distance before circling back to join the second group. Tharn stopped, caught up his bow and brought down three more of the enemy as he began a slow withdrawal. Lights were beginning to show from some of the palace windows; at any moment an arrow from above might strike him down.

Suddenly a door in the palace wall burst open and a white-tunicked figure came bounding across the lawn toward him. Tharn's bow was on its way into position to send an arrow leaping to meet this new attack when a familiar voice called out his name.

"Trakor!" Tharn shouted, astonished.

The boy bent while still running and caught up a spear from beside the body of one of Tharn's victims. Hardly had he reached the cave lord's side when a third group of palace guards appeared on the scene from behind them.

Cut off in two directions by enemies, blocked in another by the palace itself, Tharn chose the only possible avenue of escape.

"To the wall!" he shouted, then wheeled and raced across the greensward with long flashing strides, Trakor close at his heels.

Angling in sharply from two directions, the Ammadians sought to[Pg 122]overtake them. Several spears were hurled but the distance was too great.

Trakor, seeing the high walls, knew it would be impossible to scale them in the few moments before the Ammadians arrived. But his faith in the cave lord remained unshaken; if a way to freedom could be found, Tharn would find it!

WHILE still a few feet short of the wall, Tharn swerved sharply to the left, crashed through a thick growth of bushes and paused in front of a small gate. Even as Trakor was about to point out the futility of trying to force a way through those stubborn planks, Tharn drew open the barrier and leaped through.

Trakor, stricken dumb with astonishment at this new development, followed him into the street as Tharn slammed shut the gate and dropped its bar into place a split second before a heavy shoulder thudded against its opposite side.

What promised to be at least a breathing space died in its infancy as a full dozen of the white-tunicked fighting men of Vokal's guard appeared at the juncture of streets to their left, and catching sight of them, came tearing along the pavement in their direction.

"This way," Tharn said, and the two cave men raced into the night.

For nearly a quarter-hour the two Cro-Magnards fled through the black labyrinth of Ammad's streets, twisting and turning to throw off pursuit. Twice they encountered patrols from other estates along their erratic pathway, but an arrow or two from Tharn's deadly bow drove them off.

Finally the two men slowed to a walk, their feet soundless against the stone surface of a narrow street between two walls in which no gates were visible. For the moment at least, it appeared their hunters had lost them, thus giving them a chance to gauge their present position.

Judging from the way this particular street slanted upward ahead of them they were on one of Ammad's hills. Further along a huge building loomed against the night sky from squarely across their path—a building larger and higher than any they had seen thus far.

"Dylara is back there," Trakor said abruptly.

Tharn nodded without looking around. "I know," he said simply. "We must find some place to hole up until another night comes. Then I am going back for her."

"We were close to getting away—Dylara and I," Trakor said ruefully. "We were on the verge of stepping out into the open when I heard the guards attacking you."

"You were that close to freedom?" Tharn asked, surprised.

Briefly Trakor recounted what had taken place in Vokal's palace. When he had finished, Tharn shook his head in savage disgust. "That makes the second time she was almost within arm's reach of me! I suppose by this time they have her again and she is locked away."

"Perhaps," Trakor admitted. "When I saw who it was Vokal's guards were after, I gave her my knife and she crawled under one of the tables to wait for us until we had killed the guards and could come back to get her." He laughed shortly, bitterly. "We *would* have killed them, Tharn, if so many hadn't come to their aid."

"It is always thus," the cave lord said philosophically. "Tomorrow night we shall try again."

WHILE talking, they continued on up the steep rise. Now their way was blocked by the wall they had glimpsed a few moments before. A narrow roadway skirted its base in two directions, and to the right, several hundred yards distant, they could make out the faint yellow rays [Pg 123]of a lantern above a recessed gate.

"What now?" Trakor asked shortly.

Tharn shrugged. "A tree with foliage so thick none can see us. Judging from the size of the building beyond this wall, its grounds should contain many trees. Let us enter and see if we can find one large enough for our purpose."

Trakor glanced doubtfully up at the wall's edge fully fifteen feet from the ground. "Do we go over it or through one of the gates?"

"Over it. We dare not risk arousing the guards."

"How can we reach its top?"

In answer Tharn took up a position with his back only an inch or two from the wall. Cupping his hands together in front of him, he bent his knees slightly, keeping his back straight. "Extend your arms above your head," he directed, "and place your right foot in my hands, crouching a little while I support your weight. That way I can toss you high enough to enable your hands to catch the wall's edge."

Trakor nodded, a shade doubtfully, and followed directions. Like a striking snake Tharn uncoiled his bent legs with a sharp upward thrust, at the same instant jerking his locked hands up to chest level.

The youth shot upward like an arrow from a bow. Tharn heard a dull thud, followed by a low exclamation of pain. He looked up to see Trakor sitting astride the wall rubbing one of his shins.

At Tharn's instructions, Trakor lay chest down against the wall's top and extended his right hand downward. The cave lord backed away, then ran forward and leaped high, catching Trakor's fingers and swinging lightly up beside him.

There were trees—many of them—singly and in groups, their branches heavy with leaves. The grounds in which they stood were immense, with winding paths of crushed stone, winding between bushes heavy with jungle blooms. Here and there concealed jets flung graceful and shimmering curtains of water skyward, the falling drops pattering musically into stone-lined pools. In the distance loomed the gleaming white walls of a palace that, Tharn realized, was easily three times the size of any he had seen in Sephar.

Lightly the two men dropped to the closely clipped grass. Tharn would have liked to remain aloft for a minute or two, to drink in the beauty of the scene and to get some idea of just where within Ammad they were. But should some sleepless Ammadian be standing at a window in that palace, he could hardly keep from seeing those two figures atop the wall.

Side by side the two cave men strode lightly toward a cluster of eight trees arranged in a small circle.

While from the depths of a thicket of bushes bordering one of the garden pools a pair of eyes watched them in startled wonder.

DYLARA crouched beneath a table in Vokal's kitchen and listened to that nobleman's strident voice as it lashed at a group of palace guards outside the half open door.

"Do you expect me to believe," he said hotly, "that a single warrior could slay seven of you? Were their muscles turned to water at sight of him? And the rest of you—are you soldiers or children to be so easily outwitted?"

No one attempted a reply. Ekbar, captain of the guards, stood stiffly by, beads of nervous perspiration dotting his forehead. His turn would come once Vokal was through with the guards themselves. He would be fortunate indeed to escape with no more than a tongue-lashing; he might well end up being demoted in rank.

"Who was this man?" Vokal demanded. "Did any of you recognize him? Speak up, before I order your [Pg 124]tongues cut out with your own knives! You!" He pointed a finger at one of the men. "I understand you were one of those who first saw him. Who was he?"

The designated man, his trembling voice matching the shaking of his knees, said hurriedly, "He was like no warrior I have seen in all Ammad, Most-High. He was very tall, with great rippling muscles that——"

"Enough!" Vokal shouted. "I might have known you would claim no ordinary man could best the lot of you. And, I suppose, at least fifty more of these huge strangers fell upon you?"

"No, Most-High," the warrior admitted. "But there was one more, not quite so large as the first. He came from within the palace to join his friend and the two of them ran——"

"Wait!" the nobleman said sharply. "Are you sure this second man came from *inside* the palace?"

"Yes, Most-High." He pointed an unsteady hand at the door leading to the palace kitchen. "He came from there. With my own eye I——"

"Enough!" Vokal wheeled toward the captain of his guard. "Ekbar, send a detail to comb every room of the palace. There may be more of these strange intruders in there."

"At once, Most-High."

Dylara, listening from her place of concealment within the kitchen, knew she dared stay there no longer. A moment from now the room would be swarming with armed men and she was sure to be found. It was unfortunate she could not have accompanied Trakor when he raced out to Tharn's assistance, but she had known then, as now, that she would only have slowed their dash for freedom. With Tharn and Trakor both at liberty within Ammad's walls, they would eventually find a way to rescue her.

There was no point, however, in waiting around to be rescued. If she could make her way beyond Ammad's walls without help, so much the better.

Rising from her hiding place, the stone knife Trakor had given her ready in one sun-tanned fist, she crossed the kitchen with stealthy swiftness and hurried along the short hall leading to the palace dining hall.

It proved to be empty of life, although she could hear the sounds of sandaled feet entering the room she had only just quitted. Quickly she crossed the huge chamber, carefully drew open the same door she and Trakor had passed through a short time earlier, and raced lightly back up the stairs there to the building's second floor.

At the landing, she stopped and pressed an ear against the planks of the corridor door. She could hear no sound from beyond them to indicate someone was there. Carefully, inch by inch, she drew it inward until there was space enough for her to peer through.

Not ten feet away from her were the broad backs of two guards!

Despite the pounding of her heart and the almost uncontrollable efforts of her feet to break into instant flight, Dylara very slowly allowed the heavy door to return to its closed position. Then she was away, racing upward on the balls of her feet, silent as the shadow of a shadow.

She did not even pause at the third landing, for her quick ears caught the tread of feet beyond its closed door. At the fourth level the stairs ended at the corridor itself, with no door to mask them.

Fortunately the long hallway was deserted. Dylara turned to her right and hurried along, ears and eyes alert for the first sign that she was not alone. Past a score of doors and around several corners the corridor led and in all that time she encountered no one.[Pg 125]

It seemed very still here on the fourth level of Vokal's palace. The almost eerie silence seemed to press down upon her spirits like some weighty and invisible hand. She could hear her heart pounding and the whisper of her breathing. The floor underfoot was now covered with a thick carpeting of some woven material and her sandals pressed soundlessly into it.

She had reached a point only a few yards from another bend in the hall ahead of her when she caught the faint sound of voices in that direction—voices which seemed to be growing louder.

Instantly she whirled to retrace her steps, then halted again. It was a long way back to where the corridor had last jogged; the owners of those voices might come into view before she could reach it.

There was a door in one wall almost even with where she stood now. It might open onto a room filled with guards, or it might not open at all. There was no time to weigh her chances.

She released the latch and pushed lightly against the wood.

She came into a large, low-ceilinged room, lighted by candles in beautifully carved wooden brackets affixed to the walls. Polished tables and luxuriously covered chairs stood about the carpeted floor. A door stood slightly open in one of the side walls, disclosing the foot of a wide bed, the covers rumpled as though some one had been sleeping there moments before. Several windows open and unbarred, permitted a panoramic view of a large section of Ammad, and one of them came all the way down to the floor to permit entry to a small balcony.

As Dylara stood there, drinking in the beauty of the room, voices sounded suddenly loud and clear from just outside the door. A moment later the latch moved under an unseen hand and the door itself swung wide. But even as the latch moved, Dylara was across the room, through the balcony entrance and crouching there, out of sight.

"... one, then call me immediately."

"As the noble Vokal commands."

The silver-haired nobleman closed the door, muttered something under his breath, and crossed to where an earthen jug of wine stood on one of the tables. He filled a goblet to the brim, drained it with a flourish, blew out all but one of the candles and went into the bedroom.

Dylara swallowed her heart back to its usual place and straightened slowly to ease cramped muscles. Give the Ammadian an hour to fall into a deep sleep and to allow the palace inhabitants to return to their beds, and she could make a second attempt to get away.

The minutes passed with almost painful deliberateness. So complete was the silence here that she could hear the sounds of even breathing from the bedroom. It was the breathing of a man who was sleeping soundly; a few minutes more and she would make her bid for freedom.

Knuckles pounded sharply on the apartment door.

As Tharn and Trakor were on the point of swinging into one of the half circle of trees, a crepitant rustle among the nearby bushes brought their heads sharply around in instant alarm.

Six stern-faced guards in spotless tunics stood less than a dozen feet away, spears leveled at the broad chests of the two Cro-Magnards. At sight of those weapons Tharn's hand dropped from the hilt of his knife and utter chagrin filled his heart.

He felt Trakor stiffen beside him and he put out a restraining hand. "It is useless," he muttered. "The slightest move and they will cut us down."[Pg 126]

One of the six stepped forward a few paces and peered at the two intruders. "Who are you," he demanded, "and what are you doing on the grounds of Jaltor, king of Ammad?"

"We are men of Sephar," Tharn said, following the first line of thought that popped into his head. "We came to Ammad with Jotan's party and were looking over the palace grounds. There is nothing so fine in all Sephar, let me tell you!"

It was a wild, almost incredible shot into complete supposition. It was possible that Jotan and his men *had* reached Ammad by this time; and, while less possible, it was conceivable that the young nobleman had come straight to the palace to pay his respects to Jaltor, instead of postponing the visit until the following day.

What Tharn did not know, of course, was that Jotan's entire party had been met outside Ammad's gates by a force of Jaltor's own guard and brought directly to the palace and were being held there until the king got around to ordering their release.

The officer in charge of this patrol knew all that—as did most of the palace guard. He looked searchingly at the two men for a moment, then said:

"You are lying! Every member of Jotan's party is already under guard. Come with us; we shall allow Curzad to hear your story."

He made a small motion with his hand and instantly Tharn and Trakor were surrounded by a ring of spear points. Side by side the two cave men strode toward the palace, helpless to resist.

Within the huge building they were led to a guard room on the first floor, and after a few minutes the tall, broad-shouldered figure of Jaltor's captain, sharp-eyed and alert, entered the room.

He listened to the officer repeat what Tharn had said outside, then ran his gaze slowly over the two men.

"You are not warriors of Sephar," he growled. "You are not even Ammadians. I have seen your kind before. What are two cave men doing inside Ammad?"

Tharn shrugged but said nothing. Trakor, observing his reaction, followed his lead.

"Perhaps a few days in the pits will loosen your tongues!" Curzad said harshly.

Still no reply.

"As you wish." Curzad turned away indifferently. "To the deepest pits with them, Atkor," he said to the officer. "After a few suns I will see them again to learn if they feel more talkative."

JUST how many downward sloping ramps they trod on the way to the pits Tharn had no way of knowing. Further and further below the earth's surface they went, their hands bound behind them, while brightly lighted subterranean corridors gave way to others only faintly illuminated. Finally even the faint light disappeared and they moved, heavily guarded, through blackness relieved only by flames from a torch carried by one of the guards. There was the clearly audible trickling of water along the stone walls and several times Tharn felt his feet sink to the ankles in cold pools that had formed in hollows of the stone flooring.

At last the wearying procession of sloping ramps ceased and they moved along a level corridor. On either side Tharn made out heavy wooden doors with apertures in their surfaces closed off by columns of stone in the form of bars. Now and then light from the torch picked out white, heavily bearded faces containing white-ringed eyes and expressions of dull hopelessness. Not once, however, did he hear sounds from the throats of those prisoners—only the mute despair of lost souls peering into nothingness.

Finally the officer ordered a halt. [Pg 127]At his command two of the doors, almost directly across from each other, were opened. Tharn felt the cold touch of flint as a knife cut away his bonds, a strong hand thrust him roughly into the cell on the right and the door banged shut behind him.

He turned back and looked out through the bars, to see Trakor, head held proudly erect, shoved into the opposite room. Bars at the top and bottom of each door were drawn into place, a sharp order rang out and the Ammadian guards started back for the surface.

"Curzad said 'to the deepest pits!'" one of them chuckled. "There are no deeper dungeons than those!"

CHAPTER XIII
SITAB'S MISTAKE

AS the sound of knocking rang through Vokal's private apartment, Dylara, crouching on the small balcony off the central room, felt her spirits plummet to a new low. Given another few minutes of grace and she would have been out of this cul-de-sac and on her way to freedom.

Again came the knock, louder this time. She heard a muttered exclamation from the bedroom, then Vokal, tying the belt of his tunic, crossed quickly to the corridor door.

"What do you want? Who is it?" he called, impatience strong in his usually calm voice.

"Your pardon, Most-High," said a humble-sounding voice, "but a visitor, bearing your personal talisman, insists on seeing you at once."

"It must be that fool Sitab," Dylara heard the nobleman mutter. He threw open the door, then stepped back suddenly as the cloaked form of a woman pushed her way into the room.

"Rhoa!" he gasped. "What are you doing here?"

"I want to talk to you. Send the guard away and close the door." Her voice, deep for a woman, sounded muffled through the folds of cloak shielding her face.

Vokal obeyed, and when the door was shut she slipped from the wrap and dropped it across the back of a nearby chair.

She was a woman past thirty, taller than average and beautifully formed. Her hair was a dull black and she wore it long, framing the delicate features of her olive-skinned face. Her eyes were large and very black and at this moment there was anger in them.

"What are you doing here?" Vokal said again.

"It is fairly simple," she said imperiously. "I am tired of waiting, Vokal. For half a moon now old Heglar has been missing. I do not doubt for a moment but that he is dead. Why should we delay this thing any longer? You promised me that once the old fool was dead I could take my rightful place as your mate. I say the time for that is now!"

"But you don't understand, Rhoa. To acknowledge our love now would play directly into Jaltor's hands. Once our names are linked together he will realize Heglar attempted to assassinate him because I hired him to do so."

"I have given this a great deal of thought," Rhoa said coldly, "and I think you're being overly cautious. Let the good people of Ammad talk; the mere fact that we take no trouble to conceal our love will prove to them you had no hand in old Heglar's disappearance."

"You're not making sense!" Vokal cried. "The minute Jaltor hears we are together he will put enough of the threads in place to see the real picture. He will guess that it was I who hired Heglar to attempt that mock assassination in an effort to usurp Garlud's position in Ammad."

He threw his hands wide in a gesture of despair. "In the name of the God," he pleaded, "don't upset everything this short of success! Go back[Pg 128]to your home, Rhoa. Give me a few suns—seven; no more than seven—and I promise you I will have things worked out the way we both want them. Do this for me because I love you and you love me and we can be together without fear of Jaltor."

"How can you know seven days will be time enough?" she asked doubtfully.

"In a few minutes I am expecting a visit from Sitab, a high-ranking guard of Jaltor's court," he explained. "He is in my employ, secretly, and will do as I wish. I shall instruct him to learn if Heglar and Garlud are held in the pits beneath Jaltor's palace. If they are, he will arrange the deaths of both; if they are not there we can assume both are already dead and act accordingly. But first I must *know*, Rhoa."

SHE stood there, erect and beautiful in the shimmering radiance of candle light, indecision plain in her face. "When will this man Sitab get the information for you?"

"Tonight! Between the hour I discuss the problem with him and the hour of dawn. You will do this my way, Rhoa?"

A discreet knock at the door interrupted her reply. Vokal, sudden alarm plain in his face, stiffened. "Who is there?"

"The guard, Most-High," said a voice, muffled by the planks. "A second visitor, who refused to give his name, awaits your pleasure."

"It is Sitab," Vokal told the woman, whispering. "Will you give me those seven suns, Rhoa? Will you go now, and be patient for that long? What is your answer?"

Abruptly she nodded. "Seven suns, Vokal. But no more than seven."

His breath of relief was clearly audible. "Good!" He went to the door and drew the bar. "Hide your face so that none may know who you are. Goodbye."

He drew open the heavy door and the woman, her face concealed by the folds of her heavy cloak, swept regally through, past the staring guard and a short, barrel-chested man in the tunic of a guard of Jaltor's court.

Vokal, his handsome face completely without expression, crooked a finger at the latter. "Enter, my friend," he said cordially. "You have arrived at exactly the right time."

SHORTLY after arriving at the palace of his father, following the surprising interview with Jaltor, ruler of Ammad, Tamar had gone to his room and his bed.

But not to sleep. His thoughts were of his friend Jotan and the trouble that had befallen the young Ammadian noble. Tamar never doubted Garlud's innocence and he longed to take some action that would clear both father and son. In keeping with Jaltor's instructions he had told his own father nothing of what had taken place, letting him think Jotan had died beneath the claws and fangs of Sadu, the lion.

After more than two hours of fitful tossing, Tamar rose from his bed and entered the living room of his suite. He was standing at one of the windows overlooking sleeping Ammad, when a discreet knock at the door startled him out of his reverie.

"Who is there?" he called.

"The corridor guard," said an apologetic voice. "A young woman wishes to speak with you, noble Tamar. Upon an urgent matter, she says."

Tamar crossed the room quickly and unbarred the door. Beyond the stalwart figure of the guard was the softly curved form of a woman whose hair was very black and who, despite the folds of a cloak held to shadow her face, seemed young and beautiful.

"Alurna!" Tamar gasped incredulously. "What are you doing here?"

She shook her head warningly, en[Pg 129]tered and waited until Tamar had closed the door. The nobleman helped her remove the cloak and she sank down on a nearby stool.

"I thought you would be sleeping," she said, smiling a little.

Trouble clouded his fine eyes. "I could not sleep," he said huskily. "I tried. But I keep thinking...."

"Of Jotan," the girl finished. "And his father. We must help them, Tamar. We must not leave them to rot in the pits of Ammad."

"But what can we do?"

"Do you know how to reach the pits without being seen?"

He stared at her. "What difference would that make?"

"Why can't we free them, Tamar? Give them a chance to learn who is behind the plot against them." She leaned toward him, her face set with determined lines. "My uncle, it seems, is content to let them suffer until time works out the problem of who is guilty. I say Jotan and his father should be allowed to do something themselves to hurry matters!"

"But there's no way——"

"Are you sure? Have you thought about it before this?"

He hesitated. "No-o. But it could mean imprisonment for us if we fail, Alurna. Jaltor can be completely ruthless; if he learned we were attempting to interfere with his way of doing things ... well it could be too bad for us."

Color crept into her cheeks but she met his eyes resolutely. "Jotan means enough to me to risk that," she said flatly. "Do *you* feel that way?"

He rose and began to pace the floor. "You're right. Let me think. There is an entrance to the corridors housing the pits of Jaltor's palace, an entrance supposedly secret, which Jotan himself once pointed out to me."

He wheeled suddenly and entered his sleeping quarters, returning a moment later with a flint knife in a sheath at his belt and there was the light of battle in his eyes.

"Return to your room, Alurna," he said grimly. "I will go to free Jotan and his men."

She shook her head. "This was my idea and I'm going with you."

"But—but this is dangerous! If I am caught I shall be thrown in the pits myself—perhaps killed. This is no venture for a woman!"

"It is a venture for *this* woman," she replied doggedly. "Jotan is to be my mate ... even though he may not realize that yet. He must find me beside you when we rescue him."

For a long moment they stared into each other's eyes—then Tamar's shoulder rose and fell in surrender.

"As you wish," he said.

SITAB, warrior of the palace of Jaltor, moved stealthily down a steep ramp. About him was darkness more intense than that of a tomb, forcing him to feel his way with infinite slowness lest a misstep make a noise loud enough to rouse one or more of the guards in the arms-rooms here and there among the subterranean corridors.

From one of his hands trailed a heavy spear; in the other was a keen-edged knife of flint ready for the first man who should find him where Sitab had no right to be.

For whoever he came across now must die. It would not do for word to reach Jaltor on the morrow that Sitab, a trusted guard, had been seen on his way to the pits.

A miasmic odor of damp decay seemed to increase in strength the further below the earth's surface he progressed. Now and then a water rat would rustle across his path, its passage marked only by the rasp of claws on rock. Damp stretches of slippery surface proved difficult to negotiate and on several occasions he saved himself from falling only by a quick movement of his feet. Now and then he would step into ankle-[Pg 130]deep pools of chill water, bringing an involuntary gasp to his lips.

At long last his feet found no ramp where one should have been and he realized he now stood at the beginning of the deepest corridor beneath the palace. For a long moment he stood there, his ears straining to catch some sound of life. As from a great distance he caught the muffled snores of sleeping men, the faint murmurings of troubled words from a mind dreaming of the horrors to which it awakened after each sleep.

Grasping his spear tighter, Sitab inched his way cautiously along the corridor until his ears told him he was standing between twin rows of cells. From the belt of his robe he drew a small length of tinder-like wood and from a pouch in the same belt came a small ball-like bit of stone, its interior hollowed to hold a supply of moss in the center of which glowed a single coal of fire. Drawing the perforated bit of wood serving as a cork, Sitab let the bit of fire roll out onto the miniature torch. It rested there, glowing redly as he breathed against it. When a minute of this had gone by a tiny tongue of fire rose to life and within seconds the torch was fully lighted, dispelling the ink-like gloom about him.

On silent feet Sitab moved from door to door of the cells. At each barred opening he let the rays of light seep into the tiny interior of the room beyond while his eyes sought to identify the sleeping men.

Some he saw were hardly recognizable as human, so long had they lain prisoner in this awful hole. Matted hair hung over faces so thin and emaciated as hardly to be human at all. Others he saw were still in excellent physical condition: these had been here only a little while.

But none was familiar to him until he was well down the first row. As he peered into this particular cell, he saw a man lying asleep on the bare stone platform which served this cell, as in others, as a crude bunk. The sleeper's face was turned toward the wall, shadowed by a raised arm, so that Sitab was unable to make out the features. But something was familiar about the man's general build and the shape of his head, and for several minutes Sitab stood there waiting for the man to stir in his sleep sufficiently for his face to be seen.

When full five minutes had passed without this taking place, Sitab broke a small piece of the rotting wood from his torch and flipped it unerringly through the barred grating of the door. It struck lightly against the bare arm of the sleeper, and he sighed heavily, stirred, then turned his face toward the light.

Sitab stiffened, waiting for the man to awake and cry out in alarm at the glare of the torch. But the eyes did not open and the prisoner lapsed back into complete slumber. Only then did Sitab see who lay sleeping there.

It was Jotan.

A SLIGHT gasp escaped the guard's lips. Jotan *here*! But Jotan was dead! Vokal himself had said as much.

Sitab smiled. No matter that Vokal had been misinformed; Jotan would be dead within seconds. Vokal would reward him well for killing both Jotan*and* Garlud—if the latter were imprisoned here as well.

How best to kill him? Open the door, creep to the side of the sleeping man and plunge the spearhead into his heart? That would be the quietest way ... and also the most dangerous. What if Jotan were in reality awake—lying there waiting for this unknown visitor to enter the cell, then jumping upon him in a bid for freedom.

A glance at those muscles, even though apparently relaxed in sleep, was enough to give him his decision. [Pg 131]Lifting his spear, he thrust its point between the bars of the door, aimed it squarely at Jotan's exposed chest—and tensed his muscles to launch the heavy weapon.

CHAPTER XIV
AMBUSH

FOR a long time after Sitab was gone, Vokal remained seated on a low bench in the living room of his apartment. Worry was crowding in on his mind, the ambition that had led him into discrediting Garlud was proving itself a curse, and his love for Rhoa, wife of old Heglar, was now a burdensome thing that had cost him a thousand tals and might end up costing him his life.

Well, the die was cast now; there was no turning back. Dawn was no more than two or three hours away; long before Dyta's golden rays flooded Ammad's streets Sitab should have returned with word that Heglar and Garlud were dead. Everything depended on that now—it was still not too late to recoup, winning back his thousand tals and a higher place in Ammad's society.

The silver-haired nobleman rose from his chair and reached for the candle to blow out its flame. A few hour's sleep would make him better able to face the morrow....

... From her place on the narrow balcony of the nobleman's apartment, Dylara watched the candle flame perish under the man's exhalation. This time, she thought, I will not wait so long for him to fall asleep. She watched him cross the room and disappear from sight into the sleeping quarters beyond, waited for the space of a hundred heartbeats to be sure he would not come into this room again, then very slowly, her heart in her mouth, she began to move with extreme stealth across the floor toward the corridor door.

The journey seemed to take hours although two minutes were all that passed before she reached out to remove the heavy bar Vokal had dropped into place when his last guest was gone. With trembling fingers she set the thick length of wood against the stone flooring and slowly swung the door open a crack.

Light gleamed dully from down the corridor. With great care she widened the distance between the door's edge and its frame. When the space was large enough, she put her head out cautiously and looked along the corridor.

Standing there, watching her with wide eyes, was one of the palace guards!

Shock held both Dylara and the guard momentarily paralyzed—then Dylara, the first to recover, was into the corridor and running swiftly in the opposite direction.

Behind her she heard the guard shout a command. But before he could do more, she was around a bend in the corridor and racing toward the stairs she knew were further along.

... Vokal, not yet completely asleep, leaped from his bed at the sound of a sudden hoarse cry from outside his apartment. When he arrived at the open door—a door he had only moments before barred from inside—he found a knot of palace guards already assembled there.

"What has happened?" he demanded sharply.

The man regularly stationed outside his door explained in a few words.

Vokal's cheeks paled at the full implication of what had occurred came to him. Whoever this mystery woman was, she had overheard—*must* have overheard—his conversations with both Rhoa and Sitab. Were she a spy—someone who would go to Jaltor with what she had heard—Vokal was a dead man![Pg 132]

"Find her!" he screamed. "A hundred tals to the man who brings her alive, to me. Death to all of you unless she is found! Go!"

They went. They went as though the hounds of hell were at their heels. Within seconds every floor of the palace was alight with torches, every hall crowded with warriors, every room being searched. Guards at the palace gates were alerted, patrols were set to scouring the grounds between palace and outer wall.

There was no sign of the missing girl.

THARN, sleeping soundly as a man does whose conscience is clear and whose bed is no more uncomfortable than a hundred others he has occupied, awakened suddenly. For a brief moment he lay without moving, his ears searching for some indication of what had awakened him.

There! The barest whisper of leather against stone from down the corridor that ran past his cell door. A sandaled foot had made that sound. Other ears—even the ears of a man already awake—would have missed what his sleeping brain had caught.

Soundlessly he left his stone bench and moved to the door. But the darkness was such that even his unbelievably sharp eyes were helpless to penetrate it. But if his eyes were useless, his ears were not. Fifty feet further down the corridor a man was standing; he could hear his breathing and the rustle of garments. A few seconds later Tharn's eyes caught a tiny glow of light—a glow that soon swelled to a flickering light strong enough for him to see the opposite row of barred cell doors.

Again came the whisper of sandaled feet. Presently an Ammadian guard came into view, a heavy spear in one hand, a small torch of flaming wood in the other. The guard was peering into each of the cells across from Tharn, pausing at length at some, passing others quickly. Tharn wondered at the man's attempt at stealth; since it was impossible for any of the prisoners to get at him, such precautions could serve no evident ends.

When the man reached a cell almost exactly across from Tharn, the cave man saw him toss something through the opening framing the bars. He heard the unseen prisoner sigh ... and then the guard raised his spear and inserted its head through the same opening.

Tharn was on the point of crying out a warning, his reason dictated only by a desire to thwart as far as possible the hated symbol of authority represented by this white-tunicked assassin. But in that moment he saw a second figure steal into the outer periphery of light thrown by the torch—a figure of a man whom Tharn recognized instantly as one of those who had accompanied Jotan in his search for Dylara a few days before.

As the arm holding the spear tensed to send it plunging into the unseen prisoner, the newcomer leaped cat-like upon the would-be assassin. There was a startled cry that echoed along the subterranean hall and the two men became a squirming knot of arms and legs.

And then abruptly the threshing figures were still as the second man pressed the blade of a flint knife against the other's thinly clad back.

"Not a move," growled Tamar, "or you are a dead man!"

NOW a lovely dark-haired girl came into view, her face revealed by the flickering light of the still burning torch lying on the corridor's flooring. As she bent to pick up the bit of blazing wood Tharn recognized her as Urim's daughter, whose life he had saved on a long gone day.

"What were you up to there?" growled Tamar. "Who are you and what——"[Pg 133]

"*Tamar!*"

The cry came from behind the barred door from which the young nobleman had just drawn the cringing Sitab. There, framed in the barred opening, was Jotan!

Alurna, a faint cry of happiness on her lips, rushed to the door and removed the heavy bar. Jotan bounded into the narrow hallway, gave Sephar's princess a thankful pat on the back, then turned to Tamar.

"What's going on here? Who is this guard? How did you find me?"

"First," Tamar said, "I'm going to find out why this son of Gubo was about to send a spear into you!"

At Jotan's blank expression, Tamar explained what had been about to happen when he and Alurna arrived. Whereupon Jotan took the trembling Sitab by the front of his tunic and shook him until most of his breath was gone.

"Who sent you?" Jotan snarled. "Speak before I strangle you with my bare hands!"

77

"I dare not tell you! He would kill me!" Sitab cried through chattering teeth.

Again Jotan shook him. "But I will cut you into tiny pieces if you do not tell. First I will cut your toes and fingers from your rotten body, then I will dig out your eyes and chop off your——"

Sitab had fainted.

Three ringing slaps brought the man back to consciousness. In a voice made shrill with terror he gave the name of the man who had sent him.

Tamar and Jotan stared at each other in utter amazement as the name of Vokal fell from those craven lips. Angrily Jotan hurled the shrinking figure from him, Sitab fell headlong against the stone wall and lapsed into a motionless heap of quivering flesh.

Tamar said, "That's all we need! We can go to Jaltor and tell him what this coward has said; then he will free you and your father and put Vokal in your place."

"My father lives?" cried Jotan. "I thought Jaltor had slain him."

Quickly Tamar explained what had actually happened. When he had finished, Jotan said, "Before we do anything else I must find my father. Help me search these cells, both of you."

"He may not be on this level," Tamar said. "We could spend hours hunting him. The thing to do would be to go to Jaltor——"

But Jotan was already on his way along the corridor, peering in at the occupant of each.

MINUTES later there was a sizable group of men freed from the cells and grouped about Jotan and Tamar. Among them was Garlud, Jotan's father, his gaunt face wreathed in smiles, his strength, sapped by long days of imprisonment, flowing back at the realization he was free and in possession of the name of the man who had brought about his downfall. The others were those members of Jotan's party who had accompanied him from far-off Sephar, released from their brief imprisonment and ready for action.

Tamar said, "And now we can go to Jaltor and tell him what happened!"

"We shall have to take this man"—Jotan pointed to the fallen and unmoving body of Sitab—"to Jaltor as our only witness against Vokal."

Garlud said, "It is hard to believe that Vokal is the one behind all this trouble. We have been friends for many years, all of Ammad loves him, even Jaltor admires him more than almost any noble of the court."

"He is behind the plot against us, father," Jotan said sharply. "There can be no doubt about it."

"We shall need overwhelming proof."

"Our proof lies there." Jotan waved [Pg 134]a hand at the motionless bulk near the wall. "Get him on his feet, somebody; it's time he told his story to Jaltor, king of Ammad!"

Tamar bent above the fallen man and shook him. "Come! You've rested long enough!"

But Sitab did not move and Tamar shook him again, harder this time, and repeated the order. Then suddenly the young noble was kneeling beside the still form of the guard and placing a hand against the tunic over his heart.

In the silence Tamar rose to his feet and met the stricken eyes of his friends. "He is dead," he said simply.

"There dies our proof," Garlud said glumly. "Now it is our word against Vokal's."

"No!" Jotan swung around to face his father and Tamar. "There is another way. We can go to Vokal's palace, pull him from his bed and force him to confess!"

"And what of Vokal's loyal guards and warriors?" Garlud said soberly. "Do you think they will idly stand aside and permit that?"

Jotan swept out his hand in a half circle. "Here are fifty men—stalwart warriors all. And in your own palace, father, are hundreds more. I say let us go to our own palace, gather together our warriors and march upon Vokal!"

"You forget," Garlud said softly, "that I am regarded as an enemy of the State. As such, my palace and possessions are confiscated and my warriors stripped of their weapons and confined to quarters."

"Jotan," said a quiet voice from behind them.

THE group of men standing about the subterranean corridor beneath the palace of Jaltor of Ammad, turned as the quiet voice reached their ears.

Standing at the barred opening of one of the locked cells, the strong handsome face, visible in the light of the late Sitab's torch, was Tharn, a slight smile on his lips.

"Who calls my name?" demanded the young noble, stepping nearer the door of the cell.

"It is I—Tharn, son of Tharn, the cave man. Have you forgotten the times we have met in the past?"

Recognition dawned in Jotan's expression. "Of course! You are the man who claimed Dylara belonged to you."

"And she still belongs to me," Tharn said quietly.

"She lives?" Even the absence of more than dim light could not hide the sudden hope flaring in the young nobleman's eyes.

Tharn nodded. "Even now she is held prisoner by the man who has plotted against you."

Jotan stiffened. "You mean Vokal? How do you know this?"

Tharn, with a few terse words, explained what had taken place at Vokal's palace only a few short hours before. When he finished, Jotan was ready to start out for that nobleman's palace, alone if necessary, to rescue her. But others of the group remonstrated, pointing out the rashness of such a move. As they stood there arguing the point, Tharn's clear voice brought them into silence once more.

"There are too few of you to march against Vokal," he pointed out. "But all around you are men who are no better than dead as long as they remain behind bars. Free them, arm them with the weapons of the guards attached to this wing of Jaltor's palace, and they will march with you to overcome your enemy."

The idea caught instant hold. Moments later the group of fifty had swollen to three times that number as cell after cell of the lower three levels of Jaltor's pits were emptied.

There were some of the prisoners who held back, preferring to remain[Pg 135]behind bars rather than become involved in a war between noblemen; while others had spent too long below ground to be little more than empty shells of men.

It was on the fourth level that they found several rooms furnished as quarters for the guards stationed in this wing of the palace. An ante-room contained a large supply of spears, bows and arrows and knives, but guards were on duty at that point, while a dozen others slept in the adjoining room.

After a brief council of war, it was decided that Tharn and Trakor would attempt to creep up on the two guards on duty just within the entrance to the arms-room and overpower them without permitting an alarm to be given. Should they succeed in doing this, it would be a simple matter to bar the only exit to the sleeping quarters, thus effectively keeping Jotan's men from being surprised from the rear by Jaltor's warriors.

While the embryo army waited on the level below, Tharn and young Trakor crept up the next ramp and moved stealthily toward their goal. Almost at once Trakor returned, a broad grin creasing his face, and beckoned the others to join him.

THEY found both guards bound and gagged, the door into the guard's quarters closed and barred, and weapons enough for an army at their disposal. With muffled cries of joy the men swept up bows, arrows, spears and knives; and what a few minutes before had been an unarmed mob was now a small compact army of disciplined men, ready to win amnesty and a nobleman's favor by helping to expose a traitor.

So great was the excitement, so strong the exultation of them all, that none noticed one of the recently freed prisoners detach himself from the group and steal back into the corridor. An instant later this man was fleeing rapidly up the final ramp, on his way to freedom.

For more than an hour now the palace and grounds of Vokal, nobleman of Ammad, had been the scene of great activity. Every guard, every servant, scoured the four floors and palace grounds, inch by inch, in search for the girl who had fled Vokal's room.

While seemingly everywhere at once, the silver-haired nobleman spurred them on, his calmness gone, his eyes wild, fear riding him hard. He alone of them all knew what it would mean for him were this girl to escape and find her way to Jaltor with the knowledge she had gained while lurking on the balcony outside his private suite.

He was standing now in a room on the first floor, giving directions to Ekbar, captain of his guards, when one of the warriors pushed through the crowded room, a stranger at his heels.

"Your pardon, Most-High," said the guard, "but this man came to our gates a moment ago and demanded to see you. He says he has important information that is for your ears alone."

Vokal, turning to order the man aside, stopped and stared. The stranger was tall and little more than a skeleton. His hair hung in long strands to his shoulders and a heavy beard covered his face. Among a race of men who permitted no hair to mask their countenances, the beard alone made him worthy of attention.

"Who are you," Vokal snapped, "and what do you want of me?"

"I am Tarsal," croaked the stranger, "once guard in your service. Many moons ago I fought with one of Jaltor's guards and slew him. Since that day I have been confined in the pits of Ammad's king."

Ekbar, who had been staring at the [Pg 136]man closely while he was speaking, nodded. "He tells the truth, Most-High. I recognize him now."

"What do you want of me?" Vokal said again, his voice shrill with impatience.

"I came to warn you," Tarsal said. "Garlud and Jotan, his son, have escaped from their cells and have gathered together a small army taken from Jaltor's pits. They say that it was because of you that Garlud and Jotan were imprisoned by Jaltor, and they are coming to capture you and take you before the king."

The nobleman's skin turned a dirty white. This was ruin for him! Wildly he sought to think of some way by which he could escape Jaltor's wrath, once the truth came out.

"What are the plans of this mob?" he demanded. "Do they expect to win Jaltor's support in the fight against me?"

"Not that I know of, Most-High. They spoke of stealing from the palace and marching here to take you captive and bring you before Ammad's king that he may hear the truth from your own lips."

Vokal's brain was working with cold precision. There was a way out, then! Were he and his warriors able to ambush this gang of prison rats, able to wipe them out to the last man, there would be none left alive to tell Jaltor what they had hoped to accomplish.

All thoughts of the mysterious young woman who had raced from his apartment earlier that night were forgotten as he whirled about to confront the open-mouthed Ekbar.

"There is still time," he cried, "to save ourselves. Listen to me closely, Ekbar, and do exactly as I say!"

As the heavily armed force of perhaps one hundred and fifty men entered one of Ammad's broad avenues no more than two blocks from Vokal's palace, Jotan called it to a halt while the leaders conferred.

Five men comprised the leadership of the relatively small army. They were Jotan and his father, Tamar, Tharn and young Trakor. Almost from the first it was Tharn to whom the others turned for guidance, despite the fact that he was a complete stranger to Ammad.

"How many men," Tharn asked, "are likely to be defending Vokal's palace?"

"No less than five hundred," Jotan said grimly. "We shall be badly outnumbered my friend."

"We have something on our side worth hundreds of warriors," Tharn observed. "Surprise is our biggest and best ally. If we can win our way into Vokal's palace and reach the quarters of Vokal himself before his guards are sufficiently alerted to interfere, the fight will be over before it begins."

"And how do you propose this shall be done?"

Tharn rubbed his chin while his quick mind reviewed the situation. "I think," he said finally, "that it would be better if Trakor and I went ahead and removed the guards outside the wall gates. Then our entire force can enter the grounds themselves and hide in the shrubbery there until a door at the rear of the palace can be unbarred. It might serve us best if Trakor and I go directly to Vokal's room and take him captive before we give the signal for the rest of you to enter."

Garlud was shaking his head. "No. That is risking too much. If the two of you were captured, the entire palace would be alerted before the rest of us could put a foot inside it. Then indeed would we be helpless; Vokal's men could cut us down from the safety of the palace walls."

The five stood there in the silent sleeping street, stone walls rising [Pg 137]steep and bleak on either side, the entire army behind them hidden from chance view by the almost total lack of light. There was less than two hours remaining before dawn and they must act quickly or lose their chief aid: the darkness of the now moonless night.

It was finally decided that Tharn and Trakor, as a tribute to their superior experience in tracking down the most wary of prey, were the ones to remove the guards outside at least two of the gates in Vokal's wall of stone.

And so it was that the two Cro-Magnards stole away into the darkness, armed with arrows and bow and two good flint knives.

Half an hour later both were back, reporting success to the other leaders. "It was almost too easy," Tharn said thoughtfully. "Where there were four guards at one of the gates earlier tonight, I found but one—and he was sitting with his back to the gate and fast asleep. After I slew him I went on to help Trakor, only to learn he had had an almost similar experience."

"It is not uncommon for guards to sleep at their posts," Jotan said impatiently. "Let us get started before other of Vokal's guards discover the gates are unguarded and rouse the palace defenders."

"I think we should make sure we are not going blindly into some trap," Tharn demurred. "This entire thing is suspicious ... too easy."

But Jotan waved the cave lord into silence. "Can't you understand," he said crisply, "that we don't have time for that? I say let's get on with our plan and not spend time worrying about things that will never happen."

In this both Garlud and Tamar agreed, and so Tharn shrugged and said no more. He was in league with these Ammadians for only one reason: to make it that much easier for him to snatch Dylara from this strange city and return with her to the caves of his own people. What had happened to her, once he and Trakor had fled Vokal's palace earlier that night, leaving her hidden within the building, was something he could not know. But there was no other place in all of Ammad he knew where to look for her, and so he must act in the belief that she still was behind the palace walls, either hidden there or once more a captive of the rascally nobleman.

LESS than half an hour later all of Jotan's band of warriors squatted behind the belt of foliage just within the walls of Vokal's sprawling palace. In the dim light of stars they could look out between the interstices of growing things, seeing the many windowed bulk of stone rising four full floors above the neighboring terrain. No where in all that vast expanse was there a sign of life. No candle showed its brief flame at any window. Silent and dark and somehow a place of brooding danger.

After another whispered conference, Tharn left the other leaders of the band and flitted across the open ground, moving like a black shadow toward the same doorway through which Trakor had raced to join him only an hour or two earlier.

Those watching him from the shadowy foliage lost sight of him almost at once; and when, a few moments later, he seemed to rise from the ground almost under their noses, a startled gasp from a dozen throats made a rustling sound against the heavy silence.

"The door is still unbarred," Tharn reported, frowning. "I am even surer now, noble Jotan, that we are heading straight for a trap set up by the wily Vokal."

"He could not know our plans," Jotan said impatiently. "It means simply that they forgot to bar the door after the excitement you and your friend caused them earlier. Things are work[Pg 138]ing out well for us."

Tharn smiled his enigmatic smile and said no more. Quickly the five leaders moved among their eager troops, issuing orders down the line. And then, at a single word from Jotan the band of one hundred and fifty armed men stepped into the open and started for the palace walls.

Suddenly the shrill cry of a woman rose against the weighted silence. "Back!" the voice screamed from high above them. "Go back! It is a trap!"

"Dylara!" Tharn shouted, and with great bounding strides he raced toward the palace. Startled by the shrill shout, puzzled by Tharn's dash into the jaws of what might be a trap, the hundred and fifty wavered uncertainly, then charged after the racing cave man.

And as the first wave of Jotan's warriors reached the halfway mark in the clearing, a hundred flaming branches were hurled from the open windows into the courtyard beneath, their flames lighting up the entire ribbon of open ground and disclosing the pitifully small army to the waiting warriors of Vokal.

A rain of arrows, spears and clubs now rained down from those windows upon the men beneath. Men reeled and fell, some instantly dead, others badly wounded. Some of those unhit stopped in their tracks, looked wildly around, then turned to flee for the safety of the street behind them.

And it was then that Vokal's masterful plan was fully unveiled. From those same openings through the stone wall encircling Vokal's estate, came other of that nobleman's warriors, stationed in places of concealment outside, their purpose to close off the last avenue of escape for Jotan's troops.

IN all this confusion, with death threatening from all sides, Trakor had eyes only for his friend and companion—Tharn, lord of the caves.

At first he did not comprehend what lay behind the cave man's mad dash toward the palace. But when he saw Tharn leap lightly up to catch the sill of one window, then swarm rapidly up toward the second story, he understood fully what lay in the giant warrior's mind.

One of Vokal's warriors leaned from a window directly in Tharn's path and raised his spear with the obvious intention of burying its head in the cave man's defenseless body as it hung a full fifteen feet above the ground. Trakor, seeing this, fitted an arrow to his bow with unthinkable quickness and sent the flint tipped missile across space and full into the enemy warrior's exposed chest.

The heavy spear rolled from an already dead hand and the man fell loosely across the wide sill as Tharn worked his way upward past the limp body.

Three more attempts were made by those within to bring down the climbing cave man. On each occasion Trakor, standing like a rock amid a shower of deadly weapons that struck every where about him, brought down the would-be killer.

Tharn was only a few feet from the roof's edge now, his naked feet and long-fingered hands finding foot—and hand-holds where Trakor would have sworn none existed.

Trakor, watching, groaned with sudden fear. Barely visible in the flickering light of torches below, a figure appeared at the roof's edge directly above Tharn's rising form. In the figure's hands was a heavy spear and the arm holding it swept aloft preparatory to skewering Tharn on its point.

Even as Trakor witnessed this, an arrow from his bow was flashing up toward that menacing warrior. But the combination of bad light, distance and the necessity for haste was too great a handicap for success, and the arrow whizzed wide of its mark.[Pg 139]

Again Trakor groaned. There was no time for a second shot. Tharn was doomed to die.

And in that second a slender figure appeared at the roof's edge beside the would-be assassin and threw itself headlong against him. The man staggered back under the impact, his spear falling from his hand, then turned and closed with the newcomer.

As the two of them teetered there on the thin strip of stone forming the roof's edge, Tharn's strong hands closed about that same edge and he rose to his feet. He saw who it was that had saved his life: Dylara, daughter of Majok.

Even as he raced forward to save the girl he loved from being thrown into the void below, Tharn knew he was too late. Voicing a scream of fear, Dylara reeled back and toppled into space!

As her feet left the roof, Tharn threw himself headlong in a direction parallel with the edge, one arm out-thrust, the other bent to check his fall. For one agonizing second the reaching hand encountered only air; then his fingers brushed against cloth, closed like a snapped trap, and as his muscular frame crashed against the roof's edge, a sudden jerk against his outstretched arm told him he had checked Dylara's fall.

A heavy sandal thudded home against his ribs, nearly rolling him into the void and to death on the packed earth below. Before the swinging foot could strike home a second time, Tharn was on his feet and Dylara was swung back to safety of the roof.

As Tharn released the girl, the screaming, clawing figure of his enemy closed upon him. In the faint light, Tharn saw the other's hair was a silvery white and beneath it was a face once gentle but now transformed into the mask of a madman.

A GRIM smile touched Tharn's lips as one of his brawny arms snaked out and caught the raving beast that had once been Vokal, third most powerful and influential figure in all Ammad. With almost casual ease Tharn swung the human form high above his head, then tossed him, a screaming missile of terror, to the ground below.

A long eerie wailing cry ended suddenly and the thud of flesh against earth seemed to jar into silence the tumult filling the grounds of the late Vokal's palace. In the light of the still burning torches Vokal's lifeless body was clearly visible to the palace defenders.

In that hushed moment, Jotan took advantage of the miracle that had saved the remnants of his fighting force.

"Vokal is dead!" he shouted. "Vokal the traitor is no more! Lay down your arms, warriors of the dead Vokal! Lay down your arms that you may win forgiveness from Jaltor, king of Ammad!"

A wavering moment of indecision followed as the warriors at the palace windows stood with raised weapons hesitating to decide one way or the other. And in that moment a brawny figure appeared at one of the open windows.

"Death to the invader!" shouted Ekbar, captain of the late Vokal's guards. "Avenge the noble Vokal! Kill them all!"

As the last words left his lips a second man appeared beside the captain. Before the latter could realize what was taking place a stone knife flashed in a savage arc, burying its length in his heart.

Ekbar voiced a single scream of anguish and toppled across the sill and to the ground beneath, dead beside the master he had so faithfully served.

While from that same window a [Pg 140]young warrior of that same dead master smiled with grim satisfaction. Otar had made sure his bride, the lovely Marua, would never again be visited by her former suitor.

With Ekbar died the last of all resistance against Jotan's invading warriors. Scores of weapons fell uselessly to the ground and the palace defenders began to stream from the building, their hands lifted in surrender.

And it was then that a quiet voice from behind Jotan and his father said:

"Are the pits of Jaltor so shallow that they may not hold my enemies?"

The nobleman and his son wheeled about, then stiffened to rigid attention at sight of Jaltor, king of Ammad, standing at the forefront of a squad of his own guards.

CHAPTER XV
CONCLUSION

DAWN had come an hour before but the group of seven people sat about the breakfast table in the private dining room of Jaltor, ruler of Ammad.

It was a wide, richly furnished room on the top floor of the city's palace. The east wall was composed entirely of windows, barred by fluted, slender columns of white stone, through which streamed the bright rays of morning sun.

"Had you delayed your escape from the pits another two hours," Jaltor was saying, "all of you would have been freed without having to fight for proof of your innocence. For old Heglar's mate, the beautiful Rhoa, had been followed to Vokal's palace, and when she left there, my men picked her up and brought her to me at the palace. Strangely enough she was not at all hesitant about betraying Vokal; I think she believed he was trying to get out of taking her as his mate."

"Then instead of helping," Alurna said, smiling, "I nearly brought about Jotan's death. That should be a lesson to me not to mix in another's affairs!"

Jotan smiled at her briefly, then went back to his apparently careful examination of the earthen plate in front of him. Ever since he had seated himself across the table from Dylara and the broad-shouldered young cave man next to her he had little to say. But in his mind there was a welter of conflicting thoughts and emotions.

Fate had thrown the girl he loved into the arms of the man who long ago had claimed her as his mate. The fortunes of war had made that same man Jotan's ally during the night just past. Could Jotan, then, turn against his ally because he too loved the girl whom Jotan desired above all others?

He stole a glance at the radiant young woman who held his heart in the hollow of one slender hand. How lovely she was! And how closely she leaned toward the young giant of the caves who sat beside her. Her smiles were for the man of her own kind; as the minutes passed they seemed more and more to belong to each other.

Well, it was up to Dylara now. Soon she would be called upon to make a decision: to accompany the cave man back across the vast expanse of plain and forest and mountain range to the caves of his people ... or to remain within Ammad as the mate of Jotan, nobleman of Ammad.

Beside Jotan, no less lovely in a completely different physical appearance, was Alurna of Sephar, daughter of one king and niece of another. Often her eyes strayed to the handsome young nobleman next to her. She saw his eyes go to the girl of the caves and back to his plate again as a wave of color poured up into his cheeks. She knew what was going on in his mind—knew it as if he had spoken the words aloud! The next few hours would decide what her future life would be: Jotan's mate or [Pg 141]a woman who had lost her bid for happiness.

In all that room, perhaps, only two men did not feel the cross currents of emotions that seemed to make electric the very air about them. One missed it entirely because he was very young and interested in only one person—that was Trakor. The other was Tharn; and while he understood what lay behind Jotan's studied preoccupation, he was indifferent to it. Dylara belonged to him—and though an entire nation might stand between them, he would claim her for his own.

As for Dylara, she smiled warmly at everyone and said little. For she too was waiting—waiting with the serenity of one whose mind is made up as to the course her life will take.

"All of you are weary," Jaltor said finally. "I suggest slaves show you to the quarters I have set aside for those of you who wish to remain as my guests."

His eyes went to the three cave people questioningly. There was a moment of weighted silence ... and into it Tharn said:

"Dylara, Trakor and I are far from the caves of our people. I, for one, am anxious to start back. Perhaps we will sleep until tomorrow's sun—then begin our journey."

As he finished speaking, his eyes came to rest upon the cave girl.

A BREATHLESS hush seemed to settle over the room. The moment had come—and Tharn had so phrased his words that the daughter of Majok now held the key to the hopes of two men ... and the choice was hers, without pressure from either of those two.

Jotan's head came up and his eyes met the brown, sun-flecked gaze of the cave girl. A deep, chest-swelling breath filled his lungs....

"I am not tired," Dylara said calmly. "I would like to start for your caves at once, Tharn."

And with those words, and the lifting of her hand as she placed it on the cave lord's bronzed forearm, Dylara made her choice.

Pain—the awful pain of unrequited love—rose like flames in Jotan's heart. Rose until they shook him with agony ... swelled ... and broke to settle back under the man's iron control.

He was conscious, then, that a soft hand had placed itself on one of his as it lay palm down against the table. He looked down at it, not understanding, then lifted his eyes slowly to meet the troubled eyes of Alurna....

Jotan said, "I had hoped that you three would remain in Ammad for a few suns as the guests of my father and me. But I can understand your eagerness to return to your own people."

Dyta, the sun, stood two hours above the eastern horizon. On a small hillock a few yards from the edge of dense jungle and forest not far from Ammad's walls, stood a group of Jaltor's warriors flanking the king and his guests.

Silence, broken only by the voices of diurnal jungle, held those on the high bit of ground as they watched the three Cro-Magnons move lightly toward that towering wall of verdure. They moved lightly, eagerly, as though anxious to lose themselves among the riotous vegetation, a familiar world to them.

Jotan, watching, felt a strange peace come into his heart. Only now did realization come that at no time during the past moons since Dylara had come into his life did he have the slightest chance to win her love. He stole a quick glance at the girl beside him. Here was the perfect mate for a nobleman—his own kind, fit to take up the duties of mate to one of his own high station. Yes, he told himself, it was better this way.

His eyes went back to the three now [Pg 142]almost within the jungle's reach. The girl turned back and waved her hand in farewell, joined by the lifted arms of Trakor and Tharn.

Abruptly a mist seemed to form before Jotan's eyes and he bowed his head, blinking rapidly to dispel this evidence of unmanly weakness.

When he looked up again only the empty distance met his eyes.

CPSIA information can be obtained at www.ICGtesting.com
Printed in the USA
LVOW04s2021291214

420794LV00037B/2875/P